LOVE LESSONS

LOVE LESSONS

THE RISKY LOVERS SERIES, BOOK 2

MALLORY RUSH

Book and cover design by eBook Prep
www.ebookprep.com

March, 2020
ISBN: 978-1-64457-076-0

ePublishing Works!
644 Shrewsbury Commons Ave
Ste 249
Shrewsbury PA 17361
United States of America

www.epublishingworks.com
Phone: 866-846-5123

For my daughters

A NOTE FROM THE AUTHOR

While this story is a work of fiction, the sexual content is based on two primary sources of research. I highly recommend *The Yin-Yang Butterfly, Ancient Chinese Sexual Secrets for Western Lovers* by Valentine Chu (Putnam Tarcher, 1993) for anyone who would like to know more about the sensual arts. Mr. Chu generously offered his time and assistance in response to my many questions. I also recommend *The Multi Orgasmic Man* by Mantak Chia and Douglas Abrams Arava (Harper San Francisco, 1996).

A previous version of this novel was originally released as a Harlequin single title called *Love Play* in 1999. This is not the same book. It's a rare gift for any of us to rewrite the past from hindsight's 20/20 vision, and so it is true for this author. Although the time frame and setting haven't been altered for plot purposes, and the early chapters remain mostly intact, the remainder of the book is almost completely new to better tell Whitney's and Eric's story.

Story is what composes all of our lives. And what is fundamentally true in life, and in love, remains unchanged.

CHAPTER 1

MOBILE, ALABAMA - SEPTEMBER, 1997

"So...so how long do I have, Dr...." What was his name? He had delivered her, set her broken arm when she'd fallen out of a tree at the age of eight, then ten years later he'd held her hand when Mama had lost her battle with cancer, and he had even gone to the funeral, swiping away tears as her mother had been laid to rest. Only last week he'd given her a B12 shot for the fatigue she couldn't shake. She'd known him all her life. So why couldn't she remember his name?

"I'm sorry, Whitney, but I'd rather not hazard a guess until we run some more tests."

He was stalling. Didn't he realize she couldn't possibly leave this office without knowing if her worst suspicions were true? "In other words, you don't want to tell me because you've already hazarded a guess, haven't you?"

Silence. He dropped his gaze onto the lab report that held the answer he wasn't giving.

The suspense was killing her. Whitney leaped out of the chair facing his desk and snatched the report lying on it. Before he could stop her, she scanned the page. Three words stood out: *acute myelogenous leukemia.*

The paper fell from her hands and her legs gave way. Sinking back into her chair, she vaguely realized he was finally talking. Fast.

"These are only the initial results, Whitney, please keep that in mind and..." Dr. Whatever-His-Name-Was seemed to be having trouble speaking. Or maybe it was just that she wasn't hearing well. There was a buzz in her ears making his voice sound muffled and distant.

Some rational part of her mind insisted it was important she have the answer. "Is it a year? A month, a week? Do I have time to pay my bills?"

"Your bills aren't important, Whitney, you are and—"

"The hell they're not important!" Her tone was so shrill she winced. Struggling to stay calm, she managed a brittle laugh. "I mean, I've always been careful to pay them on time and I'd really hate to die with a bad credit record."

His mouth was moving but she didn't catch more than the gist of his response. Something about her being in shock, she shouldn't drive in the state she was in, he'd have someone take her home. Like that mattered when she still couldn't remember his name and he still hadn't answered her question.

So very slowly, distinctly, she repeated, "How...long...do...I have? *Tell me.*"

He plowed a hand through his thinning gray hair and, with a heavy sigh, gave in. "Six months. Maybe." Then he backtracked as if he were trying to erase his words. "But Whitney, new cures are found every day and remember, this is just the preliminary diagnosis. I want to refer you to a specialist, Dr. Goldberg. I'll call him today, get you in to see him tomorrow. He'll want to do a battery of tests to verify it is advanced leukemia before starting treatment. The sooner that's started the better chance we have of extending—"

"What?" she demanded, unable to believe this was happening to her and not to someone else. "Just what would I be extending besides some trips to the hospital, the treatments, the pain? That's not a life, it's a pitiful attempt to hang on to what's already lost. If six months is all I've got, then I'm not about to waste one precious minute hooked up to a machine."

"I know that's how you feel now, but give it a little time and you could change your mind."

"A little time?" Her voice was bordering on a shriek. Maybe she was closer to hysteria than she thought. "Time is the one thing I don't have! Think about it Dr....Dr. Clark—" yes, that was his name, and crazy as it was she was glad she didn't have to devote another priceless second to something as inconsequential as remembering a name.

"What if it was you?" Whitney leaned forward. "Would you let yourself be probed like some specimen under a microscope, then maybe get lucky and hang on another few months, after losing all your hair and wishing you were already dead? That's how bad the treatments are. And you know they are, Dr. Clark. I saw what my mother went through and so did you. Now tell me and don't you lie, what would you do if you were terminal?"

The light that always seemed to dance in his eyes was gone; they were as dull as his toneless reply. "I would get a second opinion, take any course of treatment prescribed and fight the inevitable as long as I could. As a doctor, I know that's what I should do."

"But as a person, a human being who was living on borrowed time, what would you do?"

Dr. Clark looked away, shook his head, then gave her the unvarnished truth. "I'd maybe subject myself to another test or two, then leave it at that. I'd get my affairs in order, and immediately turn my practice over to a colleague. Then I'd do all the things I never made time for, go for the dreams I never went for, laugh enough for a lifetime, and love with the heart of a fool. I'd live each day as if it were my last and squeeze them all dry for every drop of joy I could."

"And come that last day?" she asked with a quiet tremble.

"Well, Whitney," he said with paternal kindness, "let's just say that we all die with regrets, but for most of us, those regrets aren't so much for the things we've done, but for all the things we didn't do. I'd want

3

to go with as few of those regrets as possible, knowing that for at least a while I'd lived my life with a rare kind of richness."

"Then I guess that makes me pretty lucky." She gave a small, faint laugh. "I mean, anybody can get hit by a truck and boom, that's it. At least I get the chance to...to, well, do whatever before..." She couldn't say it. God, she couldn't even think it. If she did she'd surely start screaming "It's not true! It's not fair!" and turn into some kind of madwoman that Dr. Clark wouldn't let loose on the streets.

"I need to leave." Whitney reached for her purse and though her hand felt oddly detached, she noticed how smooth the leather was, how vibrant the purple-and-green-and-rust patchwork pieces were. To touch, to see, she'd always taken those senses for granted, but suddenly they seemed like a luxury, as wondrous and miraculous as the life she'd taken for granted as well.

"I'll call Dr. Goldberg first." Dr. Clark reached for the phone while she walked to the door like some zombie moving without will or thought. "Whitney, wait! Just wait a minute while I take care of this and I'll drive you home."

"Thanks, but no," she said with an eerie calm. "You have patients waiting and I need some fresh air." At his distressed expression, she gave him a wobbly smile. Not much of one, but it was the best she could do. "Don't worry, I'll be okay."

Before he could protest, she took off. She had to get out of there, walk from the office, through the building, out the exit door, and only then could she escape from this really, really bad nightmare.

As a warm September breeze licked at the heat of her skin, Whitney shivered. Huh. She was outside but she wasn't waking up. She was so dazed and distressed that she felt like she was sleepwalking, not hearing the cars whizzing past on the road as she crossed the street or seeing the people she kept bumping into on the sidewalk.

She didn't remember reaching her apartment, but somehow that's where she ended up. How long she'd been home, Whitney wasn't exactly sure. She'd suddenly developed an aversion to every tick of the clock and so she'd tossed her watch into the silverware drawer in the kitchen. That's where she'd been when it dawned on her that she wasn't going to wake up.

The bad dream was real.

It seemed a shame to waste what was left of the day and night on things that didn't matter much anymore like balancing her checkbook, doing her laundry, wondering what to do with the $33,565.32 in her savings account since she couldn't take it with her. Maybe she should try to enjoy it, throw some of it around, what with all the pennies she'd pinched and the small inheritance she'd socked away, no family to pass it on to.

She felt very, very strange. For some reason she hadn't shed a tear. Neither had she called anyone, but when she thought about it, just who did she feel like calling? A neighbor, co-workers at the library, maybe someone from the health club? Health club, hah!

A quick anger surged. How many hours had she spent at that stupid health club, working up a sweat to stay in shape? And just look where it had gotten her!

Membership canceled, as of now.

Just as she was ready to dial up Nautilus to inform them their services were hereby nixed, the phone rang. Whoever it was, she didn't want to talk to them, not even if it was Donny the Dreamboat from Davidson High, asking her out ten years too late.

The answering machine clicked on.

"Whitney, this is Dr. Goldberg. I've spoken to Dr. Clark and I have you scheduled for an office visit at nine in the morning. You might want to pack a few things and bring them along since I'll be sending you to the hospital afterward. I've already contacted admitting so we can get on to this right away. It'll be a busy day, so try to get a good night's sleep. See you tomorrow."

Well, well, wasn't he the presumptuous one? Whitney swallowed down a knot in her throat and struggled to hang on to her anger. Anger felt good, she could hide in that, so the angrier she was the better. Yes, she hoped Nautilus went bankrupt without her membership. And as for Dr. Goldberg, she'd see him when she was damn good and ready. To be exact, never. Her time was her time from now on and no way was she going to the hospital tomorrow. Once she checked in, they'd prick her and probe her and keep her until Dr. Goldberg said she could leave.

Only to come back and back and back and...

"I know you mean well, Dr. Goldberg, but nevertheless, screw you and your high-tech voodoo, too." No, she wasn't about to end up like her mother who had endured unspeakable suffering, trying to hang on for her only child.

Children. Love. Marriage. Whitney thought of how she'd been feeling cheated lately since those things had yet to come her way. She was gripped with sudden greediness for them, even while acknowledging it was a blessing to have no one but herself to worry about. No lover, no child to struggle to live for, no family left to grieve over her. Oh yes, it was much better this way.

So why didn't she feel blessed instead of mad as hell? Mad at God, at the world, at Dr. Goldberg, and—

Ring. Ring. The phone. How dare it intrude on her spiteful musings? She suddenly hated that phone, hated the greeting she had recorded when another dateless night was the worst of her worries, hated the stupid ending beep.

"Whitney? Whitney, are you there? Dammit, child, if you're there, pick up the phone....Ah hell, this is Dr. Clark. Look honey, I don't want you staying by yourself. Call a friend or get your preacher over, you can even page me and I'll be there in a wink. If I don't hear from you tonight, I'll be calling Dr. Goldberg first thing tomorrow to make sure you showed up. Be there, Whitney. Remember, I was the first one to spank your bottom twenty-seven years ago, don't give me a reason to straighten you out again, you hear?"

Whitney glared at the phone. She wanted to vent her rage on his message as if it were the disease stealing her life away. With a snarl and a snap she unplugged phone, grateful to have some control over something. For good measure she gave it a hard *smack*.

There. There, she felt much better! And what better way to spend her time—her time, all hers—than to celebrate her freedom from all the concerns she needn't concern herself with anymore? Champagne was in order. She couldn't remember the last time she'd skipped like a kid, but the child inside who insisted she was still immortal, skipped over to the refrigerator.

No reason to save the bottle of Andrés bubbly. She hadn't had need of it that last, lonely New Year's Eve when she'd sat alone in front of the T.V., watching the New York revelers and wishing fiercely for a kiss of her own at midnight. Well, she sure as heck had use for that bottle now. After today she was fully entitled to get plastered and even dance naked in the streets if she wanted to. So what if she couldn't sing worth a hoot? Just let the other tenants bang on the walls, the hell if she cared.

Singing at the top of her lungs, she wondered why she was grinning like a loon instead of sobbing out the tears that refused to come. Boy, she was a terrible singer, her off-pitch voice hurt her own ears. Maybe Dr. Clark was right, maybe she did need some company, somebody who could carry a tune.

To the stereo she went and selected her favorite CD. "Don't worry," she told Billy Joel as she upped the volume, "I like what you have to say, so I won't murder your disc."

Music on, champagne uncorked, she guzzled straight from the bottle. She'd never done that before, never gotten smashed except for that once in college, little Goody Two-shoes that she was. Was, as in the past tense. The rebellious nature she'd never had was finally getting its due. As the ever so astute Mr. Joel was pointing out, "Only the good die young."

"Sing it, Billy!" Whitney took another swig, looked at the bottle and laughed. Laugh enough for a lifetime, that's what Dr. Clark had said. Well, by golly, she was laughing. Some rich life she'd led. Why, she hadn't even downed a third of the bottle and here she was, three sheets to the wing. Or was it the wind?

Didn't matter, starting tonight she was gonna rip through life with the gusto she'd never had. After all, she only had six months to pack in the sixty years she was getting robbed of. Spend those six months at the library, working for a boss she couldn't stand? Forget it. One of her most beloved fantasies would be realized tomorrow when she marched into the Mobile Public Library and told that little weasel to take her job and shove it, along with as many books as he could cram up his you-know-what.

"The word is *ass*, Whitney," she slurred. "Gotta work on your... hic...bad language."

With a tipsy giggle, she wove her way into her neat-as-a-pin bedroom and pulled her one nice piece of tapestry luggage out of the closet. After sniffing in disdain at the buttoned-down, no-frills wardrobe hanging in neat order, she rummaged through her dresser drawers, found a few things, threw them into her suitcase, and deemed her packing done.

There was lots of room left for all the naughty, sexy, daring dresses and nighties she was gonna buy to take with her...where? Someplace...exotic. Yeah, exotic. Someplace where there were lots of guys. Yeah, guys. Not that she needed many, one would be plenty. A hunka-hunka-burnin'-love who would make her feel like a love goddess. That was her other big fantasy and by God, she deserved to have it before...

She'd rather think about her fantasy man—some handsome, mysterious stranger who didn't know she was really a mousy children's librarian who got her kicks from reading books out loud to kids.

At the thought of children, of those she would never read to again, of those she would never bear, Whitney felt her throat tighten. There was a sting behind her eyes that she blinked against as she returned to the dresser, for what she didn't know. Just something to focus her attention on, like the brush she picked up and put to her hair.

She had pretty hair, long and dark and wavy. She had pretty blue eyes, too. They were looking back at her from the mirror, but they were so empty and hopeless and frightened that she couldn't bear to meet her own gaze.

She lowered it to her breasts. The brush fell from her fingers and she worked loose the buttons of her plain white blouse. Then that was gone and so was her bra and she was staring at her bare breasts, and how pretty they were too. So pretty that she touched them, cupped them in her hands, and wondered what she had ever done that was so terrible she would never nurse a newborn babe.

Her hands trailed over her arms, traced the neat groove of her waist, the flare of her hips. And then she pressed her palms to her belly, that place where no new life would ever grow because her own had been cut short.

Despite its flaws, her body was beautiful. Beautiful and *sick*. The care and respect she had always shown for it meant nothing. Her body had betrayed her. God had betrayed her.

She had betrayed herself.

Tears welled in her eyes and spilled onto her cheeks. A sob caught in her throat as she whispered, "Whitney Smith. You're kind and you're decent, but what have you really done with your life? Not much and that's a terrible shame because you're twenty-seven years old. And you are going to die."

CHAPTER 2

"*Y*ou're late." Mr. Andrews looked over his reading glasses with a scowl. "One hour and forty-three minutes late, Ms. Smith. And what might be your excuse?"

She had never been late for work, not once in nearly five years, but did he care why she was late today? Was he even capable of caring that she'd spent the morning on the phone she was glad not to have destroyed, speaking to a lawyer and a funeral director, for reasons she had no intentions of sharing with him? Did he have enough of a heart to care that she was wearing sunglasses in the library because her eyes were so swollen, anyone who saw them would surely guess she'd been sobbing all night?

He couldn't care less. He was a cold little man who must have some virtues she didn't have the time left to detect.

"I asked you a question, Ms. Smith. What's your excuse for being so late?"

"And what's your excuse for speaking to me like you're my whip master and I'm your slave?" Whitney felt a little thrill at the flippant retort she wouldn't have dared speak before.

"Because I'm your boss, that's why!" he sputtered. "Now I suggest you get to work before I write you up for insubordination."

"Feel free to do just that, Mr. Andrews, but you'll only be wasting your time. You see, the reason I'm late is because..." Her heart raced. This was it, she was really going to do it! She smiled and said, "I quit."

His shocked expression was so comical Whitney struggled not to laugh. But hey, she needed a good laugh, and what was he going to do about it, fire her? So laugh she did before informing him, "The only reason I stayed this long is because of the kids, they're so special to me. You, however, have been terrible to work for, Mr. Andrews. You must be a very unhappy person to treat others as meanly as you do, and I really hope you can change that. After all, life's too short not to enjoy to its fullest and smile as much as we can. You made me smile today. Thanks."

Whitney strode away and was aware of a euphoric lift, as if she'd just let go of all the rules and responsibilities and resentments that had kept her weighted down. She knew it was a rare liberation she'd claimed, but how she wished it hadn't been won by having nothing to lose.

Two days later, Whitney marveled at the peace she felt as the plane bound for the Caribbean island of Dominica kissed the clouds and promptly hit a pocket of air. Where had her fear of flying gone? Somewhere between her flight out of New Orleans and the layover in San Juan her white-knuckled fists had relaxed and she'd bid her fear good riddance, along with those irksome matters she'd dealt with to simplify her life.

Her insurance, which the library would no longer cover, was paid in advance. The next six months of rent, ditto. And her final residence after that, secured.

Whitney shuddered. *Don't think about it, don't you dare. If you do, you'll get depressed and then you'll spoil the moment and the moment is all you have.*

And just what did she have in this moment? That was the little game she'd begun to play with herself, one she wished she'd thought up a long time ago. Better late than never, though, and for now she had a seat by the window in the first-class section, the taste of Wrigley's Spearmint gum in her mouth, a *Cosmo* magazine on her little airplane tray, a new floral sundress on, and an attractive man sitting beside her. His nose was firmly planted in a book.

"A room without books is like a body without a soul," she quietly mused.

"Cicero." His low-pitched voice was crisp, and pleasant to the ear. Though she hadn't expected a response, he looked directly at her for the first time—unless she counted a cordial nod when he'd rushed to his seat, laptop and leather backpack in hand, the last passenger to board on their hour and a half island hop flight. "Of course he also said, 'There is nothing so ridiculous but some philosopher has said it.'"

The man's smile was infectious. Whitney found herself smiling back despite her vow to avoid conversing with other passengers since her last seatmate had been a motor mouth.

"You seem to know your Cicero. Do you teach philosophy?" If so, Whitney was sure he didn't lack for students, particularly of the female persuasion.

"Hardly. I had to write a paper on Cicero in college, oh how long ago was that?" He tapped his temple and she noticed he had the most remarkable face. There was an arresting quality to his prominent cheekbones and gleaming black hair, combed straight back from a widow's peak. His eyes, an exotic, slightly almond shape, were a medley of dark-and-light brown, flecked with amber. He reminded her of that actor in *The Devil's Advocate*—not Al Pacino, but...Keanu Reeves? That was it!

Guessing him to be a little older than she, but not by much, he surprised her by saying, "I was a freshman so it's been nearly twenty years. But it only took me all of two minutes to forget most everything about the class—except for the prof, that is. He was nearing retirement so the university kept him on despite this little problem with narcolepsy that made him fall asleep in the middle of his own lectures."

"That's awful!" Laughter bubbled from her throat and she silently thanked him for that.

"Yeah, it is," he agreed, chuckling himself. "But at the time, I thought it was pretty cool since he'd wake up and say, 'Now where was I?' and we'd all reply, 'You were about to dismiss us,' and then—"

"Excuse me," said a flight attendant, "Would you care for a beverage?"

Though the question was directed to her flying companion, he turned to Whitney and asked with the courteous finesse of a tuxedo-clad date, "What would you like?"

"Hmmm...how about time in a bottle?"

He smiled that smile again, warm and comfortable as an old pair of jeans molded to a familiar body. He had very nice lips. "I'd arm wrestle you for possession if I thought they had one to serve."

"In that case, I'll take champagne."

Another flash of that smile before he ordered a champagne "for the lady" and an imported beer for himself. After the drinks were promptly served, he asked, "Now where was I?"

"Class was just adjourned."

His expression was somewhere between a rueful grin and a wince. "And to think the first thing I do on a plane is open a book so I don't get stuck listening to some stranger go on and on about stuff I couldn't care less about." He offered his book to Whitney. "Feel free to hide in there for the rest of the flight, but I will need it back when we land."

After glancing at the title, *Volcanology: A Retrospective Analysis of Earth and Man,* Whitney shook her head. "I wouldn't dream of stealing your pleasure reading, and besides, I was really enjoying your story. So, did you pass?"

"Can you keep a secret?" he whispered.

"Cross my heart, hope to..." Her smile faltered, but she quickly reminded herself to think only of the moment and in this moment she was with a man whose eyes imparted equal measures of somber reflection and quiet laughter. They held the maturity of one who had seen a lot, and the alertness of one who missed nothing—including the hand she'd laid over her heart.

"Sure you can trust me," she whispered back, aware of a tingling sensation arcing from crown to nape. "So what's the secret?"

"Nothing I'm proud of, believe me."

She leaned slightly closer.

So did he. "When the prof was asleep," he confided, "we revised some of our grades. Nothing too drastic, but I pulled a B-plus when I should have gotten a B-minus. It was a stupid kid trick and I'm lucky I didn't get caught. As it is, it's one of those things I really regret having done, but not enough to turn myself in and risk losing my reputation. Even worse, they might make me retake that god-awful class and I can't imagine a more fitting punishment than that. Anyway, there you have it, and why I told you, I have no idea since I swore silence with my fellow criminals and you're the first to hear me rat us out."

"I'm...flattered," Whitney said. "But really, who better to tell something like that to than a stranger? There's a certain safety in anonymity, don't you think?"

An expressive dark eyebrow drew up and he tapped his lips with his finger. Generous and firm, she had the wildest impulse to find out if those lips were as kissable as they seemed while he simply looked at her. Looking at...that wasn't quite right. He was studying her.

"What I think is," he replied, "that's an astute observation and I like the way you think."

The inflection of his tone made it without doubt the sexiest compliment she had ever received.

Lifting her drink, Whitney said brightly, "Here's to airplane confessions."

"And to charming travel companions who listen as well as they think."

As glass tapped glass, Whitney had to wonder just who this woman was, sharing a toast with a handsome stranger who was setting off all sorts of deliciously illicit thoughts in her head. As light as her head felt, she couldn't blame it on the champagne she wouldn't have dreamed of ordering a week ago. A diet soda had been more her style —a style which had gotten her nowhere but stuck in the rut she was plowing out of in high gear.

All the more reason to savor a long sip of champagne in the first-class section of a plane flying over the Caribbean Sea, with a delightful man whose sensual half smile prompted her to say, "You have a wonderful smile. It's very sincere and natural."

"Glad you like it since it's the only smile I've got."

"I don't know about that. I've seen at least three different kinds of smiles from you in the little while we've talked."

"I'm intrigued." And he was. Eric couldn't remember when he'd felt so immediately comfortable with a woman, especially one as attractive as his flight companion. Not that she was *whata babe* gorgeous, but that was part of her allure. This perfect stranger, who had somehow induced him to share a totally silly yet nonetheless condemning blight on his past, had a natural prettiness that was as unstudied as the tilt of her head, the swish of coppery brown hair over her shoulders, a bit pale but ever so touchable beneath the tropical sundress she wore, and wore well.

A very pretty package on the outside indeed. But there was more to her than that. Just as he was an observer of geographical hot spots, whose expertise had taken him to all corners of the world, he was an observer of its inhabitants and he was drawn to what he had observed so far of this woman.

She radiated a rare love of life in the way she listened, savored her champagne, and made a person feel good on an otherwise sucky day.

"I'm waiting," Eric prompted.

"For what?"

"To get my ego stroked." Oh yes, this woman most definitely had a way of inspiring a man to bare his soul. "I want to hear your take on those three smiles. If you noticed anything less than complimentary, just do me a favor and lie."

He'd made her smile again and, man, she had great teeth. Unlike his own. They weren't unsightly but he regretted putting up such a stink as a kid when his parents wanted to fit him with braces. Yet here was this pretty stranger, looking closer to beautiful by the moment, who found his smile worthy of comment.

"Okay," she said. "The first time you smiled, my impulse was to smile back. Since I didn't intend to talk to you or anyone else on this flight, consider that first smile to be disarming."

"Disarming. I like that." Her, he liked. She was different than Amy, his ex who wanted a feathered nest, not a husband who practically lived out of a suitcase and was happy to keep it that way.

"Your second smile was even better than disarming." Upon dangling the carrot she took a languorous sip from her glass and sighed in pure pleasure. "This is really good."

Eric hailed their flight attendant, took note of her name tag. "Sonja, might we have a refill, please?"

"Of course."

While Sonja was quick to top off the glass, Ms. Straight-Pearly-Whites with the knockout smile and a personality to match faintly protested, "I really shouldn't."

"Really, you should," he insisted. "After all, if one doesn't carpe the hell out of the diem, what's the use of living, right?"

She stared at the bubbles as if they were a crystal ball, before taking a small but quick drink, then with a short laugh agreed, "Right."

"Good. Now hopefully you're inebriated enough to tell me that second smile could charm the pants off a nun."

She looked over the rim of her flute and grinned. "Nope."

"And to think I've been practicing that smile since junior high, when the most it netted me was a rap on my knuckles from Sister Eustacia who surely would've been a lot nicer if she'd just gotten laid." Had he said that? Had he actually divulged his heartfelt opinion about the old grouch?

"I can't believe I said that," was all he could say to excuse his totally inexcusable comment about Sister Eustacia. "I don't know what's come over me. First I tell you about cheating in college, then I foam at the mouth about poor Sister Eustacia who had every reason and then some to hit me with her ruler in seventh grade. Here, take my book," he insisted, placing the tome on her little tray. "Even if it's not your thing it has to be an improvement over the seatmate from hell."

He hadn't meant to be funny, it was just the truth, but she threw back her head and laughed. Great as her teeth were, they had nothing on her neck. Her neck was made for stroking and kissing and…How old was he anyway? Thirty-seven supposedly, but at the moment, sixteen seemed closer to the hormonal count.

"Oh, you are fun!" she exclaimed with a light touch to his wrist. Impulsive, warm, unselfconscious, a touch so frank and frankly arousing he wanted to pull her out of her seat and land her on his lap. "That's actually the second smile I saw, a really fun, easy-in-your-own-skin kind of smile, very inviting and laid-back and…well, you get the idea. Now as for that third smile…" She slyly grinned.

"If you think I'm going to ask after embarrassing myself, no, I won't do it, I swear I will not."

"Okay." Still grinning, she offered him her magazine. Eric placed it next to his beer, glad the tray was hiding his growing response to her close, but not nearly close enough, proximity. While he pretended interest in the contents of *Cosmo*, she began to flip through his textbook.

Literally *his* textbook. Besides some much needed R and R, the purpose of this trip was to update his research on the Caribbean's volcanic activity. Even before it went to print, his findings could be subject to change. Volcanoes were unpredictable, fascinating, and potentially fatal when they took man off guard, as they were wont to do.

A lot like women.

The one beside him stirred the same adrenaline rush he got when a mountain heaved up its earthy guts, and lava flowed. Such an intensity of reaction was too rare to ignore. So was the fact that he wanted her eyes—come-hither eyes, soft and inviting and blue—to be on him rather than on his book. It wasn't a long flight and the longer their silence, the less time to get better acquainted.

Fortunately she didn't take long to comment, "What an interesting subject."

"Do you really think so?"

"A lot of it's over my head but yes, I do find this interesting. Whoever wrote the book is brilliant. I mean, complex and scientific as it is—and believe me, science was to me in school what philosophy was to you—he, or she, makes it seem approachable. I like this author's style."

"I'll be sure to pass that on the next time I see him."

"You know him?" She looked at him with surprise, looked at him with those blue-aqua eyes that reminded him of the ocean beneath. Forget the teeth, forget the neck, yes, the eyes had to be the best of her best features. As for pretty, as for beautiful, no, no, no he had been wrong about that, too. Definitely gorgeous—a catcall whistle, oooh-baby and more. "I'm impressed. Is he a colleague, a friend?"

"Let's just say we're close," Eric hedged, enjoying the unguarded sentiments this anonymity was providing him with.

"Then please tell…" she glanced at the author's name, "Dr. E. D. Townsend that—" She paused, slowly smiled. "Tell him that if his way with women is as impressive as his way with words, he must have them lined up for more than his autograph."

Eric had to wonder if it was the champagne talking, given her little "hic" and another giggle. No matter, this was one hot babe who was fanning a sensation he knew a lot about: Fire.

"Tell you what, I can always get another copy from my friend, so why don't you keep it?"

"I'd hate to put you to that bother—"

"No bother, I insist."

"In that case, I accept. I could use some extra beach reading while I'm in Dominica."

"That's my island, too. How long will you be there?"

"I'm not exactly sure." She paused, then offered, "I'm staying at a place called The Bird's Nest Lodge. In Roseau. You?"

"I'm meeting up with my brother in the Prince Rupert Bay area. No telling where he has us booked, it could be a tent." Damn. If Roseau was her stop they wouldn't be getting off at the same airport. There went suggesting they share a cab. As it now stood, they had a logistical problem and very little time left to share. "Enough about me. What brings you to the Isle of Beauty, Isle of Splendour, as the anthem goes?"

Another thoughtful pause. "I decided it was time to get out of the rat race and take a shot at having a real life. Go where I've never gone before and let adventure find me."

"Just you?" he asked to be sure.

"Just me," she confirmed.

"Solo travelers and road scholars, we must be kindred spirits. As for getting out of the rat race, you couldn't have chosen better."

"So I gathered from reading the brochures. Not too touristy, not too remote, black sand beaches, rain forests, waterfalls and crystal lakes. It sounded perfect. Of course, so did rates on a bungalow compared with other parts of the Caribbean."

Though he chuckled at her candor, something about her struck him as guarded. Or maybe it was just that he'd been so uncommonly open about himself that he wanted her to be equally forthcoming with some private revelation.

But beyond her immediate destination she didn't offer, he didn't press, and much too soon their easy banter was interrupted by the pilot announcing the plane's decent.

"Then you don't have a lot of plans lined up once you land?" he prompted.

"My plans pretty much come down to seeing what comes my way and exploring the world from a whole new perspective."

"Go. See. Do. Be. Sounds like a great plan to me. As for perspective, it's everything. We can complain because rose bushes have thorns, or rejoice because thorn bushes have roses."

"More Cicero, or did you come up with that little gem by yourself?"

"Honest Abe gets all the credit." If he was as honest himself he would be telling her she had the most gorgeous blue eyes, a mouth made for kissing, and he wanted her to be the mother of his babies. Oh yeah, that should get her running—as fast as possible to another hotel where Stalker Boy couldn't find her.

The moment was lost, their time had run out. As glasses were collected and trays put up, he silently damned the brevity of their encounter, cut even shorter by the drone of the pilot announcing their landing at the Canefield Airport. She was getting her purse, getting to her feet, smiling as if anticipating his company, at least to the luggage pickup. Perhaps she was even thinking they might share a cab and dinner as he had earlier hoped.

Eric reluctantly stood.

"I get off at Melville Hall Airport, next stop." *Stop,* his brain shouted, *stop her from leaving, stop your trite goodbyes, just say something, do something to make sure you see her again or you're gonna regret it for the rest of your life.* Where that thought came from Eric didn't know, but it was a bone deep certainty that caused him to block her exit. "Even short flights seem to take too long for me, but this one wasn't long enough. I really enjoyed talking to you." He offered his hand.

"Same here. Thanks for the book." She tucked it under her arm and met his grip. The fine hair on his nape prickled and his groin, semi-hard throughout their flight, fully extended. The connection between their eyes, their hands, was electric. Surely she felt it, too. Nonetheless she let go, glanced at the crowd lined up in the aisle behind him before saying in a breathy whisper, "By the way, about that third smile?"

"Yes?" he asked expectantly.

"That was the smile that could charm the pants off a nun." The smile she gave him was so sensually simmering, it left him speechless. As she moved past him, time ceased to exist. All he could feel was her shoulder breezing against his chest, her hip lightly brushing his erection.

Was that her sharp intake of breath he heard as she walked on, or was it his own? He was only vaguely aware of the de-boarding passengers she joined, urging her closer to the exit. And all he could do was watch as she paused, turned, waved. Desperation to find her again kicked his brain into gear and his tongue into action.

"My name's Eric," he called to her. "What's yours?"

She glanced at the book as if it might provide some inspiration for an adieu befitting their chance meeting. With the blow of a kiss, she called back, "Anonymous."

CHAPTER 3

*T*he breathtaking scenery, wrapped on either side of the taxi, was enough to steal her breath. Lush foliage, an unbelievable emerald-green, contrasted with crystal clear waves lapping against black sand. The air tasted of salt and blended with the scent of rich, fertile earth that smelled like just cut grass. Even Pierre, the spritely old taxi driver, was a delight to hear speak, a Creole patois flavoring his English.

Despite her vow to exult in each moment, Whitney knew the grandeur of all this deserved a better relishing. It made her a little sick to think of how often she'd dwelt on the past and might have beens, rather than embrace the present. But here she was, doing it again, kicking herself over a mistake she couldn't reverse.

"Anonymous," she groaned, "Whitney, how could you say something so stupid?"

"What you say?" Pierre asked, swiveling his silver-haired head to glance at her in the back seat.

Whitney's immediate reaction was to reply, "Nothing," and keep her distress to herself. But why? She could use a listening ear, and chances were they wouldn't see each other again.

A lot like her and Eric.

Whitney leaned over the front seat, not wanting Pierre to take his eyes off the road. Short as her life expectancy was, she didn't want to give up what she had left with a plunge over the ribbon of cliff the taxi was hugging.

"Tell me, Pierre, have you ever done something you thought was clever only to realize you'd give anything not to have done it?"

"Sure," he admitted. "We all think we so smart sometimes then see we not smart at all." He took a dark, weathered hand off the wheel long enough to give a pat to hers, draped over the beat-up vinyl upholstery. "What you do? You tell Pierre and he won' tell nobody, he swear."

Sympathy from a stranger. Before today she'd tended to shy away from people she didn't know, and wasn't quick to open up to those she did. How many friends had she failed to make because she hadn't reached out or met someone halfway?

"I screwed up, Pierre." His understanding nod was all the incentive she needed to go on. "I met this incredible man on the plane. There was something between us I can't even describe and—and he felt it too, I know he did."

"Ah, *frappeé par le foudre*," Pierre said knowingly. "Struck by the lightning."

"That's exactly how it felt. I looked in his eyes and my head actually had this strange tingle and we were talking and laughing and I felt like I'd known him all my life. I thought he was getting off the plane with me, but it turned out he was flying to another part of the island, someplace in the Prince Rupert Bay area. I could tell he didn't want to say goodbye, either, the way he kept standing there until I made myself go on and…"

A shiver went through her. The sensation when he gripped her hand—she could still feel it. And then, the brush of her arm to his chest, the press of her hip to his pants. He had been hard, hard for her. Just thinking about it created that hot sliding response all over again, reminding her that she was still very much alive.

She could feel her cheeks flare when Pierre observed, "This man, he touch you."

"Yes," she whispered.

"And his touch, it like fire, no?" At her nod, he concluded, "You have the magic. You must see him again."

"If only I could. The problem is, we'd had this conversation about feeling safer with strangers sometimes than people you know and so when he asked me my name, I didn't tell him." *Why?* Pierre seemed pretty sharp about such stuff; maybe he had some insights. "What would make me throw away a chance to see him again?"

"The heart," Pierre tapped his chest, "it know only two things." The taxi slowed as they neared the main guest house made of stucco and wood. It nestled cozily in the shadow of a mountain and near the river where her private bungalow should be. "Love and fear. That all the heart know, just love and fear."

"Then you think I was afraid?"

"Could be."

"But what's to be afraid of?" Besides death, that was.

They rolled to a stop and as Pierre turned to her, she saw the wisdom of the ages in his brown, brown eyes. "Love."

Whitney considered that. For all of two seconds.

"Love takes time, Pierre. It doesn't happen in an hour or even a month. Maybe in fairy tales, but not in real life."

"With love, anything possible. Could be your heart know something the head say 'no' to and it make you so scared, you run away."

It had been a very long day and this conversation was taking the last of her energy. She suddenly felt too tired to think beyond getting checked in and hitting the sack.

"I left the way I did because I wanted him to remember me," she decided. "I wanted to be one of those women who enter and exit a man's life with their mystique intact and live on forever in his mind." It had been a form of immortality she couldn't resist. Made sense.

After a shrug that seemed to imply "So you say, but sounds like bullshit to me," Pierre opened her door. As he retrieved her suitcase from the trunk of his seen-better-days cab, Whitney couldn't help but wonder how much wisdom he'd dispensed to other riders like herself, heading to a new destination while seeking some guidance as to which way to go.

Despite her need to rest, she was sorry when Pierre deposited her bags in the terra-cotta tiled entry, and with a simple farewell, turned to leave.

"Wait," she called, reaching into her purse. "I need to pay you."

"No charge," he said, waving aside the bills she held out. "But I let you buy gas if you want to go to Prince Rupert Bay area. He probably in Portsmouth. I take you there and we drive till you find him."

"I can't do that!"

"Why such a big no?"

"Because..." Because she was too tired? Or maybe because there was such a thing as *frappée par le foudre* or love at first sight? Not that she would ever know. An affair she could have, but the love boat had sailed before she'd had the chance to climb on board. Love, the kind she had once dreamed about, was for the living, not the dying, even if they needed love the most. "Because he was meeting his brother and they could be hiking in the mountains for all I know. Besides, I don't even know his last name and...just because."

"See?" Pierre drawled with a shake of his finger in the direction of her chest. "You scared. Look in your heart, you know why. Be brave and we go find him."

Fatigue washed over her and she wasn't certain which was the more to blame—the illness itself or the deep sense of loss she felt for the second time today as she hugged Pierre goodbye.

After checking in and getting her key to Bungalow #1, she wheeled her partially filled suitcase out of the main villa where most of the guests had rooms. She had been too busy taking care of details to do much shopping. Her new sexy wardrobe consisted of two sundresses, a pair of swim shorts with a tank top, a pretty pink bra, some white silk hip-hugger panties, and a box of condoms she had brazenly purchased last minute at the nearest Walgreens.

A handful of patrons sipped tropical drinks at the outdoor cantina she passed as she followed a faded arrow sign pointing in the direction of Bungalow #1 and Bungalow #2.

Lush foliage hugged the path to her very own front porch with a macramé swing, potted palms, a weathered rattan settee with fat, muslin cushions. The raised wooden porch slightly creaked beneath her feet; the floor that greeted her inside was an aged bamboo, covered with a bright red rug. Her small living room was simply but delightfully furnished with a breezy tropical motif. So was the efficiency kitchen. In the few hotels she'd stayed in she had immediately made use of the closet and dresser, making it her home away from home even if for only a night. Now she was too exhausted to take a minute to unpack.

Whitney immediately flopped onto a blessedly comfortable mattress, fluffed both pillows under her head, and flapped a light blanket over her travel-weary body. The closest thing she had to a man in her bed was the book Eric had given her, which she promptly opened—only to just as promptly drift into a deep sleep.

When she finally stirred it was to the swish of her heart racing in her ears, her chest. Or maybe it was the sound of waves, rhythmically beating out two words:

Love. Fear. Love. Fear. Love…fear…

The image of a golden-eyed man surrounding her with warmth and laughter blended with a heavy pulse between her thighs while the echo of love…fear…slowly receded.

It was dusk, close to dark, as the remnants of an arousing yet disturbing dream left her feeling empty, alone. Strange.

"It's okay, you were just dreaming," Her voice shook. So did her hand as she reached for the lamp on the nightstand.

The bedroom, bathed in a soft glow, was all soft white and bamboo tan; an unfussy, relaxed Caribbean interior. She didn't have a watch, had sworn to herself not to even think about time or checking a clock, but the one on the nightstand called it…

Whitney unplugged the clock. She opened the drawer of her nightstand and stuffed the enemy inside. A ceiling fan overhead stirred the fragrant air, as well as the pages of the book she'd conked out with. Picking up Eric's gift, she flipped through a section on seismic shifts and laser beam technology.

When that had her yawning again, she went for the pictures. Now *these* were worth staying awake for. One in particular caught her attention. Not because of the smoke rising out of a crater, but because the person who'd struck a pose nearby looked familiar.

The caption beneath confirmed it.

She read his name again, just to be sure, and yes, there it was, Dr. Eric D. Townsend, the author himself, a leading expert in the field of volcanology.

Her gaze settled on his face and what she felt was...

Fire. That's how it had felt when he touched her. It's what she felt now, just looking at his picture. Pierre was right. She had been afraid. Afraid to play with fire. So little time left, she couldn't squander it on fear.

Somehow she had to find Eric. But it was dark and despite her nap, she was still tired.

Her stomach growled. She hadn't eaten since breakfast unless she counted champagne and an eye candy man.

Whitney peeled herself off the bed, freshened up, and left the bungalow, book in hand. The path leading to the main villa was enveloped by all manner of wildflowers, tangled vines and reaching trees. Exotic. Untamed. A little spooky alone at night.

"Everyone comes into the world alone and they die alone," she reminded herself. "Think of it as practice." She made herself take the first step, then the next, imagining that Eric would be waiting where she could just make out a line of tiki torches and hear a reggae beat.

Of course he wasn't at the outdoor cantina she passed. Or in the cozy, coastal dining room filled with fragrant hibiscus. But here she was, taking risks she never would have dared before, like ordering *crapaud* instead of shrimp scampi.

As she dined on mountain frogs, surprisingly delicious, Eric's book proved good company. The passion he brought to his text made Whitney wonder if he was an equally passionate lover.

She plucked the little umbrella from her mai tai, stuck it between the open pages, and closed the book with a wistful sigh.

Eric had been all over the world. As exotically handsome and personable as he was, he'd surely had women throwing themselves at him from every corner of the globe, probably picked up all kinds of bedroom tricks.

She wasn't worldly or successful, and as for sexual experience, she was embarrassingly limited—thanks to her Southern Baptist mother drumming it into her head that nice girls didn't and bad girls did. Mama had been bad once, that much she knew as a by-product of a shot-gun wedding that had ended worse than bad.

Well, Mama had made her own mistakes and the good daughter was entitled to make some herself while there was still time enough to make them. She just needed to add some juice to her squeeze with a plan of seduction before going on a potential wild goose chase around the entire Prince Rupert Bay area in search of Eric.

Tomorrow she would rest up, make a plan. The day after? No excuses.

"Hi. I noticed you were sitting alone and I wondered if you'd like to join me in the cantina for an after-dinner drink?"

Whitney made herself smile at the man who was attractive enough, but something about his tight fitting black jeans and the gold necklace against an open white shirt displaying a carpet of curly black chest hair suggested it was time to make an early exit.

"Thanks for the offer, but I'm calling it a night."

"Then what about tomorrow, make it an early happy hour instead?" Before she could answer he rushed to add, "My name's Richard Kincaid. Dick to my friends, so that's Dick to you, too. Mind if I join you?"

He pulled out a chair and Whitney sprang to her feet. Gripping Eric's book to her like some talisman to ward off a tropical snake, she quickly said, "Have to get my beauty sleep, bye!" and made her escape.

Whitney was halfway out of the restaurant when she realized she'd left her mai tai behind. She really wanted to finish it, maybe while she soaked in the tub. Normally she'd just cut her losses rather than return to a table where she had probably come off a little rude. Then again, if anyone was rude, it was Dick, sending her running from her own table.

With an assertiveness she'd always longed to have, Whitney squared her shoulders, returned to the table, and retrieved her glass from Dick, who apparently intended to dump the remains into his mouth.

"I believe that's mine," she told him. Boy, did it feel good to stand up for her right to drink her own drink and spend the evening as she pleased! Forget calling it a night, she wanted her table back.

Sitting back down, she said with a crisp politeness, "Actually, Dick, I'm not ready to leave, but I would appreciate you doing so yourself. The truth is, I have a date later. You should hit on someone else." She took a sip, then two. "By the way, you might want to tone down the bling and work on another pick-up line to up your chances elsewhere."

Dick held up his hands, gave her a thoughtful look. "You sound like my sister."

"You should listen to your sister. She's a smart girl."

"Yeah," he conceded. "You, too. I wish more women would say what they really think. It would save us guys a lot of second-guessing about what's really going on in your pretty heads."

Pretty girls turn heads. Me and my bitches break necks. Whitney couldn't remember where she'd seen that quote, maybe on a poster when she visited the French Quarter in New Orleans, a hop-skip-and a jump from Mobile, and yet a world away.

She should visit New Orleans again and let the good times roll. There might be time still before the clock ran out, but for the time being she was reclaiming her space with a self-empowered, "Good-night, Dick."

Well, Whitney thought as he left, what a revelation! Not only did Dick seem to respect her more, she felt better about herself. The positive changes she'd made in her life in a matter of days were no less than amazing.

Seducing a worldly man had once been the stuff of fantasies, but her growing lust for life wanted nothing to do with that. Fantasizing wasn't enough. She wanted, needed, the real thing, and Whitney Smith was going after it the day after tomorrow.

CHAPTER 4

"*A*re we having fun yet?"

"Huh? Oh sure, this is great, Adam." Eric hoped his reply didn't sound as distracted as he felt. Despite evidence to the contrary, he was still on yesterday's plane rather than chilling with his brother whom he hadn't seen in nearly a year. "Ready to do some more snorkeling? The scenery's beautiful down there."

"It's not bad up here, either." Adam nodded toward a topless sunbather, lying on her stomach, her breasts partially visible from the sides. "I think I want to come back as a beach towel in my next life. To be exact, that beach towel in this one. She's hot, isn't she?"

After a glance at the sunbather in question, Eric shrugged. "She's okay."

"Okay?" Adam repeated, his perfectly chiseled features a portrait of curiosity.

Though he made his living as a model, Eric knew his younger brother thought such physical perfection to be more of a liability than not. Perhaps that's why he'd never been envious or wanted to trade bodies despite some very unattractive scarring beneath the tank top he wouldn't be taking off before diving in. Nobody wanted their nice day on the beach marred by a bared back that resembled a raw piece of bacon.

As Eric reached for his goggles, Adam casually asked, "So, what's her name?"

Gazing into the horizon of endless sky and sky-blue sea, all Eric could see were her eyes, her unforgettable face; in the gentle lapping of the waves to shore he heard her lilting laughter. The reactive clutch in his groin and uptick in his chest left no doubt as to the mystery lady's ongoing hold.

"I wish I knew," he replied with a heavy sigh. "She got off in Roseau and wouldn't tell me when I asked. Maybe because I had foot-in-mouth disease the whole time we were together."

"You?" Adam scoffed. "I don't believe it."

"Believe it. And the funny thing is, I was having the time of my life hearing her laugh, so I didn't even care if I was making a fool of myself—until she walked off." Eric lifted a handful of sand and watched it trickle through his fist like so much time in an hourglass. "She worked some kind of mojo on me, bro. I can't get her out of my head."

"Did I just hear what I think I heard?" Adam wiggled a finger in his ear as if to unclog whatever must be affecting his hearing. "Can it be that Indiana Spock is crushing on a girl?"

"Indiana Spock only crushes on a goddess."

While Adam ribbed him some more Eric let him have his fun. He didn't mind the silly nickname since his logical nature often clashed with his Indiana Jones thirst for adventure. But neither persona was a hopeless romantic who lost their hearts along with their heads.

Like Spock and Indiana, he was too analytical for that. Unlike them, however, his thirst for knowledge extended to his one quarter Asian ancestry and a fascination with certain intimate activities his research had turned up regarding what went on behind closed doors in ancient China. Nothing he would discuss with his beloved Grandmother Ming, of course. Or his half-Chinese, half-American mother, married to his four star general dad. God no!

As for Amy...he couldn't deny that his intellectual curiosity, which had extended into sexual experimentation, had contributed to their divorce.

Nevermind it was monogamous; he wasn't into swinging.

Nevermind he was a scientist of the highest order who saw an opportunity to infuse some variables into their love life once things started to go stale—only for Amy to groan, "Are you kidding me? You want to do *what?* That's just weird."

He was amply chagrined to let the subject drop. So much for The Art of the Bedchamber, as the ancients called it, with the wife who had finally split the sheets with him five years ago. Other lovers had followed with more than enough interest, but something was always missing. Maybe that was the Indiana in him, along with the Spock, holding out for a soulmate/bedmate he'd begun to think didn't exist.

Until yesterday. Their meeting was so brief, yet he couldn't stop thinking about every insightful word out of her beautiful mouth, her lilting laughter at all his faux pas, the light in her eyes that made a rising Caribbean sun look dim, while the sweet slope of her jawline, the fine arch of her neck, led his gaze to the scooped top of a sundress where she placed a hand over her—

A punch to his shoulder was followed by Adam raising his beer bottle in a salute. "Here's to your goddess, my man."

With a tap of bottle to bottle, Eric took a swig, choked, and spit the gritty foam out. Swiping the back of his arm over his mouth, he demanded, "Did you put sand in my beer?"

Adam roared. "I didn't have to, you were doing just fine by yourself! The whole time I'm talking you're staring out at the water and sifting sand, over and over—straight into your beer!"

And with that, Adam started packing up the cooler. "So what are you waiting for? Get off your ass and go find her." Parroting their highly decorated father when his two military brats got out of line, Adam snapped, "Hop to and that's an order!"

Eric sprang to his feet, put up his fists and did his best De Niro, *"Are you talking to me?"*

They feigned a few punches before Eric slapped Adam on the back. "Sure you don't mind me leaving you on your own?"

"Nah. But if the lady loses any of her mojo, I'll be around for another week before I take off for the next assignment."

"Paris?"

"*Oui.*"

Since Adam didn't mention Jolene, Eric didn't ask. Theirs was one of those turbulent on-again-off-again relationships he'd never understood. It was as if they were hooked on the chemistry between them—never mind it kept going bad. Which it obviously had, again, given Adam's offer.

"You take the Jeep and I'll introduce myself to the babe. I'm sure she won't mind keeping me company while you find that goddess who makes her look just okay."

It was dusk when Eric pulled up to The Bird's Nest Lodge. The whole time he'd driven, his heart had been racing. It was still going a mile a minute as he got out of the jeep and approached the front desk in the main villa. "Anonymous" had mentioned a bungalow. It would be irresponsible of management to direct him to the quarters of a single woman whose name he didn't even know. Which meant his best course of action was to simply become a guest himself, and how fortuitous they had a vacancy—in Bungalow #2.

He took a detour to the lodge's restaurant—she wasn't there—before surveying an outdoor cantina. It resembled an overgrown tiki hut where a reggae band set up for the night's entertainment and a small crowd sipped tropical cocktails. No luck there either.

As he walked past lit torches then down a shadowy path leading to Bungalows #1 and #2, Eric considered his next move. He parked his things inside his cabin, flipped on the porch light, and sat on the stairs so anyone around could see him. He wasn't very good at waiting. It was simply a part of his nature he would always have to work on.

"Knowing others is intelligence; knowing yourself is true wisdom," he whispered by rote. "Mastering others is strength; mastering yourself is true power."

Lao Tzu had that right. Eric deeply admired the wisdom dispensed by the ancient Chinese philosopher, and as a devoted world student he agreed with Lao that *"A good traveler has no fixed plans and is not intent on arriving."*

So much for that. He had arrived. Now he needed a plan.

A sweet smelling breeze that hinted of nearby water moved through the palms. Their big, leafy paddles of green shifted to reveal a light twinkling of lights strung past the far side of the first cabin, the one to his right. And there, in the middle of the lights, Eric noticed another path had been carved with just enough illumination to see where it might lead.

Knowing himself all too well, he didn't wait to find out.

The river after dark was a tad too cool, but it soothed the heat of Whitney's skin. Time, which she'd become all too aware of in her determination to ignore its march, had ceased to exist as she'd basked in the sun earlier in the day on a deserted stretch of sand.

The outing had been a tonic for her. She felt better than she had in ages. Of course it had been ages since she'd taken a day off to do nothing but pamper herself. Reading, resting, eating without a care to calories, and thinking of Eric while she planned her grand seduction —that was her whole day. Unfortunately she hadn't gotten further with her plan than fingering the card Pierre had given her to call for his taxi, deciding to wear the other sundress Eric hadn't seen along with her new underwear, and bringing along her box of condoms from Walgreens.

Oh, what the hell, she would call for Pierre in the morning and wing it from there. For now she was still pleasantly buzzed from the two mai tai cocktails that had encouraged her to return to the river minus a flashlight, only the glow of the moon and some distant lights that had clicked on in the direction of her bungalow to lead her back.

Tho...whatever would possess her to leave when no one was around to see her do something she'd always secretly wanted to try?

Such a no-no in her previously up-tight, do everything right according to Mama's world.

Whitney peeled off her tank top, flung it to the shore. It landed near the big beach towel she'd been sitting on. Next came the swim shorts, *plop*, hitting the terrycloth guest robe she'd found hanging in the closet.

The river slid like liquid silk against her skin. Gliding along on her back, her bare breasts bathed in moon glow, she felt like a water nymph, some magical being of the fairy tales she had loved reading in her youth. Only now she was part of the story, making it her own, and singing "Twinkle, twinkle" to the glittering stars overhead.

It was a glorious nude awakening she would remember for however long forever might be. Refusing to let the inevitable steal her joy, she plunged down, touched sand, and surged up with a pretty shell in her hand. Whitney kissed it then flung it skyward with a wish she could sail as free into the mighty unknown. She whipped her hair back and fro so it stung her cheeks. Her nipples dripped water and beaded up as fresh island air licked their tips. They were cold. How good would it feel to have a man's mouth, Eric's mouth, lave one and then the other with a warm tongue?

She shivered. A gentle breeze whispered over the chill of her exposed flesh. She pretended it was a human touch rather than air caressing her as she emerged from the river, her arms raised to give alms to the night sky that had witnessed her private pleasure.

Skinny dipping. Check. Off the bucket list she hadn't realized until tonight deserved to be on it.

Foregoing the wet clothes she had stripped off, Whitney picked up her robe, slipped it on, and was about to tie the sash at her waist when her hands froze.

She was not alone.

She could smell the scent of citrus and spice he'd worn on the plane, carried on the light breeze. She could hear the sand shift as his feet stopped mere inches from her bare toes. So close, her head tipped back to meet his searching gaze.

And then there was silence. A silence so absolute that the world seemed filled with the catch of her breath as his hands slowly lifted to her face and touched her as if she were made of the most delicate porcelain.

Somehow her hands found their way to his face as well. The amber flecks in his irises nearly disappeared into the dilation of his pupils. Smoke in his eyes, in the pleased curve of knowing lips. He had seen her, for how long she did not know, but he had seen her as no one else had before.

They spoke in some silent language that went beyond the explicable. Without hesitation or even awareness beyond the rightness of how he felt, her palms slid over the sloping plane of hard muscle and crisp cotton covering his shoulders.

His fingertips slid down, over her throat, then further to the slight gape of her robe. She thought he would part it and yes she would let him...only for Eric to pull her lapels together as his mouth descended.

Is it all right that I'm doing this? Was what she heard in that tentative, first brush.

She answered with a deeper press of her own lips, slightly parting, breathing him in. He tasted of mint and lemon, tasted divine, as they embarked on an earnest search of just who they were getting to know.

He was a playful tease, a curious seeker, thoughtful of his findings while urging her to do some exploring herself. His mouth was as warm and inviting as home, yet had an exotic taste, a chameleon texture that was alternately sleek and rough and made her feel as if she were courting danger.

She wanted the danger.

Whitney twined her fingers in his hair—so thick, soft, lustrous. Then that wasn't enough and she hungrily roamed her hands over the expanse of his back. His skin, she wanted to touch it, feel flesh and muscle under her palms. She released one, then two buttons of his shirt, and was going for the third, wondering if she dared go for his belt as well, when his hands were suddenly on hers, stopping her in mid-release, urging her arms around his neck.

Had she done something wrong? Whitney eased up on her kissing and as if divining her thoughts he moved his lips to her ear and whis-

35

pered, "The way you touch me, I love it a little too much to stop if this goes any further."

She could feel the quick, steady beat of his heart pressed against her chest. And his hips, flush against her belly, imparted the assurance that he was very much a man. One who wanted her as much as she did him.

How much time passed as they stood there in the sand with her arms looping his neck and his hugging her waist while he breathed deep and she struggled to catch her breath, Whitney had no idea. It didn't matter anyway since she would gladly stay in this moment for an eternity and beyond.

"Since I met you on the plane," he said, softly breaking the silence, "all I've been able to think about is you and damn myself for letting the most unforgettable woman I've ever met get away. I must've thought of a thousand different things I wished I'd said or asked, but for the life of me I can't remember what they were. Except for just one question."

Whitney cupped his cheek, stroking the shadow that had lightly abraded her skin. "And just what would that question be, Dr. Townsend?"

He pressed a lingering kiss to the center of her palm, then gave her that smile that could charm the pants off a nun.

"Besides Anonymous, have you got a name?"

CHAPTER 5

*T*he woman who had haunted his thoughts for nearly two days now had a name.

"Whitney," he whispered. Her name emerged as intimately as the quieter setting they had retreated to after a shared dinner of tapas, wine, and non-stop conversation in town.

Their two bungalows shared a small courtyard illuminated by a full moon, distant tiki torches, and a flickering taper candle in the middle of a small outdoor table. She sat across from him, the fragrance of tiger lilies gently blowing through her untamed mane of river bath hair. Her shoulders were draped with a light shawl, accentuating the heart-shaped bodice that covered perfect pale breasts, the perfect everything he had seen as she sang to the stars then kissed a shell and sent it sailing before she emerged like Aphrodite from the water, arms raised to the sky.

Conscience had dictated he not steal more than a glance but he'd been held in thrall, consumed by a rush he could only liken to a full body orgasm, circulating around vein and muscle and rocketing through his brain. Just looking at her now, he still felt high.

"Penny for your thoughts," she said, sliding a hand over his.

"You'd have to pay me a million to incriminate myself like that."

She raised a finely shaped brow. "You saw me."

"It wasn't intentional, but yes. I did. It was a moment that not even a lobotomy could make me forget."

Back went her head to better expose her neck and out came that amazing laugh of hers. Whitney didn't seem to take life, or herself, too seriously. A quality he greatly admired, he couldn't always say the same for himself.

He was, in fact, ready to have a more serious conversation.

"If you had seen me in the same state of undress you wouldn't forget it either, but not for the same reason. And not in a good way." Yes, better to get it out in the open and not wait to ruin the perfect moment when it happened. They were going to sleep together and both of them knew it. "There was a reason I stopped you from unbuttoning my shirt. I had an accident in the field about five years ago. Galeras, in Columbia. I lost several close colleagues to an unexpected eruption. I got lucky. But you should be aware that I've had a number of skin graft operations on my back."

"Does it hurt?" One of her hands squeezed his.

"Only to look at. That's why I always wear an undershirt, unless I'm alone."

She looked away in thought, then directly at him. "But what if I asked you to make an exception. Would you?"

"For you?" He gave a curt nod but quickly warned, "It's something I would caution you against asking, however. Fire and flesh don't make nice companions."

She passed a fingertip through the candle's flame then put her finger to his lips. "Maybe I like playing with fire."

Eric caught her wrist. "Careful. Curiosity is not without its consequences." He nipped her fingertip to let her know he meant business. "Just ask the cat. And I don't mean the one that ate the canary."

"Are you trying to frighten me away?"

"Hardly. There's just a lot you don't know about me yet. And there's everything I still want to learn about you." He raised his hand and she did the same, meeting him in a parallel connection, fingertip to fingertip, palm to palm. "Who are you, Whitney Smith?"

Who are you?

Whitney studied the contrast of her soft, lighter skin to a man's who was deepened by a love of the outdoors. She wished she had an answer for Eric, but what could she say when she didn't know herself? Over dinner she had told him some dressed up basics—that she was living off an inheritance and had been in the book distribution business before deciding it was time to reinvent her life.

She could tell Eric many things, but not that her life would be dwindling to an end while his continued on. If he knew she was sick, he wouldn't see her as the healthy, vibrant woman he thought her to be. And for now, that's who she was. It made no difference who she had been. That woman was gone.

"Who am I?" Whitney repeated, having found an answer that was true enough. "I am becoming."

He tilted his head, studied her with undisguised fascination. "And just who or what are you becoming?"

"I am becoming who I want to be and charting my course as I go to get there."

"And do you know where 'there' is—where you want to arrive?"

"Not yet." She suddenly recalled a quote she'd seen stenciled on the wall of an import store. The reason it had stuck with her was because it seemed so ridiculously bohemian. Now she got it. Boy did she. "But even if the writing's on the wall when I find out, 'A good traveler has no fixed plans—'"

"'And is not intent on arriving.' Lao Tzu." He shook his head in disbelief. "What you just said, it's...wow. You amaze me."

Whitney proceeded to amaze herself with what popped out next. "Just stick around and there's no telling what I'll become."

"Oh, believe me, I'm sticking around," he assured her. "When I look at your mouth I can hardly think, and then you say something like that and all I can do is think."

"About what?"

"Stick around if you want to find out. Care to dance?"

He was out of his chair and pulling her from hers before she could form a reply. She'd thought most men didn't like to dance, and most of her own practice was limited to solo moves with the radio playing. Now a bass guitar was joined by a keyboard, the beat of a bongo in the background, a soulful croon emerging from the cantina. Her feet were awkward at first, only to seemingly sprout wings as a man who definitely knew how to move firmly turned her this way and that until she found her own rhythm and swayed sinuously against him. Some part of her brain insisted she was tired but Whitney told it to shut up, she would dance until she dropped before losing a moment of the magic they were making together.

The magic continued until the music stopped several dances later. She was breathless and giddy when her feet left the ground. Eric held her in his arms as if she were weightless, her body the substance of air.

"I don't mean to be presumptuous, but the band seems to have packed up and what's left of the night will seem even longer if you prefer that, for tonight at least, we go our separate ways." He nodded in the direction of her bungalow #1, then his next door. "Your choice."

She didn't want the night to end and she did not want to sleep alone. But it did take two for a night of wild passion and the fact of the matter was, she did feel ready to drop.

"Would you be open to a compromise?" she asked.

"I'm open to anything with you."

"Then would you be willing to spend the night together as cuddle buddies and get better acquainted when we wake up?" Hoping to encourage his agreement she added, "I don't snore. At least I don't think so."

"Even if you do, consider it music to my ears."

He gave her a soft kiss and deposited her at the threshold of Bungalow #1. "You go on in and I'll get my things. Be right back."

"I'll be waiting."

CHAPTER 6

*W*hen Eric returned to Whitney's quarters half an hour later, thanks to an emergency consultation call since live volcanos did not sleep, he came to two conclusions: She was as beckoning in slumber as she was wide awake. And, despite her assurances otherwise, she did snore. Nothing loud or obnoxious, more a soft, open-mouthed deep breathing, punctuated by a cute little snort.

Putting down the satchel he'd returned with, Eric leaned over the bed and pushed aside a tangle of hair to brush a kiss to her temple. Her only response was a puff of air blown through slack lips.

She looked so vulnerable, so innocent, sleeping without awareness of his observation that her dress was on the floor, or that he lifted the covers to see a pretty pink bra and pretty white panties were still on beneath the sheets. His body's response was immediate and insistent. Lucky for Whitney he understood the value of delayed gratification. Even a guy like him who wasn't very good at waiting had come to appreciate that much with age. He was older than her, though not amply so to feel like he was robbing the cradle.

Cat's in the cradle with a silver spoon...

Her reaction to his earlier warning about the consequences of curiosity had told him something about Whitney. It wasn't anything she said but the look in her eyes. She was far more a kitten when it came to the workings of the world than she was a seasoned feline when it came to men who favored danger.

Whitney had taken a risk to ask of him what she did, but only naiveté would have compelled her to plunge into a place so dark as a yet-to-be lover's disfiguration.

Well. She had asked. And should she regret it in the light of day, the consequences would not be hers alone to pay.

His shoes were by the front door by habit, thanks to his Grandmother Ming. He tossed his shirt over Whitney's dress. Next his belt, his pants. He debated on removing his boxers. Left them on. But it was the tank top that would leave him truly naked and he wanted to give her a chance to reconsider once moonlight and wine had lost their influence.

Under the covers, his chest nuzzled the fine curve of her spine and he draped an arm around her waist to pull her even closer. God, she felt good. Familiar. Right. As much as his hands insisted he roam north and south, east and west, Eric contented himself with the pure sweetness of spooning the woman he instinctively knew was destined to be far more than a bedmate.

Mmm...Such a marvelous sensation. Whitney felt as if she were floating on feathers while the tingles in her neck tripped down her spine. Her skin felt slick, warm, gliding through a tunnel of rubs. Or was it a tunnel of love? Kisses, husky murmurs, stolen touches in the dark...yes, she must be in one of those love tunnels at the fair. She'd always wanted to ride in one of those boats, they'd seemed so romantic.

Only how had she gotten here? And why did the light filter onto her eyelids? Was the ride over already?

If so, the kisses weren't stopping, the murmurs were getting closer, and the stolen touches were becoming bolder as they moved up her legs. Surely her date wasn't touching her panties! But he was and she was letting him, not even a whimper of protest when he slid a palm between the knees she should clamp closer together since she wasn't that kind of girl.

But it felt so good, better than anything she'd ever felt before and maybe she was that kind of girl because she obeyed his whispered command to, "Relax, *yuan-pao*, your scarlet pearls are safe with me."

Yuan-pao? Scarlet pearls?

Wherever she was, it was not the Tunnel of Love, though she felt loved by the hand that was palming the barrier of a very moist pair of panties she was urgent to take off.

Another whisper in her ear stopped her in mid-peel.

"Sorry if I woke you up...actually, no, I'm not sorry at all. Good morning, kitten. How did you sleep?"

His breath smelled like fresh mint. Her own tasted like the dregs of dinner and drink. *Ugh.* So disgusting!

"I need to brush my teeth." On automatic pilot she started to spring from the bed only for Eric to land her back on the mattress and plant a morning kiss on her morning mouth.

"Umm," he decided once he was done with the kiss she hadn't returned, "Tastes as good as last night to me, but if you're determined to freshen up, have a sip of my *ling-chih* tea. Eternal life, Grandmother Ming swears by it. I have at least two cups a day. Can't hurt the way I figure, especially since she looks closer to 60 than going on 90."

Were they really having this conversation? With her panties nearly off her behind while Eric tutored her on the benefits of his Chinese grandmother's herbal tea?

Whitney took a sip. It wasn't bad, just half bad. But anything that even hinted at a promise of enteral life? Sign her up.

She gulped down the remains of his offered cup. And still wanted to brush her teeth. But that meant getting out of bed fully awake now and letting him watch her try to look comfortable prancing around in her underwear to the adjoining bathroom.

As free and breezy as she'd felt the night before, the morning after wasn't proving quite as comfortable in her New Whitney skin.

Eric retrieved the empty cup, placed it on the nightstand where she had stuffed the bedside clock inside a drawer that now shared space with her box of condoms.

"I've traveled the world," he told her, "But damn if I can remember ever seeing anything as breathtaking as Whitney in the morning. And for the record, I have a very good memory."

"Eric, I..." She had no idea what she was going to say.

He saved her the trouble by placing her right hand on his chest. "Feel that?"

What she felt was his steady heartbeat beneath a light growth of dark chest hair, mostly covered by a clean white tee-shirt that had somehow acquired the ugly connotation of "wife beater."

"I don't tend to sleep too well, not since 'the event' with Galeras. After losing three of my best friends, and coming very close to joining them, I lost my marriage, too. And I don't blame Amy for it, just to keep everything honest between you and me. But last night, when I came back here thinking something might happen that didn't, it turned out that something even better did. I curled up behind you and before I knew it, I was out like a light, had the best sleep I've had in years. No nightmares. No night sweats. I don't know if I dreamed. All I know is that you excite me like crazy, then you give me peace—and on a personal level that ranks right up there with discovering quantum theory."

The need to cleanse her mouth was suddenly paltry in the scheme of this wake-up call from a man who had nearly died and had no idea she was walking in the same green mile shoes he had narrowly escaped. But even if he could commiserate more than most, had unknowingly provided her with the perfect opportunity to purge the secret she was desperate to share with someone who would under-stand, she would not tell him. To do so would completely change everything between them and she was not about to rock the boat before they set sail.

Seeking the common ground they could safely share, Whitney unhooked her bra. The ease she felt was remarkable as she bared her breasts without the painful shyness she had always felt washing up after a gym class in a girls-only shower. No wonder she had yet to strip down for a man.

"My god, you're beautiful," he whispered.

"Your turn," she whispered back.

While his gaze remained locked on her breasts, his hands hesitated to pull off his own white cotton.

"Let me." And she did.

His chest was perfect. Worthy of a Michelangelo carving.

He tipped up her chin so their eyes met, his questioning, hers as certain as her short nod. He turned, showed her his back.

She managed to stifle the immediate gasp that surely would have escaped had he not warned her.

It was bad. A patchwork travesty of what had no doubt once been as perfect as his chest.

Whitney traced what looked like a map of various continents pieced together to form a Salvador Dali view of the world.

She laid her cheek against the skin he always kept covered but had revealed to her. It had been important somehow that he would grant her an intimacy that he did not share with others. Even once she was gone, perhaps he would never make himself as vulnerable to another woman as he just had with her.

"You're too kind," he finally said, his voice gruff.

"No," she told him. "It's not kindness. It's want."

"Of this?" He turned and his face was etched in pained lines, as if she had offered pity to the proud. "Whitney, how could anyone want such an unsightly thing? I don't need your sympathy, and even less do I want your lies."

Yes, she had lied about herself, and to herself. But at least she hadn't lied about this. "You can't tell me what I do or don't want, and what I want is you. Not the abbreviated version you show to everyone else. I want all of you—especially what no one else sees."

Then she did something so unlike her old self, it was like watching another woman take over her body and pull down her panties, throw them to the floor.

She insistently tugged at his waistband. And then she wasn't thinking, not thinking at all. He had her back to the mattress and was straddling her hips. His boxers were still on but did little to restrain his protrusion.

"You want all of me?"

She managed a nod.

"Better be careful what you ask for little girl because it just might be more than you bargained for."

Why she had thought her outreach of compassion would be met by a more sanguine response, Whitney didn't know. What she did know, as his underwear joined hers, was that if she had a major deflowering on her bucket list, this would be one check mark that deserved at least three. Maybe breakfast at Tiffany's could be deleted. Climbing a pyramid in Egypt, too.

But then he did something unexpected again. Just when she was sure he would pounce and plunge, Eric moved to the end of the bed and grasped her left foot. He began to massage it, focusing on areas that shot straight up her leg and into her groin. Languorous moans that sounded like they belonged in an X-rated movie came out of her throat and she tried to retain some dignity by not writhing all over the bed in response. When her best attempts proved futile, he turned his attention to her right foot, and once the same results were had, he worked his way up from there.

At some point she had closed her eyes, had given up any pretext of control, but when his mouth came down between her legs and his finger crooked to hit a point of no return, her eyes snapped opened. Only to nearly roll back into her head as she grabbed wildly at his hair and shrieked, "Oh! My! God!"

She was still shaking when his head lifted and so did his body, until it lay flush over hers.

His eyes, in the morning light, were like prisms of a palate, and his voice, a quiet respite assuring her, "I'm no god. I'm just a man. One who's made his share of mistakes. But you, *yuan-pao,* are not amongst them."

That name again. *Yuan-pao.*

Before she could find the coherence to ask him what it meant, his hand found her again while his mouth latched onto a breast that didn't give a damn what he called her.

Whitney forgot about God. She forgot about dying. She forgot about everything except the man responsible for her cry of: *"Eric!"*

CHAPTER 7

*T*he waves increased in momentum and dizzying velocity as he pressed firmly and rubbed against a spot so sensitive that she felt as if she were imploding.

She heard herself wailing an almost inhuman sound and her nails were like talons, clawing blindly at his shoulders while her heels pounded the mattress until she was certain there would be nothing of her left but a heap of bones if he didn't stop.

"Enough," she gasped. "Please, I can't take any more."

Eric stopped and simply held her, limp in his arms, until her breathing was almost normal. But once it was, he kissed her hand and urged it down.

"Touch me," he told her.

She gave a tentative first pump. His skin was warm and soft; cloaking what was hard and faintly pulsing beneath. She didn't have a lot of practice at this but all those romance novels she'd read were highly instructive. And, as it turned out, so was he—until Eric suddenly gripped her wrist.

Whitney felt his contractions in her hand; she felt a surging thrill within herself. Power, that's what she felt, knowing it was she who made his eyes close tight; it was she who was responsible for his face pinched into a grimace suggesting pain, though it was obviously rapture that she, yes she, was giving him.

She had never seen a man orgasm before. It was truly a riveting sight. One that propelled her gaze down. He was still, very quiet, and his erection was no longer quite so erect. But he wasn't as flaccid as she expected him to be and strangely, no fluids were to be seen.

And then she thought no more of it. All that mattered was the way Eric held her, so close and tight against him that she felt a oneness that neither words, nor touch, could capture.

With the sort of awe reserved for the Sistine chapel, he whispered, "I think I just died and went to heaven."

Whitney knew such a statement should depress her, but Eric looked so sublime she was more inclined to savor the moment, albeit with a bit of black humor.

"If that's what going to heaven is like, I can hardly wait."

"And I can't wait at all for a proper good-morning kiss."

A brief one and Whitney turned her head. "You taste funny."

"I taste like you and you taste like nectar. Look at what you do to me."

Look she did, only to see him defy the laws of nature. Her throat felt a little dry as she imagined accommodating what was bound to be uncomfortable at first, maybe even a little painful. Hopefully he would be too preoccupied to notice.

"Shouldn't you be smaller than this? I mean, that is normal for most men after, well afterward, so...why isn't it happening to you?"

He wound a hand through her hair and pulled until her eyes met his.

"Because, my dear, I'm not most men."

For a moment she could only wonder what she'd gotten herself into by getting into bed with Eric.

"It's an old secret from the Far East," he explained. "It goes back centuries, when Chinese emperors had lots of wives. Sometimes hundreds. When I read that some of these emperors were trained to satisfy ten of their women in a night, all I could think was, wow. *Wow.* How did they do it? How can I do it? That's what I wanted to know, so

I dug deeper until I turned up their secret. It's a mind-body technique that takes patience, discipline, and a lot of practice to perfect."

"And partners to practice with, right?" How many had Eric had? Plenty, no doubt, and she envied them all.

"Actually, it's better to practice alone, especially at first. It's easier to concentrate when there's not so much to sidetrack the attention." Softly he milked a breast.

He had a wonderful touch. Soothing, sure, arousing. Though she was obviously having the same effect on Eric by simply running a fingertip over the impressive evidence of it.

"But there is a purpose to all that practice," she persisted.

"Of course. Not that my goal was ever to have a harem."

"Then what was it?"

"To have mastery over myself, to walk a fine, disciplined line between ultimate physical pleasure and mental control that wouldn't just be to my benefit. My reasoning was, and is, that if any man had the ability to satisfy multiple lovers in a night, how much pleasure could he bring to just one? I can be a little obsessive about the things that interest me, and frankly I've yet to find a subject as fascinating as what was once called..." he paused, giving his next words a certain gravitas—"The Art of The Bedchamber."

He was watching her closely, waiting for her reaction.

She wanted to sound worldly. She wanted to sound smart. She wanted to respond as if she were in his element instead of him being in the pro leagues hitting a ball out of the park while she sat in the nose bleed stands for those who were too cheap, too poor, or too disinterested to buy a better ticket.

She was not disinterested, that was for sure.

As if an epiphany fell from the sky, Whitney recalled the Chinese fortune cookie she had cracked open a few days before her ominous summons from Dr. Clark. Little had she known just a week ago that the little scroll of paper that had tumbled out would come in so handy now.

"You know, Eric, in some of my reading I came across a bit of wisdom I think an inquiring mind like yours would appreciate:

`When the student is ready, the teacher will appear.' According to your bio, your credentials include a visiting professorship at MIT along with a lecture series that, I gather, makes you something of a rock star in the science community?"

His smile, his nod, was supremely satisfied. "Not only does she quote old Buddhist proverbs, her subtext is sly. What a smart girl you are. Now I think we should extend your vernacular." He folded her hand around his erection. "Jade stalk." Then he led her to fondle his testes. "Orchid bags."

"Jade stalk," she repeated. "Orchid bags. How—" Before she could say "poetic" the slide of his hand between her legs accompanied his whispered:

"Dark garden." He lingered long enough to make her wetter than the river she had bathed in, before slipping a finger into the passage where she ached. "Moon grotto."

She was still panting when he rolled her onto her stomach, followed by a single word: "Lesson."

As he pressed into a triangular hot spot at the small of her back, the pure pleasure that radiated from her nerve ends left no doubt she was indeed in the presence of a sensory master who was more than qualified to teach the universal laws of cause and effect.

"What are you doing?" Her voice didn't even sound like her own.

"It's called the *Ming-Meti*. Your life gate. Do you like it?"

Her response emerged more creature than human.

"I'll take that as a `yes.' Now come here. Let's talk."

"About more lessons?" She wasn't sure she had the wherewithal for another just yet as he pulled her up until she lay half-draped over him with her head on his chest.

"More lessons later. I want to talk about something more fundamental to relationships."

As if he'd hit a light switch, her languor abruptly toggled into what felt closer to alarm. How had they gone from a steamy encounter to something even more intimate? Relationships, even bad ones, represented a tie between people with past experiences and the expectation they could have more.

She darted her gaze to the nightstand where her box of condoms kept company with the clock she had unplugged. Even if she and Eric couldn't have a long-term relationship, that didn't rule out a hot and heavy fling. Flings were relationships, too. Maybe that was something she should get settled with Eric up front, make sure he understood she wasn't permanent girlfriend material, just a transient affair.

Transient affair. The thought made her wince. It cheapened something between them, whatever this thing was they were sharing while she was in the process of "becoming."

Whitney decided it was better if she just let him do most of the talking.

"Okay," she said with a feigned lightness. "Just what sort of fundamentals do you want to talk about?"

"Needs."

"Well, it seems we're doing just fine thus far in that department!"

Instead of laughing along with her, he brushed aside her hair and got right to it. "I want to make sure you realize that my intentions are sincere. And I want to be sure that we're honest with each other about what our needs might be. I didn't do very well at that in the past and I don't want to repeat my mistakes. Not with you. So, you first."

If only she could be honest and tell him her needs. *Give me hope, Eric. Give me a lifetime of laughter. Let me learn what it means to love so much it hurts. Make time go away and don't let this moment ever pass because what I feel is bliss. What do I need? I need more than you can possibly give but I'll take whatever you've got.*

"I…I'm not really sure how to answer you. Because right now, in this moment, I feel as if I have everything I could possibly need while I'm laying here with you." She smiled up at him and put the ball back in his court—though it felt closer to a ticking bomb. "What about you?"

"My needs are a little more extensive. I need to share what I've learned and explore what I haven't with a special partner. I need to be able to speak freely together and feel comfortable when there's nothing to say. I need to laugh and get crazy. I need peace and anything but. Those are my needs, not just wants."

Whitney took a steadying breath. And then another. For all the good it did since she still didn't feel steady at all. She was getting in over her head, she just knew it, and all these intimacies and lessons were bound to deepen their emotional bonds. This was dangerous. *Dangerous.*

But the new Whitney, the one she was becoming, seemed to like a little danger. She just couldn't forget the potential risk to them both if things got out of hand. But they weren't there yet. And, as it now stood, his offer was too enticing and her time too short. With so little remaining, how could she throw this away?

"Then we need the same things, Eric. Today, at least. But you never know what tomorrow might bring, so let's not look too far ahead and simply appreciate what we have for now."

"Works for me," he agreed, only to add, "For now, *yuan-pao.*"

She kissed his chest. His lips. He looked at her as if she were something priceless that had fallen from the sky and into his waiting for her, and only for her, hands.

"What does *yuan-pao* mean?"

"Prime treasure." He put index fingers and thumbs together, making a longboat-shaped sign. "Instead of ingots and bars, it's the shape gold and silver used to be cast into in China."

Silver and Gold. Their time would almost certainly run out before they could sing such carols at Christmas together. Holidays were something they wouldn't be sharing but spending the last one alone wouldn't be so bad when she could remember the day she'd been dubbed the finest riches any man or king could claim. Prime treasure.

"*Yuan-pao.* I like it."

"And I more than like what the shape symbolizes." Bending his knee then rubbing it between the apex of her thighs, he named what he touched. "The vulva. And yours, like the rest of you, is finer than gold."

The condoms she had felt so brazen buying were wrapped in gold foil. If Eric really wanted honesty, there was something she could tell him regarding the prime treasure she had tried to lose once only to regret it. She knew she had daddy issues, trust issues. Maybe if she opened up a little about those he would better understand the personal choices she had made if the truth came out that she was a 27 year old virgin—which might have proclaimed her a virtuous old maid a century ago but in today's world it just made her a *freak*.

"I think there's more you should know about me, Eric. My mother died from cancer when I was eighteen. She worked too hard and didn't play enough. My father deserted us when I was still pretty small. I don't remember much about him except that Mama cried for a long time after he left and for a long time I thought it was my fault. It took me awhile to realize he was an irresponsible jerk and we were better off without him."

"Bastard." A muscle ticked in Eric's cheek. "Do you distrust men because of him?"

"Somewhat," she admitted. "At least historically." Should she tell him that was why her hymen was still intact? That the boyfriend in college who wanted proof she loved him proved how little he loved her when he couldn't push in and she got cold feet, so he dumped her? That she hadn't trusted the few other love interests that followed, who inevitably tired of waiting and moved on, confirming her fear they would use her then lose her, just like her father had her mother?

Just as she was about to take the plunge, a phone rang.

Eric groaned. The expletive he uttered wasn't nearly as romantic as his metaphors for personal body parts.

As he grabbed a cell phone from his overnight satchel, he made his apologies. "I am so sorry, but I have to take this. There were specific instructions not to call me unless it was an absolute emergency."

CHAPTER 8

Though she couldn't hear the other end of the conversation, Eric's intense expression and muttered, "Okay…okay. People on alert? Good. No, don't send Fields in to fix it, he's got three kids. Yes, I realize time is of the essence but keep the chopper; you might need it to get out. While I get a charter plane—of course, ASAP —keep an eye on the tiltmeter data and gas readings…." told Whitney something dangerous that had to do with volcanos was going on and that dangerous something excited him. Not a "whoopie, oh boy!" sort of gladness, but an anticipation that relayed itself in his voice and taut posture as he signed off with, "On my way. Oh, and Grayson, I'll be pissed if you take that smoker on without me like you did at Kilauea."

Kilauea. In Hawaii. Where rain hitting the soot mixed up a cocktail so acidic it was between lemon juice and battery acid. Whitney remembered that from his book. She also remembered a picture of a pretty woman scientist whose name had just struck a bell.

"I can't apologize enough about this, Whitney. I'll be back as soon as I can—hopefully tonight." Leaning down, he kissed her then called the airport.

As he reached for his clothes, Whitney struggled to keep her voice casual. "So, you're going to Montserrat."

"It's only a hop, skip and a puddle jump away—which is why I'm elected despite being on vacation. Unfortunately they don't have time to get someone else in for an emergency repair on the crater."

"An emergency repair on the crater?" she repeated, laying a hand over her throat.

"Right. A seismometer shut down and it's crucial to get it up and running so we have a better chance of evacuating in time if that baby decides to throw more than another temper tantrum."

Eric was tossing on his shirt. If the worst happened, she might never again see the back it covered.

"You love the rush, don't you?"

Eric stopped in the middle of tucking his shirt into his pants. Her gaze was drawn to his open fly. He was aroused. Did the thrill of danger do that to him? Or was it a reaction to her naked body, still draped on the mattress he had abruptly deserted?

"It's addictive," he conceded. Eyes slitted, he touched the length of her with his hooded gaze. Hot. Yet coolly assessing. "And so are you."

He would stay a little longer, let her make him late for his plane even though minutes counted. Eric would allow it now. But maybe not the next time—if there was one—and she didn't have the time to squander on chewing her nails while he jousted with the Grim Reaper today.

Rising on unsteady legs she wobbled over to her mostly empty dresser and asked, "Jeans and a T-shirt okay?"

"Okay for what?"

"For Montserrat."

Eric pulled her around, his hands firm on her shoulders. "You are not going with me."

"Okay, then I'll go by myself. The same plane you're taking won't have any misgivings about accepting my fare with yours. If you don't want to sit by me, fine. But Eric, I am going."

"It's too dangerous."

"Not too dangerous for you."

"I'm an expert. You're not. And I can't watch after you while I'm working."

Though she was tempted to remind him that he bore the proof that being an expert didn't give him special immunity, Whitney knew that would not get her on the plane with him.

"Of course not. That's why I'll stay out of your way while you do what you do best." She patted his fly. All her new bold moves were proving addictive themselves and she deepened her pat to a full frontal massage. "Well, almost best."

With a groan Eric moved her fondling hand to press it over his heart.

"If anything bad happened to you I would never forgive myself."

"I will be fine, Eric. I'll go where the islanders are waiting it out. Maybe I could even do something to help. You think?"

"I'll tell you what I think. I think it's never been so hard to leave. And by no means should you go with me. But I'm selfish enough to want you there anyway. If you're determined to do it, The Red Cross can always use extra help."

An hour later, as they boarded the charter plane, Eric hoped he hadn't miscalculated in his snap decision to bring Whitney along. He thought of the way she had chirped, "Will do!" when he told her to pack a change of clothes just in case, so happy to be coming along you would've thought she was on her way to a Club Med instead of taking off for a homeless shelter. Little did she know what she was walking into, or that he had immediately cut to the chase to find out if she had the grit and the guts it would take to deal with his profession. Amy had come to loathe it. Apparently it was a bit too much like being married to a race car driver who'd had one too many close calls.

It had been sweet torture watching Whitney get dressed and do that little jiggle thing into her bra that he wanted to jiggle her right out of, all the while wondering about the dichotomy she had proven to be in a shared bed. The kitten was curious and playful and amazingly responsive in her unstudied abandon. She was also incredibly tight. But clearly she hadn't taken some kind of vow of chastity, not with the box of condoms she had produced from the nightstand when he suggested they pick up breakfast, as well as some protection for later, once they were en route to the plane.

Also interesting was their little conversation when he offered to make her a to-go cup of tea. *"This is the fountain of youth that you and your grandmother swear by?"* She had gazed at the ling-chih as if the powdery contents in a vial might actually be a genie in a bottle.

"It is. The ling-chih is a huge mushroom that grows wild in China. It's too tough to eat, so I buy it ground for soups or tea. As you probably noticed it doesn't taste like much, but lore has it that ling-chih has healing powers."

"Do you really buy into that?"

"Let's just say I don't discount the possibility. The 'plant of immortality' as the ancients called it, has some modern researchers thinking it helps prevent cancer and does wonders for the immune system."

Whitney had slightly winced before placing her order: *"I'll have a double, please."*

That's when it struck him how alone in the world she was: Not only had she lost her mother to a terrible disease, she had never really had a father, and apparently there were no siblings or other living relations. He could not imagine it—a life without his brother, his Grandmother Ming, his parents, their big, boisterous family reunions with cousins, uncles, aunts, and seemingly always a new baby to join the Townsend/Liu clans.

He could share all that with Whitney. And as she flashed him that dazzling smile of hers while their plane took to the sky, he had no doubt that he would, it was only a matter of when.

It was just a twenty-minute hike, a mere seventeen hundred feet up that he and Marcia Grayson had to climb, but when they stopped to don their protective garb, Eric couldn't help but mutter, "Damn, I wish we were taking these off already and making tracks back to camp."

"You and me both." Marcia zipped up the flame-retardant suit and adjusted a boot—one that made feet sweat but kept them from getting too toasty from the leap of an unexpected flame. "How long do you think this'll take us?"

"Too long." They hadn't even reached the bubbling crater and already the overpowering stench of sulfur was assaulting his nostrils. Blinking against the sting in his eyes, Eric quickly donned the head covering that made him resemble a cross between a beekeeper and an astronaut. Both professions were a safer bet than the one he'd chosen, and at the moment he'd rather be tackling a hive bare-handed than preparing to dig up a broken seismometer with asbestos gloves. They limited his dexterity and would slow down the process, but better to take the precaution than risk losing his hands to a spurt of lava.

"Ready?" Marcia asked.

"Let's do it." Taking a determined step forward, he wondered where the thrill had gone. He should be zinging from the pump of adrenaline, not feeling a queasy twist in his stomach and thinking about Whitney when a single wrong step could land him in the hospital. Or worse.

Yet even as they neared the crater, seething with activity and gaseous fumes, his mind wandered back to their lingering kiss goodbye. He wasn't one for shows of public affection, but it had been impossible not to kiss her and hold her, to fill his senses with the scent of lavender and Ivory soap, fill his hands with the hair he'd tugged free of a rubber band. And he hadn't wanted to stop, to leave her behind in a camp that looked like a little tent city, populated by people who lacked the means to make a fresh start elsewhere.

Where was she now? Was she having second thoughts about coming? Or was she thinking of him, remembering this morning? He liked that idea a lot better. Especially if her thoughts included some visions of what the night might bring.

"Eric, watch out!" Marcia's sharp warning coincided with the flinging of her arm against his chest, shoving him back.

Though he didn't need to look down to know what he'd nearly walked over, Eric put his eyes to the ground he should have had them glued on. This particularly treacherous area of Galway's Soufrière hid dangerous fissures beneath thin crusts of earth—which he could feel cracking beneath his feet.

"Oops." What else could he say as he carefully backed off while Marcia shot him a hey-watch-where-you're-going glare?

"Once we're finished you can tell me all about that woman Larry mentioned you'd brought along—and I do feel perfectly entitled to hear everything after saving your ornery ass. Till then, Eric, do us both a favor and keep your head in the game?"

"Right," he curtly agreed as they neared the familiar site. He'd installed the equipment himself when his head had been in the game, and his life had been devoted to a calling that was so much more than a job.

The winds of change were upon him. He could feel them blowing sulfurous and hot where he stood, but it was the sweet smell of lavender and Ivory soap that was whispering a seductive command to get this job done so he could haul his ornery ass down to the woman who was waiting and the comparative safety of fertile ground.

CHAPTER 9

"Would you like some stew?" Whitney asked.

"Stew?" repeated the little boy who held out his bowl. Sniffing at the ladle she scooped from a vat, he exclaimed, "Goat-water! It's me favorite!"

Whitney filled his bowl to the brim and handed it back. "I didn't realize that was goat in there."

"And mountain chicken, too. *Rrribit, rrribit.*"

"Well, I hope yours is as good as what I had the other day." Two days ago to be exact, but it seemed a lifetime had passed since she'd eaten alone and taken her mai tai back from Dick. Dominica was so close, and yet so far away. These islands shared the same ocean but were oceans apart when it came to the people, the culture, the placid mountains there, the smoking peak Eric was on here....

She couldn't think about it. If she did, she'd give in to this terrible urge to throw down the ladle so she could get the latest progress report from headquarters.

"There you go, buster."

"Me name's not Buster." He flashed her an endearing snaggle-toothed grin. "It's Mickey."

An Irish name, spoken with a brogue by a child of African heritage.

Such a great big world was out there, chock-full of people and places she'd yet see. If only she'd ventured outside her own backyard sooner. If only it hadn't taken a lab report to cannonball her out of it and send her flying here. Here, where she couldn't cry over her own spilt milk when these people had the whole damn cow tipped over in a disaster zone kitchen.

"Okay, Mickey," she said, making herself match him grin for grin. "Enjoy." Thinking of the delicious eggs Benedict she'd scarfed down in Eric's rented jeep, Whitney's smile faltered. She couldn't help but wish she'd saved some leftovers to share with Mickey. And all the other children displaced from their homes. Given the number, she might as well have a loaf of bread and two fishes to feed the multitudes.

"Thank ye, bonnie lass."

"And you're welcome, me handsome laddie." As Mickey turned to go, dressed in raggedy clothes and no shoes for his feet, an idea came to her. "Wait! Have you got brothers, sisters? Friends?"

"One brother there," he said, pointing his bowl to a table. "Two sisters down there." After nodding to somewhere in the middle of the line that had snaked outside, he proudly proclaimed, "And lots of blokes. We camp out, just like G.I. Joe!"

Thank God for the imagination of a child consigned to a crowded shelter filled with cots. Maybe she couldn't change that any more than she could work miracles, but there was something she could do.

"Do all you G.I. Joes and Janes like hearing stories?" At his big nod she instructed, "Sunset. Your campsite. Spread the word."

Judging from Mickey's race to the table where his brother sat, the whisper in one ear, then passed on from there to another, and another, Whitney was sure she wouldn't be lacking an avid audience.

As self-appointed commander in chief of entertainment for the evening, she issued invitations while serving up the grub to the other children who passed by. What kind of future would they have? And their parents, was this the future they had imagined for themselves in their own days of innocence?

The meal line was long and each bowl served represented yet

another person who'd had to migrate to safer ground and desert the crops many of them tended for a living. While she was a visitor, everything these people had—their jobs, homes, families, lives—hinged on the mood of a volcano with a major-league case of PMS. Two volcanos actually. Ever since Chance's Peak had opened up and spewed ashes onto the south end of the island, putting Montserrat on Orange Alert— one step away from evacuation—its bitchin' twin had got in on the act.

Galway's Soufrière was its name. It towered over the island like some mercurial lord of the land hurting its own economy with its hissy fits to keep the tourist trade away. And its subjects, these native islanders, had built their humble homes in the shadow of the tyrannical ruler who threatened to turn their tropical paradise into sinking sand.

"Do you know what time it is?" she asked the Red Cross worker who was handing out bottled water beside her. When it turned out to be only fifteen minutes since the last time she'd asked, Whitney told herself that being a worrywart wouldn't make Eric any safer or get him back quicker, so the best she could do was to dole out as much cheer as she did goat-water.

After pitching in with cleanup, Whitney knew she should be too tired to think further than the nearest spare cot. And she was tired, only not as tired as she should be by now as she watched the kids dancing to reggae in the dirt streets and playing hide-and-seek.

They wouldn't be hiding behind trees, at least not the ones with a red circle around them. Those trees dripped acid. And when acidic trees were considered safe ground, what kind of danger was Eric confronting on the higher turf he'd yet to return from?

Deciding enough time had passed, Whitney commanded herself to walk, not run, for any updates.

"Larry," she addressed the father of three who'd been relegated to keeping track of the data coming in. "What's the latest?"

Looking up from the graph he was tracking, he said distractedly, "The new equipment we ordered this morning, just in case, is on its way. Good thing, too, since Eric threw the old one into the crater and wasn't mincing any bleeps on getting the replacement when he radioed in a little while ago."

"Did he..." How could she say this without sounding like her personal concerns were more important to her than the lives depending on the installation of a new seismometer?

"Yeah, Whitney, he sent a message for you. I wrote it down...now where was that paper?"

Larry located the message, skimmed the lines, and had the tact to say no more than "Heh, heh" before handing it over.

The island might be safe enough for now but you are terribly mistaken if you think you're safe tonight. Meow.

Whitney fanned her cheeks with the note responsible for their heat. "When do you think he'll be finished?"

"If the goods arrive soon..." Larry cupped his ear, stuck two thumbs up in the air. "Yes! I do believe that's a chopper I hear. Assuming that's the new equipment, and knowing they'll be working like maniacs to get it in before they can't see their way off the crater, I'd give 'em a few hours to finish up and hightail it home."

"That long?"

"Could be longer if they run into problems and have to pick their way down with only a flashlight and the moon to see where they're going. Whenever he checks in, want me to pass on the point of zee rendezvous?"

As she tried not to envision Eric tripping in the dark and tumbling into a bubbling vat of lava, Whitney shook her head.

"That's okay, I'll find him once he gets back." She'd make sure the storytelling session was over by the time he returned, something she'd just as soon keep a secret between her and the kids. And thank goodness for them to take her mind off this gnawing apprehension. "Well, guess I'd better be going and let you work."

As she turned for the door, Larry called to her, "Hey. I know it's hard, but try not to worry. When he gets back—and he will, you have to believe that—don't let him see how afraid you are. It's poison to relationships with guys like us. Of course even guys like us can get smart once we have a reason to play it safer than we otherwise would."

"Words of wisdom from someone who's been there?"

"There and back. I'll always be back for more, just like Eric, but you see where I'm sitting." He bounced on the chair. "Close enough to take in the action but not so close I won't make it home. I'd rather kiss my kids goodnight and catch Late Night with my wife than stick around for the show."

The show. Slang for the visual, life-threatening effects that could only be had by hanging around to see a pyrotechnic display that made Fourth of July blowouts seem on a par with fizzling bottle rockets. Eric had become very animated when he described some of the shows he'd seen, but much as she'd begun to crave adventure, running for what life she had left was something she could do without.

She had to accept that Eric was in his element. And an hour later, she found a welcome comfort in returning to hers. She didn't have a storyboard with felt figures to move around or even finger puppets. But ratty-haired Barbie dolls and dilapidated stuffed animals made fine characters to enact the sort of story the children had voted for. A scary story and one better told with a white sheet around her face and a flashlight Mickey shone on her as dusk descended and goblins moved closer to the tent they sought refuge in....

Pouring enough sweat to keep a rose garden blooming in Desert Valley, Eric stripped off the outfit only an alien would consider trendy while Marcia did the same.

"Yes! Yes, Yes! Mission accomplished," she jubilantly proclaimed. "Gimme some skin."

As they slapped palms together, Eric had the satisfaction of knowing they'd done well. They weren't pushing up daisies yet, and the populace of Montserrat didn't have to worry about it either now, thanks to their efforts. So, why wasn't he feeling like a war hero, just like his dad whose shoes he'd done his best to fill? Not in the military

—he was too independent for that; but he had managed to make Dad proud, and his intellectual gifts count, by waging war against a force more destructive than man.

Such derring-do usually gave him an incredible high, and that was the addiction, but all Eric felt was disappointment that Whitney wasn't around to greet him the moment he and Marcia returned to camp.

"Time to party!" she whooped with a fling of her sooty jumpsuit into the air. Catching it, she spun the thing around the way he'd imagined reuniting with Whitney.

As for Marcia's expectations to celebrate in their typical fashion, he had other plans and they didn't include staying here to party with his pals.

"Sorry, Marcia, I won't be joining you and the gang. After we brief Larry, I'm finding Whitney and we're outta here."

"Whitney this, Whitney that," she teased. "Jeez, Eric, I said you owed me the scoop but remind me to get some earplugs the next time you get a crush on—"

"It's not a crush," he cut in. "Have you ever heard me run my mouth about a woman before?"

"No. Otherwise I might have already offered you up as a human sacrifice to the volcanic gods. As it is, we've got a lot of history between us and I love you too much to do you in because you're all ga-ga over a woman you met last Thursday. It's Saturday, Eric. Saturday. You've always had a good head on your shoulders, but if you're head-over-heels after three days, that's not the head you're thinking with."

"It's more than that. A lot more. She even quotes Lao Tzu. Remember how you felt when we got called in here a few years back? You'd just met Luke and as I recall, you said—"

"Don't remind me of what I said after half a bottle of Jack Daniel's when I was nursing third-degree burns. And keep Luke out of this while you're at it."

"No," he told her flatly. "No, I won't. And why? Because if anyone should know how I feel, it should be you. C'mon, Grayson. We've been buddies since grad school. Can't you at least say you're happy I've met someone?"

"I'm happy for you." Marcia pushed up her lips with two fingers.

"If that's the best you can do, fine. What's up with you and Luke these days anyway?"

Marcia dropped her fake smile along with her suit, gave it a kick. "He left me, Eric. The same way Amy left you. It always comes down to that final ultimatum, and I guess that's why I'm not predicting great things for you and this Whitney who came along to help out."

"It's more than Amy or Luke ever did."

"True, but people do crazy things to impress each other when they're infatuated. Once reality sets in, lines get drawn. Those lines separate us from what most people can't stomach for the long haul. We're not most people, Eric. Maybe Whitney isn't, either. But you've only known her a few days and I've known you for how long? Almost fifteen years. I don't want to see you get hurt."

"As much as I appreciate the concern, we both know I'm not the one most at risk. That's why I'm being careful with Whitney—certainly more careful than Amy felt I was with her."

"Or me?"

Eric met Marcia's challenging gaze. They both knew it wasn't a fair question. He had never misled Marcia into believing they were more than the best of friends and trusted colleagues. As for that one night after his divorce when they were both in a bad place for different reasons and found some solace together, he had owned his mistake. Immediately, the next morning, he had professed his regrets. True, Marcia hadn't been so immediately regretful, but despite their different takes on the encounter they had remained important to each other personally, professionally, and until just now he'd thought that part of their past was behind them. Especially since Marcia had gone on to marry Luke...who was now out of the picture.

"I never meant to hurt you," he told her with all the truth in his heart. "I only want the best for you. Always."

"Same here." Marcia tapped his chest, twice with her palm, good buddy style. "She'd better be good to you."

"And if she's not?" Eric raised an eyebrow in question.

Marcia pecked his cheek, turned on her heel and threw over her shoulder, "Lucky me."

Eric didn't like the way Marcia's concerns and their resulting conversation mingled with the sulfur and sweat he couldn't wait to wash off in the shower tent. His instincts were usually right on the mark and they had been in high gear since meeting Whitney. It was true he had agreed to let her come along to better judge how she might handle the white-knuckle demands of his profession. And there was a chance she hadn't fared well in his absence, giving fuel to the doubts Marcia expressed and he simply did not want to hear—

High-pitched shrieks pierced his ears, abruptly stopping his thoughts along with his fast track to the shower. Children screaming inside a dark canvas shelter. Had a wildcat sneaked in, hunting for dinner? Eric raced to the enclosed tent, but just as he reached it, all became silent.

Except for the eerie sound of a ghostlike voice. A voice that dipped and swayed, along with a stuffed rabbit that seemed to float in the air, held aloft by a sheet-covered phantom who dramatically intoned, "Who has my golden hand?"

Whitney was encircled by a crowd of kids scooting back and shaking their heads.

"You have my golden hand! Give me my golden hand, Mickey. Give me my golden hand!" Whitney snarled, pointing a finger at the accused.

More shrieks. It was the sound of kids scared half to death and loving every second of their ghost story terror. Who could doubt it amidst shouts for "One more, please one more!" when she tossed the sheet she'd been wearing on top of a group huddled together.

So much for Marcia's concerns, he smugly decided.

Eric clapped along from his post outside. But he didn't make himself known. It wouldn't be right to steal Whitney away when so many were begging for an encore.

Thus, he kept his anonymity and faded into the dark. As he did, Eric could only wonder how his life had seemed so full before they'd met, only to realize how empty that life would be without her.

CHAPTER 10

*W*hitney reluctantly made her escape. If the kids had their way, they'd keep her all night. Bless Mickey's heart, he'd even offered to let her sleep on his cot in exchange for one more story. Just one more, he'd begged so earnestly, it had been a struggle not to hold him in her arms and tell him stories until he fell asleep. But she'd already stayed much longer than intended, and she wanted to find Eric before he found her.

Hurrying out of the tent lit with lanterns, she promptly collided with a woman.

"Sorry!" Her eyes adjusting to the lesser light, Whitney realized just who she had bumped into. The picture hadn't done Eric's colleague justice. She was Amazon tall, a lithe, bronzed beauty who bore a striking resemblance to another Whitney.

That would be Houston.

"You're Marcia Grayson, aren't you?"

"If you're with the LAPD and looking to collect on those parking tickets, I'm not. Otherwise, that's the name I saw on my license the last time I checked." Cocking her head, she looked Whitney over then said, "I know who you are. You're Whitney."

"How did you guess?"

"Doesn't take much guessing after the description I got. Only I don't see those auburn highlights that really come out in the sun and it's too dark to tell if your eyes could actually make the ocean look murky on its best crystal-clear day."

Though somewhat embarrassed, Whitney couldn't contain her pleased smile. "I can't believe Eric said that."

"Neither can I. Which is why I'm glad he's still getting cleaned up and we're out here. We don't have long to talk and I know plenty about you already, so I hope you don't mind if we skip the chitchat. I'd like to speak frankly. While we walk. Jeez, it's loud in there." Hooking her arm through Whitney's with a surprising comradery, Marcia's forthrightness was equally startling.

"Are you in love with Eric? After knowing him three whole days, are you?"

"I...well, I..." Was she? According to Pierre, the answer was in her heart, not her head. Shutting out the clamoring sound of its beating, she heeded the voice of reason that would protect her and Eric from a rash and painful mistake. "It's too precipitate to answer you that. So let's just say, not yet."

"Not yet," Marcia repeated. "But given more time, even a little, you could be."

She didn't phrase it as a question but a statement to refute.

Whitney remained silent.

"Look, Whitney, I've never seen him happier than he was today but he was more preoccupied than usual, too. I'm worried you might be bad for his health. Then again, you could be good for it. Much as I hate to lose the best partner I've ever had, Eric needs someone who means more to him than this—" Marcia nodded toward the smoking peak. "Even when he was married, Eric didn't have that someone. After what he said about you, it's obvious he thinks he just might have found her."

Whitney wasn't sure what to say. There were no magic words to change the state of her health or any impact she might have on Eric's well-being. But that didn't stop her from relishing a secret thrill—or from wondering if there had been an undercurrent of envy in Marcia's tone.

"I'd like to be that someone," Whitney confessed. "What woman wouldn't?"

"None that I've yet to meet."

They exchanged a look and that's when Whitney knew: Marcia Grayson had a thing for Eric. More than a thing. Even after listening to him rave about another woman while her own feelings were probably getting trampled, Marcia genuinely cared about his happiness.

Although she couldn't bring herself to say, "no worries, I'm temporary," Whitney managed to offer, "Well, as you pointed out, Eric and I haven't known each other long and it's too soon to even guess where we'll be a month from now, much less a year."

"Eric said he feels like he's known you for years." Marcia let go of Whitney's arm, turned to directly face her. "I've known him for years. We've been through a lot together. And I can tell you this about Eric— as fun and friendly as he seems when you first meet him, he is one complex dude. Deep. Doesn't get too close, too fast. He asks a lot of questions but doesn't give up a lot about himself or the relationships he's in. For him to go on and on about you is totally unlike him. I'd like us to be friends, Whitney. But I think you should know that if you break that man's heart…"

They both looked in the same direction.

"Yes?" Whitney prompted.

"I'll be the first to try to pick up the pieces."

The sight of Eric walking, and then sprinting toward her with arms open, made Whitney greedy to have those pieces for her own. Keenly aware of the borrowed time they were on, she brushed aside any sympathies for Marcia and raced to him; only to feel her feet take to the air as he spun her around and kissed her like a soldier returning to his sweetheart after a long and arduous war.

Until Marcia cleared her throat. "I hate to interrupt this Kodak moment, but it's time for me to say my goodbyes." She offered her hand to Whitney, and with a succinct grip, a significant woman-to-woman glance, said, "I'm glad we had a chance to talk, Whitney. Till we meet again?"

Her buss to Eric's cheek was distinctly familiar. "I know you need some time off so I won't be calling again unless it's a do-or-die emergency. If you need me for anything, you've got my number since it works both ways. Ciao, baby," she said, then walked off with a backwards wave.

"What was that about?"

Whitney bit her bottom lip, which still felt pleasantly plundered. She knew she should proceed carefully, should already be giving some thought to an exit plan considering the warp speed at which things were progressing. That would be the responsible thing to do...only she didn't want to be responsible and a quick, sharp anger surged at the unfairness of it all. Why was she only now meeting this amazing man? And how dare Marcia taint what happiness she could still have with an open warning? Excluding an accident, Marcia had decades of living ahead. Ditto for Eric. Whitney Smith, however, didn't have that luxury, and if holding on to what she could have while she could still have it made her selfish, then that's what she was:

A selfish woman who desperately needed to laugh enough for a lifetime, and love with the heart of a fool.

At least for a few more days. Maybe even a few weeks if her energy levels didn't take a drastic dive.

"I have no idea what that was about," Whitney replied. Quickly changing the subject, she asked, "So, where to from here? Back to the bungalows or a little detour to Argentina first for a Tango lesson? By the way, you're a marvelous dancer."

"Ah, the Tango." He placed one hand in the small of her back, and raised her arm high with the other. With a neat twirl, he dipped her. "No need to go further than the Virgin Islands for a private lesson. Say...Saint Croix? Dominica might be beautiful, but come midnight we'll be plunking change into a jukebox and after today I'm more in the mood to celebrate into the wee hours than turn in early." He gave her a devilish wink. "The plane I booked takes off in half an hour. We'll go wherever you want, just tap your ruby slippers and consider us there. We have all the essentials, I believe. You. Me. A box of Trojans."

Whitney clapped her hands, showered him with butterfly kisses between exclamations of, "The tango! Saint Croix on a whim! Eric, you make my wildest dreams come true. Where have you been all of my life?"

As he absorbed her outpouring of affection, Eric knew an even wilder dream was coming true for him. He had been all over the world, met all manner of both woman and man, had enough adventures to keep a conversation running with Mark Twain, and yet he had never had a moment quite like this.

With crystalline clarity he realized that for the first time in his life, he was really, truly, falling in love. The absolute, once in a lifetime, head over heels, *I can't believe this is happening to me* kind of love that poets waxed purple about, creating equal measures of envy and disbelief and an urge to gag from too many hearts and flowers. He had intuited that Whitney was destined to be all that he could hope for, but what he felt now ratcheted up to an even more unfamiliar realm.

As they grabbed their few belongings, raced each other to the plane, laughing all the while, Eric knew he was officially a goner. Indiana Spock was not only in emotional Terra Incognita.

He was *all in* for the greatest adventure of his life.

CHAPTER 11

"*T*ime to wake up."

Snuggling deeper into her big cuddly pillow, Whitney asked groggily, "Where are we?"

"Saint Croix. The plane just landed and I'd carry you out if I could but the cabin's too small."

Waking up more fully, she realized her head was in Eric's lap and he was stroking her hair. "Sorry, Eric. I didn't mean to fall asleep on you again."

"I'm glad you did. You needed a nap after putting in such a long day. Besides, I enjoy watching you sleep."

"Please tell me I wasn't snoring."

"Just a little, but it was more Brahms than heavy metal."

Whitney thanked God for small favors as they exited the plane and, as if he'd brought Pixie Dust along with his *ling-chih*, less than an hour later Eric was ushering her into the lobby of what had to be a Five Star hotel with a key to the penthouse suite.

"Seriously?" she asked, as he swept her up and carried her into the most magnificent accommodations she'd seen outside of a Conde Nast travel magazine.

"Oh yeah, I'm serious. About you. Otherwise we'd be at the nearest Holiday Inn fighting over rights to the channel changer."

As he deposited her in the middle of an elegant, sprawling, Caribbean-style great room with a grand piano that made her wonder if Billy Joel had checked out just before they checked in, Whitney could hardly believe this was real.

Real enough was Eric's full on her mouth kiss. Real enough was the sound of a champagne bottle uncorking with enough force for the cork to hit the elevated ceiling before Eric made a good catch and, with a short bow, extended it to her.

"Here's to us, *yuan-pao*. May all of our tomorrows be as promising as they are tonight."

Her hand closed around the cork and she knew it had just become one of her most prized possessions, something she would keep for the rest of her...

No, she was not going to go there. For now they were here where she openly gawked at the room they were in as a worldly host extended a flute of Dom Perignon with the familiar ease of another Coke served from a McDonald's drive up window.

How they could come from such different worlds and somehow end up here was the stuff of fantasy. One that continued into a bedroom where he brought the Dom along to go with flowing white drapes and a white bearskin rug on marble floors that accentuated the centerpiece—a big heart-shaped white bed with canopy curtains against a mirrored wall. And beside that bed was a basket overflowing with ripe, tropical fruit.

"A little over the top," he chuckled, "but I think we can make-do." With a sexy grin that would have convinced Eve if the serpent hadn't, Eric tempted her with his offering.

"Care for a mango? You must be hungry."

And she was. Hungry for him. She was also nervous now that the big moment was at hand. Not only that, while Eric was all cleaned up, she couldn't say the same for herself and she wasn't about to get in that bed after removing her soiled clothes and wondering if her underarms might stink. Not to mention the prime treasure she had saved that was about to be cashed in.

Her seemingly random meeting with Dick came back to her with a resonance that made her wonder if any meeting was truly random. *"I wish more women would say what they really think. It would save us guys a lot of second-guessing about what's really going on in your pretty heads."*

Eric wanted honesty from her, too. And that's what he was going to get.

"Honestly, Eric, I am a little hungry and if it's not too late for room service, even a burger and fries would be great. I also feel pretty grimy and would love a nice, long soak in the tub since something tells me we've got more than a shower stall to go with the rest. It's a little overwhelming because, well, I've never stayed anyplace as luxurious as this. And...I'm a little nervous about going to bed together, which is so silly I know, given this morning, and it's not that I don't want to, I really, really do, but..."

She should just tell him. Only the words weren't coming out, and somehow they didn't have to while he nodded, smiled as if she had indulged him in some delightful way. "Okay," he assured her. "Anything else?"

It was like he had handed her a "Get Out Of Jail Free" pass while he topped off the flute she had chugged down during her honesty-is-the-best-policy meanderings.

No reason to stop now, she may as well pull out the big guns. "I'm not completely without experience—especially thanks to this morning—but just like you always wear your tee-shirt to cover up what you don't want others to see—and it meant so much to me that you would allow me that—well, now I'm bringing you into my confidence, too. I don't want you to think I'm weird or somehow abnormal, because I'm not. At least I don't think so. But I have a confession to make." She took a deep breath. Another chug. Looked him square in the eyes and delivered the news: "I'm still a virgin. Kind of."

He didn't blink. In fact his pupils visibly dilated. His head tilted. And the way he had studied her on the plane had nothing on the way he studied her now while his lips formed into an intrigued smile and an eyebrow arched up.

"Really?" he said. "Wow. And just when I think you couldn't amaze me more than you already have."

"So, you're not put off by it, you don't want to ask me if I'm secretly frigid or part of a religious cult?"

"Hell, no!" He clinked his flute to hers. "Are you kidding me? I don't know your reasons for waiting this long and you can tell me if and when you want, but suffice it to say that I've never been any woman's first. It's an experience I've always wanted but gave up on years ago. Now that you've turned that forgone conclusion on its head, that's a game changer. It's a first for both of us, and we're going to do it right."

"Do it right?"

"Um-hmm. This is too good not to savor. Forget burgers and fries from room service. We'll make it caviar and foie gras with a whatever your heart desires chaser. A bath? Let's make it for two, see where it leads. And in between all that?"

"Yes?" she asked, relieved, and a little breathless already.

"I saw the way you looked at that piano. You play, don't you?"

"Not very well, but I've had some lessons." Five years of lessons that her mother had worked overtime to provide, along with an old upright that was still in her modest and nothing like this apartment.

"I play piano, too. One song. A duet my grandmother taught me. But I know both ends."

Just as they perfected their timing to *Heart and Soul* a tap at the door signaled their culinary delivery. In wheeled a cart with silver domed trays atop white linen.

"Picnic in the tub?" Eric asked. "Unless you'd prefer a blanket on the floor."

Thinking of Mickey and the soup kitchen where she'd met him, Whitney knew she should feel at least a little guilty with so much indulgence. But she didn't. Not even a little.

Never before had she imagined a sumptuous picnic in a whirlpool tub by candlelight, where Eric fed her strawberries dipped in dark chocolate; where she had her first taste of briny little black fish eggs that crunched then popped between her teeth, topped with a dollop of whipped sour cream. As for the duck liver that tasted nothing like liver, spread like butter on a thin, artisan cracker that melted in her mouth...

There were no words to describe it beyond a sensory orgy.

He washed her hair, his fingers massaging her scalp with just the right pressure. Her spine curved into his chest, dusted with dark, silky hair brushing her skin. His thighs rode hers and their kneecaps peaked through soapy white foam, swishing up and over her breasts.

He palmed one. "Did I mention I love your breasts?"

"Feel free to repeat yourself."

"I'd rather help myself to what bears repeating." And help himself he did, stroking and kneading until her sighs turned to moans as he whispered a decadent request in her ear. "That is, if you're open to the idea."

Whitney slid his hand down and down, past her breasts, over her belly, and to her resounding response. "What does that tell you?"

"Bath time's over."

Before either could dry off, they were on the floor, both of them wet and slithering all over each other as they licked and kissed their way from smooth marble to the soft, plush bearskin rug beside the bed.

They didn't make it to the bed.

Her back to the rug, Eric straddled her torso. Looking down at her with those exotic almond eyes and hers looking back, full of wonder that she felt so free yet so bound to this man making hot, wanton love to her breasts.

She pushed them closer together, sealing the tunnel through which he slid back and forth. The faster he went, the more intense his expression grew, and all the while his eyes burned into her, even as he groaned on a final thrust.

She could feel him shaking, hear the heave of his breath, the ragged utterance of her name. There was no doubt of his coming, though yet again, no fluids to suggest it.

There was only Eric slumping over her, whispering *"yuan-pao,"* into her ear. "I'll never get enough of you. Not enough of your taste, your touch, your voice. You're incredibly generous, giving me that release, and it will help me with what comes next."

Eric rose above her, looking for all the world like Atlas, thoroughly capable of carrying the entire globe on his shoulders. He swept her up from the rug and then she was on the mattress, so was Eric, and so was her box of condoms, getting some immediate use.

"I want this to be right for you." His voice was husky, intimate. "And that means we need to work together, like partners dancing— only this time, you lead."

Rather than gathering her close as expected, he lay supine, closed his eyes. His voice had a mesmerizing quality, like music coming from a distance, while he told her he could not look at her, or touch her, lest he break the meditative state he needed to sustain. He told her what she needed to do so her body could become accustomed to his without the risk of tearing.

After several deep breaths, he spread his arms out as if in surrender and appeared to go limp all over. Except for his partial erection, just inches away from the dark garden she explored more freely than she ever had alone. And as she did, Whitney studied this man, who excited her imagination and stimulated her senses as he laid in repose. His lessening arousal only increased her own until she couldn't bear not to touch the pliable flesh he had warned her to maneuver as little as possible.

Whitney soon realized this was easier said than done. Her initial touch caused him to jerk. Though he was dry, she was slippery, and without Eric's assistance, she ultimately had no choice but to simply stuff him in, taking care not to dislodge their protection as she did.

She felt his immediate rise but only a small distance. No discomfort where he claimed space, just this terrible ache where he did not. Needing more, she slightly rocked her hips and he responded, giving her all she could take without gasping, and stopping the moment she did. His attunement to her every nuance of movement made her feel as if he truly had become one with her, knowing what she felt, inside her head and under her skin.

Did he feel like a virgin again himself? She hoped so. He gave her so much now, taking nothing, and it was now that she truly understood the depth of what he'd wanted to give her—an undiscovered part of herself that he could help guide her to, but ultimately it was up to each individual to claim who they were, for until they did, how could another claim them?

Stroking her breasts, exploring the dark garden of her desires, Whitney claimed her own body and in so doing, felt as if she were taking her own innocence. Silently she blessed this man she claimed as well, then not so silently as she whispered, "Eric. Open your eyes and see who I am."

As if from far away, Eric heard her summons. He knew if he did as she asked, what Whitney easily accommodated now wouldn't be so manageable.

"I know who you are. You're my *yuan-pao.* My priceless pearl." Even speaking wasn't wise; the sound of his own voice was disturbing the altered state that was enabling him to keep her safe from a total unfurling that could—

Damn. What was he thinking?

"Oh, yes," she moaned. "Oh, yes, much better. I love the way you feel."

"Stop moving. Please stop. Don't say anything else."

"Don't move. Don't talk. Don't touch. Eric, that's exactly the opposite of what I want right now. Please look at me. See me as I've never seen myself before."

Were he a saint he might have denied them both that. But he wasn't a saint. Just a man who was already in love with the woman sliding her hands over her breasts, down to her belly. She caressed herself there then dipped lower, to the place of their partial joining.

"God, help me," he groaned. Heaven lent not an ear and neither did Whitney as she bore down, refusing his attempts to save her from what she apparently didn't want saving from. Her head swung from side to side. Her hair whipped over the face he did see as he'd never seen another woman before, leaving him to wonder at this marvelous creature who held him in thrall as he watched her play, let her tease...

But there came a point when a man couldn't just lie there and do nothing.

Eric rolled her onto her back.

"You took yourself, you took me," he said, his breath hot on her face. "Now we take each other."

There was a rawness in his voice, and in the way he swiped his mouth over hers, that Whitney knew she'd find alarming were she still an innocent. Any naïveté she'd had about her sexual self was gone. She spread her legs wide to invite him further, hooked them tight around his thighs and demanded, "Take me. Take me there." *There*. She suddenly knew where it was—away from the place where she was empty, hurting, alone.

Stillness, utter and absolute, above her. Writhing beneath him, raising up, her hips arched toward the sky, and then, his soft command.

"Hold my hand." Both of his spread over hers and she felt their palms meet, their fingers lock. A pause, then *whoosh*. Her breath rushed out on the stunning force of his thrust. It vaulted her over the edge and now she was airborne, suspended above that place she was falling into. Falling...falling....

Falling hard and fast and into his hold, being carried to a place too beautiful to belong to this earth, yet grounded in the warmth and nurture of...

Home.

Did he see where she went? Did Eric go there with her?

She searched his eyes and knew they were intimate companions on the same path that lead to a climax so intense she felt in the grips of a seizure.

Its aftermath was no less stunning, tumbling her down and reducing her to tears now that the most extraordinary experience of her life was over, as would her time with its provider inevitably be.

"I made you cry after all." He traced her tears. "I'm sorry I hurt you."

"Never that, Eric," she assured him.

"Then why are you crying?"

"Because I want..." She couldn't say it.

"We've shared something beautiful and rare, Whitney. Something I've never experienced before. What I feel is...it's a closeness I can't describe. What about you? We're safe here, safe together. You don't have to hide anything from me."

How she wished that were true. But to reveal her dark secret was to mark the beginning of the end, if not the end itself. That left her needing something to explain the leaking tears she dashed away with an impatient swipe at her eyes.

"You made this so wonderful, I wish I could relive it all over again. Only maybe reverse our positions and imagine what it was like being you. I'm sure it wasn't easy."

"Torture." His chuckle mingled with a pained grimace. "Sheer torture. Some of those ancient bedchamber secrets should probably remain secrets. At least this is one game I can honestly say doesn't bear repeating."

Given his ancestors' penchant for naming body parts and the recreational uses of them, Whitney was sure this particular exchange had a title to go with it, too.

"And just what did they call this game we played?"

"Dead Entry." He prodded her hip with the remains of his own game piece as he kissed her softly and swirled a finger into her grotto, making it weep for her inevitable, "Live Exit."

CHAPTER 12

Three days later they'd yet to leave the suite, unless he counted the private veranda that looked out over cresting ocean waves. Eric could only marvel at his reluctance to take the Do Not Disturb sign off the door. Once Whitney finished getting dressed in the other room they were supposed to finally emerge to do a little shopping. In the meantime he was supposedly updating some research notes and getting absolutely nothing done.

Gazing at his laptop, parked on a large slab of beveled glass near the piano, he shook his head. Indoor surroundings didn't get any posher than this, but rooms had a way of closing in on him and so did people if they didn't give him his space—though if anyone needed some room to breathe, it was Whitney.

He needed to start giving her some alone time, make sure she didn't feel suffocated. Especially since he kept catching himself crowding her a little, pushing for more than the immediate. Only each moment with her was so memorable, he just couldn't get enough.

Today would not be enough. Tomorrow, even filled with plans to go parasailing and out on the town so she could practice some of her beginner Tango moves, wouldn't be enough. The day after wouldn't be enough either when a coin flip would decide between Bonaire or going back to Dominica and a visit to Boiling Lake, then possibly a sweep through the Lesser Antilles over the next couple of weeks.

He had gotten that much of a commitment from her. But when he'd mentioned a lecture at The University of Oxford in early December, the most she would say was, "We'll see. Could you make me another cup of that *ling-chih* tea?"

She sure did like that tea—and other herbals such as ginseng that his favorite apothecary, Uncle Lee, kept him supplied with. She liked naps, too. Not that they ended up doing a lot of actual sleeping. The Tang dynasty's answer to Dr. Ruth, known as the Mystic Master, had determined there were thirty positions and fifteen coital movements, which came to 390 variations of intercourse, foreplay not included. He and Whitney had made an impressive dent in the number but they still had a looong way to go—and not just in bed.

She didn't know it yet but Whitney would be going with him to England. Just as he would win her agreement to accompany him on the lecture circuit through Europe—after the family's ritual New Year's Eve party at Grandmother Ming's. He couldn't wait for them all to meet the newest member of the family. No, he wasn't good at waiting. Time was a precious commodity, the most precious thing anyone had, and he didn't need time to debate a foregone conclusion:

This was it. Whitney was The One.

But, since she hadn't yet come to that realization herself, he would give her a proper courtship, along with something besides a ring to wear in the meantime.

"Eric," she called from the bedroom, "Would you mind zipping me up? This sundress seems to have gotten a little tighter since I wore it on the plane. I can't believe I've put on weight given all this exercise, but, oh well! Maybe you can help me pick out a few things that fit better while we're in town."

He loved how she didn't count calories any more than she watched the clock. Whitney ate whenever and whatever she wanted, relishing each bite as if it might be her last. She valued every second of life in a way few people ever did—which had a lot to do with why they were so perfect for each other.

The moment was perfect, too, for the special something he had to give her. Something he always took with him on the road because the road was more his home than the house boat and office he kept in Portland. He'd been thinking of selling since a single guy really didn't need a three story floating home, but now that he had someone to share it with…Maybe a visit to Portland was in order before San Francisco.

With a decisive snap of the laptop, Eric retrieved a small leather pouch from his satchel, and made tracks to the bedroom. A breeze fluttered long swaths of sheer curtains, transporting him back to the vision of Whitney draped in a sheet and telling a ghost story, only to cascade into that moment of absolute clarity when he knew he was six feet under in love.

And getting worse by the day. He didn't need a doctor, doctor to give him the news. He had a case so bad it was terminal, and it sure wasn't the blues.

She stood in front of the mirrored wall behind the perfectly mussed bed that housekeeping hadn't touched since the Do Not Disturb sign hadn't budged. Whitney had quit trying to straighten the sheets he didn't want washed anyway.

He came up behind her and moved her hair to one side so he could press his lips to the other side of neck exposed. There was a sweet, intimate domesticity that came from the simple act of sliding her zipper up when already he wanted to slide it back down.

"I have something for you to wear with this."

"You do?" As she began to turn, he cupped a shoulder, stilling her movements.

"Just stand like that. And look in the mirror."

Whitney did as he bade her, watching as his hands brought a dainty gold chain over her head and around her neck, where she could feel his fingers slightly tickle her skin as he secured the clasp at her nape. A circular pendant the size of a silver dollar hung from the chain's center and rested just above the area of her heart. A lazy *S* curve divided the middle, one side onyx, the other alabaster, with a small ruby on each side; one at the top, another at the bottom.

It was both delicate and substantial, a priceless piece of art that was truly beautiful, definitely antique.

"It's a Tai Chi symbol. Yin-yang. I'm sure you've seen it before."

She had, but nothing like this. Moving closer to the mirror, she touched the pendant, the set ruby stones. "How old is this?"

"Very old. Do you like it?"

"Eric, I…yes, of course. It's gorgeous. Where did you get this?"

"My grandmother. It's been in the family for some time. She gave it to me after the accident to ward away disaster…and to bring me luck in life." Leaning in, he added softly, "And in love."

It was hard to tear her gaze away from the first piece of real jewelry she'd ever had, unless she counted graduation rings. And the tiny diamond studs from Mama's jewelry box. She glanced up to see him smiling in the mirror, looking very, very pleased.

While her heart danced, her throat went dry. Eric had used the "L" word, even if indirectly. This was a significant gift. A family heirloom bore more emotional weight and attachment than anything bought new, even from a display at Tiffany's.

"The symbol is more ancient and meaningful than most people realize." His voice was hushed, the way one spoke in a church or a temple; she felt his breath on her neck, whispering near her ear. "Yin is female energy, yang male. Opposite, but complementary. When they're opposed, the world is off-kilter. But when they mate, all is in harmony. The Tao was created by their mating."

"The Tao," she repeated.

"The Way that can't be charted, the Name that can't be described, the Truth that is unknowable. It's the underlying principle of the universe where nature, humanity, and the spiritual meet. And, you could say it's a metaphor for the way men and women relate—Mars and Venus, mysteries as we are to each other, yet there's this drive that keeps us searching for that perfect complement to our opposing selves."

The sound of his voice, the way she couldn't take her eyes off the pendant, left her feeling almost hypnotized, in some kind of altered state. She shook her head, trying to break the spell. She had no right to accept such a treasured piece of his heritage when her own future was so uncertain. Or, rather, too certain.

"I can't tell you how much this means to me, Eric. But...I'm sorry, but I shouldn't accept this. It's too much."

One glance at his expression and she knew three things: He was injured. Not completely surprised. And he was determined.

"No," he countered. "It's not. This was given to me. It's mine to do with as I wish, and I wish for you to have it. You'll honor me by wearing it, *yuan-pao.*"

She was not sure if that was a dictate—as in, you *will* wear it—or a humble entreaty to gain her acceptance. Given the endearment, she chose to believe the latter.

Nevertheless, as much as she longed to lay claim to the most beautiful, meaningful gift she had ever received, Whitney knew it was a stolen delight. She didn't want to insult him by insisting he take the necklace back. Nor did she want to give up the connection it signified for as long as she could have it. Somehow she had to find a compromise that would allow her to wear it temporarily with a clear conscience.

"Why don't we consider it a loan," she suggested. When Eric frowned, she revised, "I mean, since we're taking each day as it comes, let's think of it like we're going steady and I've got on your class ring. So if anything happened to change between us, then it would still be yours, not mine." *Yours to give to someone else—even Marcia who would love to pick up any pieces I might leave behind.*

His fingertips brushed the V of her cleavage as he lifted the pendant, studied it a moment before meeting her hopeful gaze in the mirror. A curt nod and he said, "I can live with that today as long as you can't live without me tomorrow."

Whitney arched her neck to the side and watched him feast where her jugular pumped the blood that ran hot and fast for him. *He's yours for now,* she told herself. *And so is the necklace—even if you have to give it up, anyone else will only be getting your castoffs.*

She took what comfort she could from that and banished everything else from her mind. There was only the thrilling reflection of his heirloom necklace riding her skin, the smooth metal warm and getting warmer as she watched his hands and mouth possessively roam over her.

"You smell like heaven," he murmured, "And you taste like sin."

"Dr. Townsend, are you trying to seduce me again?"

"What an astute observation."

"I think you should unzip me now."

"Oh, I do like the way you think."

Whitney sorted through the postcards she had collected, debating on her favorite. As for what to pen her first note on, she couldn't decide between the postcards, the fancy hotel stationery she had confiscated, or the handmade paper Eric had bought her in beautiful Bonaire.

Ah, Bonaire, where flamingos outnumbered humans.

Now they were back in Dominica and officially sharing a bungalow for however long they were here. Eric was out, somewhere, for a couple of hours. That was their new routine. He had insisted on giving her some alone time every day, which would be even more critical, he had pointed out, if she agreed to accept a part-time position as his assistant. Even if just temporarily, she could take notes, help him catch up, and he thought her presence might help his focus improve.

Whitney couldn't believe she was actually entertaining the idea. Then again, she did have some practical considerations that were financial in nature, thanks to digging in her heels when it came time to check out of the hotel, which in turn resulted in their first spat.

"I've got this, kitten. You watch our luggage and I'll settle up at the desk."

That's when she had thought of the shopping spree he'd taken her on, wanting to pay for whatever her heart desired. And how he'd passed the charter planes off as a business expense, and wanted to take care of their future transportation, especially considering he was the reason she was doing all this unplanned travel. He insisted on paying for every meal.

Being raised by a single mother, she had been taught the importance of independence, the potential consequences of being too dependent on a man. Eric was not the deserter her father had been, but there was going to come a time in the not too distant future when Eric wouldn't be there to depend on and it frightened her a little—a lot—to be so dependent on him already.

And so, she had asserted that independence, informing him, *"WE will settle up together at the desk, Eric. You've been extremely generous and thoughtful, but I insist on splitting the cost of what all this has added up to."*

"No," he said stubbornly, *"I am the one who selected the accommodations. I am the one who placed the orders with room service. And I am the one responsible for the bill."*

Now it had become a matter of principle. Drawing herself up, she had lightly tapped his chest. *"Excuse me, but as I recall, we both enjoyed the accommodations. We both enjoyed that marvelous food—actually, I think I ate more than you. And by no means did you polish off all that champagne by yourself. No. No. We are finished with this conversation. Now let's be civil about this and—"*

"I don't feel like being civil. I feel like hauling you back upstairs where we can get this settled in private. And trust me, there would be no dispute by the time I let you off that mattress again."

That had made her mad—and part of what made her mad was how much his chest pounding was turning her on. Rather than give him the satisfaction of knowing she was ready to tear his clothes off right there in the lobby, she had spun around in the new sarong dress he had bought her, and in her new designer sandals marched to the expansive desk where she promptly pulled out her wallet from her new, exquisite seagrass tote, and asked for their bill.

It had been presented by the time Eric caught up with her, their new luggage and shopping treasures in tow.

She prayed he didn't notice her jaw had literally dropped and her eyeballs were bulging out of their sockets. Did she even have that much credit on her Visa? There was enough in her bank account and she did have her checkbook...but her home address and phone number would be clearly visible on the check and she had been careful not to give Eric any specifics regarding her actual residence.

She had, in fact, lied. Just a little. Since she had flown out of New Orleans, 150 miles west of Mobile—with limited flight options and two states away—he had presumed she came from somewhere in the lower Louisiana region. She had not corrected his assumption.

So, when he produced his credit card beside hers, she did not argue. As far as Eric was concerned she had gotten her way by splitting the bill and he even apologized in the taxi for his behavior.

They kissed and made up.

So here she was now with her pride and relative anonymity still intact, along with a budget-busting bill that would further drain the resources that seemed like plenty that crucial night she decided to live with a rare kind of richness while she still could. The $33,565.32 had taken a nice dip even before she left Mobile, taking care of all the essentials she wouldn't have a paycheck to cover once she returned to...

Die.

There it was, what stood between them. The one big mother of a sleeping mountain that was bubbling under the surface and could erupt without warning, just like Eric's Galeras.

He had only barely survived the first event. She would not taint their precious time together with an ominous dark cloud, nor would she re-subject him to the trauma he had witnessed with the loss of three friends, followed by his marriage to a woman who wanted a home and a baby, not "a volunteer for death row" as Eric had related.

He had taken all the responsibility for his failed ten year marriage to Amy, an affluent lawyer's daughter he married straight out of college. Manning up for his shortcomings, and refusing to badmouth his ex, only made Whitney love him more.

She wasn't certain when it became official—maybe after he stripped her down to nothing but his family's heirloom necklace and made mad love seem a sane way of putting it —but there was no lack of certainty that she *loved* him with the kind of completeness that made another person's happiness, your happiness; their sorrow, your sorrow; even the thought of living without them, an actual physical pain.

Eric could be aloof, she had seen that in his courteous yet occasionally detached dealings with others. But not with her, and she didn't want another woman to ever have such sway again.

How selfish.

She should be figuring out the exit plan she would inevitably need. Only, since she'd met Eric, everything seemed like a miracle. Maybe there were more miracles to come? Maybe his necklace was really an amulet with magical powers to protect its wearer from harm?

Whitney kissed the yin-yang pendant for luck then stacked the postcards in order of their appeal. They were destined for the P.O. Box she had rented for her extended absence, as was the hotel stationery that joined the postcards in the bedside table where an unplugged clock in Bungalow #1 still resided. Her box of Trojans, way gone, had been stepped up to something higher end that Eric called lambskins.

And just whoever thought Whitney Smith, that buttoned-down, uptight librarian, would become a connoisseur of condoms? Or of exotic herbs and teas that must be doing something since her need for sleep had been lessening, despite their seemingly insatiable activity?

"Knock-knock." Eric stood at the bedroom door as if awaiting an invitation they both knew he didn't need, especially with a bundle of tiger lilies wrapped in florist paper, tied with a big raffia straw bow.

"You're back!" Bounding out of bed, where she'd meant to write herself a postcard or a letter to receive when she would need it the most, Whitney relegated that intent to tomorrow. If she had learned anything, all anyone had was now. And for now she had an embarrassment of riches:

Eric opening his arms, florist paper and raffia pressed to her back with tiger lily blooms in her hair. The heirloom necklace his grandmother had given him sealed between them, chest to chest.

"You missed me?" he asked hopefully.

"If you have to ask, maybe you should go back to school. I think there's a philosophy class you might need to repeat."

"And here I was worried you might not have missed me as much as I was missing you. There's such a thing as too much togetherness and

I keep waiting for it to happen for you—because it sure hasn't happened for me—so all I can say is, if home is where the heart is, it's good to be home."

Home. Where you went to be nurtured, accepted, safe. She felt all that in his presence. But still there was that bubbling secret between them that was like a boil on the tip of your nose that no amount of Clearasil could disguise on too close an inspection.

"Hey," Eric suddenly asked, "are you okay?"

He never just looked at her; he studied her. And the longer they were together, the more attuned they were both becoming to the nuances of their voices, their looks, their moods. She mostly prized it, but she didn't like the complications that kind of intimacy presented in moments such as this. His B.S. detector was a little too sharp when it came to her, and it wasn't easy to be mostly honest while allowing for any necessary wiggle room.

"I was just thinking about an old friend of mine while you were gone." True enough. She could think of herself in the past tense while opening hell's door just a tiny crack. "In a way, she's the reason I'm here with you now."

"Then I'd like to meet this friend of yours so I can personally thank her for whatever she said or did to send you my way."

Whitney shook her head, dipped it to make sure he didn't see anything her eyes might too openly relay.

"I'm afraid that's not possible. She...she got some really bad news. It just came out of nowhere, and it was so unfair. She was young, like me, and thought she had her whole life ahead of her. But when she found out she didn't, she told me that her biggest regret was that in all the years she'd existed, she had never really lived. She'd been too chicken to ever take a risk. Too concerned with other people's opinions about her and trying to do everything right, always coloring inside the lines and making sure she didn't step on a crack lest she break her mother's back—and just look where it got her. She told me that the worst thing about dying was knowing she had squandered the time she had taken for granted and it was too late to take all the chances she hoped I would myself. So I told her I'd do enough living for us both. What I didn't realize when I made that promise was that I actually would."

Eric lifted her chin. His eyes searched hers and she knew he would only see truth.

"Well," he said gently, "that explains a lot. I'm so sorry about your friend. But I'm not sorry at all that it was someone else who got so damn cheated. That it was anyone, *yuan-pau,* other than you."

CHAPTER 13

Dear friend,

Where do I even start? It's hard to believe so much could happen in a matter of weeks. We continue to island hop while retaining the bunga-low, but no matter where we are I can only wonder…What have I gotten myself into? How am I ever going to reconcile this impossible situation that is quickly getting completely out of my control?

I don't know. I don't know, I don't know. I only know that I cannot give him up for as long as I can possibly have him. And I can't bear the thought of putting Eric through the unthinkable. There is a dangerous question in my mind: What if? What if I don't have to give him up? What if the ling-chih tea and herbals I've been downing like a chocoholic on a Godiva binge really have healing properties? What if the energy that keeps increasing when I should be exhausted, what if it's because heaven decided to cut me a break and

I'm in remission? What if the monster went to sleep and doesn't come back for a year, two, five or maybe forever?

There. I said it. My greatest hope. I know how dangerous, how foolish it is, but even just thinking there might be an alternative to such a cruel fate gives me…hope. And hope, it seems, makes it harder to simply live for the day.

I took Eric up on his offer of a job. Since I told him I wouldn't feel comfortable accepting a paycheck, we came to an agreement that he can cover all of our travel expenses that involve his research. You could call it a win-win for us both. I won't have to worry about draining my account completely dry after paying the Visa bill (thank goodness I hired that lawyer to handle my finances) and Eric can do some more chest pounding. I did include the stipulation this would be on a trial basis. God, I get so sick of all the maybes and we'll sees.

But…maybe if it turns out I'm not so sick, those days will be more numbered than mine. And there won't be any pieces for Marcia to pick up.

He'll be back soon from morning errands so ciao for now, pal—W

*W*hitney folded the stationery, added a few pictures of her and Eric on their various adventures, and stuffed the contents into a matching hotel envelope.

A lick and it was sealed.

She pushed her private therapy session into the bowels of the seagrass tote that didn't quite match but perfectly coordinated with her designer sandals, all of which Eric had spotted first. He had the eye of a serious designer with the flair of RuPaul. For a moment on their shopping spree, she had wondered if Eric had a little gay gene mixed in with his one-quarter Asian heritage.

He put that fleeting theory to rest with his appearance at their Bungalow #1 bedroom door and the jangle of his rented jeep keys.

"Ready for a ride? We've still got time to hit Boiling Lake so I can do some updates. In your new position as my assistant, I could use your help in navigating us there."

"What if I want to drive and have you navigate?"

"It's a stick shift. In a rain forest. On bad roads."

"When the student is ready, the teacher will appear." Her hand went up, ready to catch. "Pitch!"

"You want to drive through a rain forest? Those roads get pretty rough, Whitney."

"So? I can give it a try, can't I?"

The determined set of her jaw assured Eric that not only would she try, Whitney would come, she would conquer, and those roads would eat her hell-on-wheels dust.

"Consider the jeep yours."

As Whitney pumped air, Eric recalled the affectionate title his father had given his mother—the boss's boss.

"Hang on!" Whitney gleefully yelled as she took a hairpin curve that nearly landed Eric in her lap.

Gazing at her profile, listening to her lilting laughter, he wondered if she would ever cease to amaze him. Not only had Whitney taken on the road with a vengeance, she'd mastered a stick shift and right-hand drive in next to no time.

Time. Forever wouldn't be long enough to get his fill of her. He'd packed a lot of living into thirty-seven years, but always there had been something missing, something that kept him on the move while he searched for...her. With Whitney he was complete, seamlessly intertwined with the other half of his Tai Chi whole.

His grandmother's pendant bounced between her breasts as she flew over another rut and hit a bump that sent her several inches in the air.

Glancing over at him, she exclaimed, "I love this!"

"And I love you!"

Their eyes locked. Time seemed to move not at all, only to speed forward with the screech of brakes as they nearly careened into a tree.

Silence. Except for the squawk of a startled parrot, the rustle of wildlife scurrying into the protective cover of rain forest vegetation. And the tick of his heart waiting...waiting...

Waiting for more than the shallow wisp of her breathing and the slight shake of her head, which he countered with a decisive nod.

"I do love you, Whitney. I thought I'd say so in a more intimate setting, when the time seemed right. But it just slipped out. You know what, though? I always thought that's how it should be. I've never felt anything as right as we are together."

"I..." She gripped the steering wheel as if it were a life preserver that would keep her afloat in a tsunami. "I don't know what to say, Eric."

"You don't have to say anything. Do I want some assurance your feelings for me run just as deep? Sure I do. But I can wait. Because Whitney, if you say you love me, I want it to be because what you feel is so strong you can't keep it in, not out of some sense of obligation." He covered her hand and squeezed. "So don't say anything unless you're ready. As for me, I stand by my words but I'll try not to repeat them until you let me know that's what you want to hear."

While no verbal admission was forthcoming, the kiss she gave him was as wild as the rainforest surrounding them; a reckless, hungry kiss that required no words to confirm what he already knew.

CHAPTER 14

My dear friend,
Hope you've been enjoying the postcards. But
today I decided it's time to write a letter again
with more than updates on all our Go. See. Do.
Be. adventures in the lower and upper Antilles
islands. Now we are in Jamaica, maan, and staying
in yet another hotel. Not as fancy as our first,
but so very nice.
Eric spoils me. Recently I had some terrible cramps
(yes, that time) and he wanted to take care of me,
make me special tea with a combination of Uncle
Lee's herbs—and it worked! But mostly it was being
cared for. I'm not used to that. I had to take care
of Mama while other girls were worried about what
to wear to prom—not that I'm complaining. I was so
lucky to have her and to be there in whatever
capacity I was able. But I was young and she was so
worried about me ending up in foster care if I
didn't turn 18 before the inevitable happened. It
was hard. It was scary. Yet I know Mama was more

afraid for me than she was for herself. I miss her
so. But I have to guiltily admit that it's a relief
she can't see me now. Well, maybe she can, but I
hope she's closing her eyes and not listening in…
Except for when Eric said he loved me. That much
would make her happy. It's been two weeks since,
but I feel his love all around me, even when he's
not here. And he must feel all that love more
than returned, though I have yet to speak the
obvious.

I saw a ring, a gorgeous ring with two hands—one
platinum, one gold—clasping a pearl like a globe
between them, in a jewelry store window yesterday. Eric suggested I try it on and I forced
myself to decline. There is a difference in
wishing for something you desperately want and
knowing the folly of wanting too much. But that
hasn't stopped me from the crazy idea that I
could marry the man of my dreams in a princess
bride dress, after he whisks me away in Cinderella's coach to exchange vows that are meant to be
forever, even if forever is an illusion.

Truly, all any of us can count on is the now. If
only I could commit beyond the fear of mortality.
It stalks me. It stalks us all. I think Eric
understands that. It's one of the ties that binds
us. Who knows, maybe he'll ask me to marry him
with one of my ongoing contingencies as part of
the deal. Uh-huh. Yeah right. Dream on, girl.

Fantasies aside, I've decided that some additional birth control is in order. Pregnancy is
absolutely not an option. Given the precautions
we've taken and Eric's "training" it didn't occur
to me to even be concerned until I was two days

late. Never have I been so relieved to nearly be
doubled over…only to receive such genuine
concern, it truly drove home that for the first
time in my adult life, I am not alone.
For however long that might last, I am grateful
for each moment. And that said, I'd better be off
to the appointment I made at the clinic the front
desk suggested for medical needs.
Will get pictures developed while I'm out!
Love ya, pal. I'll see ya again when I see ya and
hopefully none too soon.
Hugs—W

~

*A*fter reading Whitney's letter, Eric tapped it against his lips as he considered what he had just learned. His curiosity about the letters and postcards Whitney kept stuffing into her tote bag then mailing out had finally gotten the better of him. Temptation had won out over trust.

He was not proud of that, not proud of it at all.

Yes, he trusted Whitney. It was her secrecy that had troubled him. And now that he had unveiled the proof any concerns he should possibly have were misplaced, he felt like a suspicious KGB operative checking up on his potentially double agent girlfriend.

Whitney deserved better. She deserved the best of him and he had not delivered.

He should come clean about his snooping, but he knew he wouldn't. It shamed him and he didn't want to give her cause to believe he might be less than trustworthy himself. Besides, it wasn't all bad, was it, if some good might come from having certain knowledge that he wasn't exactly sorry to now be privy?

Eric returned her letter to the unaddressed envelope from one of the lesser hotels where they had stayed. Whitney thought it great. She was so unspoiled. So appreciative of any little thing he did and now he had a better understanding of why.

He rubbed his forehead, thinking. Trying to. Ever since meeting Whitney his thinking wasn't what it used to be: Objective. On point. Critical logic his trusty guide.

If he had a theory now, it was that grand passions were on a par with quantum physics; that absolute love was the Tao personified. That being cognizant of its unfolding process was like being a brain surgeon fully aware he was in the midst of having a stroke.

That's how he felt—at the mercy of something he was incapable of stopping and no amount of analysis was going to save him.

Not that he wanted to be saved. What he wanted was to make his invasion of privacy and breach of Whitney's trust count for something.

He was going to make this right.

"You're sure about this?"

"Positive, Adam," Eric confirmed. "I've never been more sure about anything in my life."

Watching Whitney frolic in the surf with a child she'd befriended, Adam could understand his brother's decision. What didn't make sense was the rush he seemed to be in. Eric had never been obsessive over anything but his work. And all that heritage research he was so fascinated with but never really wanted to discuss. And, true, he did have a sort of hyper-focus when it came to applying himself to a special project or personal intention.

Adam had to concede that maybe Eric did have some obsessive tendencies, but they had certainly never extended to him being in a white-hot heat to get married.

"Then you really do plan to pop the question."

"Absolutely."

"And you intend to tie the knot today?" It was already ten a.m.

"Correct. That's why we're in Antigua. Same day nuptials. Which, by the way, I really appreciate you scooting down here to be my best man."

"Hey, I wouldn't miss this for the world." London to Antigua wasn't exactly scooting, but what was an eight-hour flight to witness something as incredible as this? Eric's eyes were positively glued on Whitney. It reminded Adam of their brief get-together six weeks ago, when Eric had stared out at the sea, transfixed by the memory of a goddess who'd worked some kind of mojo on him. That old black magic had apparently cast one helluva spell, and since most of Eric's left brain seemed to have been affected, Adam gave it a nudge.

"The folks and Grandmother Ming aren't going to be happy they weren't invited."

"They'll get over it. Once they meet Whitney they'll understand why I didn't want to wait."

"But what about her family? Won't they be upset when they find out she got married before they even met you?"

"Whitney has no family." Eric glanced at Adam and in that glance Adam saw flint. Shit. Eric would kill for this woman. "Actually, that has something to do with my urgency to make things legal. You know I'm in a dangerous line of work, that I could get called in for an emergency any time, day or night."

"Yeah, we all know that Eric." Adam knew there had been more than a few lectures canceled as a result, not to mention his brother could disappear for hours in the midst of a family gathering to handle a call. But that wasn't exactly what Eric needed reminding of now. "Your line of work didn't do much for your first marriage. What makes you think this will be any different?"

"Two reasons. I'm not as young and stupid as I was the first time around, and what Amy couldn't tolerate, Whitney can. She completely gets it that any of us could go"—he snapped his fingers—"like that. But since I have a few more occupational hazards than most, I want to be sure that she's well taken care of should anything happen to me. I have a number of benefits that would go to a surviving spouse, and it's extremely important to me that she never has to worry about the kind of security her sorry excuse for a father failed to provide."

"Oh, yeah?"

"Yeah. What a dirt bag. Ran out on Whitney and her mother when she was just a kid."

"What about her mother, what happened to her?"

"Dead. Cancer. I'm not sure we would have seen eye-to-eye about certain things."

Observing Eric in profile, Adam realized there was something different about his brother. As kids they had played Rock 'Em Sock 'Em Robots with Eric always the Blue Bomber and him, Adam, the Red Rocker. Eric would let the Red Rocker beat up all over him, only with one sudden punch his Blue Bomber would knock Red Rocker's head off. Every time. Strategic, analytical, invulnerable; a larger than life big brother who simply could not be beat.

This was not the same man. Eric not only seemed to have tumbled out of the sky and hit his head on a rock, he seemed to have grown an extra layer of humanity. He might even let a kid brother beat him at a game for once; actually, the kid brother might be able to win all on his own under the circumstances.

"About this mother of Whitney's," Adam prompted. "What makes you think the two of you could have had some differences?"

"Let's just say she had a lot of influence over her daughter and while much of that influence was clearly good, she placed too much emphasis on self-reliance, and on abiding by certain restrictive ideas. Whitney was devoted to her, and I think that glorious, free spirit you see in the water suppressed a lot of that spirit to please her only parent. But just look at her there—" Eric blew a kiss and she pretended to catch it on the cheek so hard it knocked her back into a wave. "When I see her like that, the way she embraces life, so unafraid to seize it and shake it for all that it's worth..." He shook his head. "It's a long stretch of the imagination but there could have been a time when Whitney may have been more like Amy in certain ways. Clinging to the familiar; more comfortable living inside the lines than venturing outside them."

"Like Amy," Adam repeated. "There's a divorce just waiting to happen."

"But it won't happen to us."

Adam patted his brother's shoulder and hoped to hell he was right.

As Eric and Whitney walked hand in hand through the streets of Saint John, Antigua's capital, Eric navigated their seemingly aimless stroll in the direction of the Ministry of Legal Affairs. A civil ceremony was only a signature and a license fee away. Simple as that.

Getting Whitney to agree wouldn't be such a piece of cake. He'd ordered one anyway—along with a chapel and all the other trimmings Adam was seeing to while he went about the business of convincing Whitney to be a willing bride.

"And what do you think of Adam?"

"He's lovely. I wish he would have joined us for lunch."

"He'll join us later." As their destination came into sight, Eric slowed his pace. "He's a handsome devil, isn't he?"

"Is he?" Whitney gave Eric the once-over, head to toe, with blatant appreciation. "I didn't notice. Apparently I was too busy checking out another guy who could be the Devil's advocate."

"Can I get that in writing?"

"You silly man." She pinched the cheek he had shaved extra close that morning. "You know that I'd take you over Adam or any other man alive any day of the week."

"Or any week of the month?"

"Yes!" She giggled, apparently thinking this conversation to be heading nowhere but to the fishing of compliments.

"What about extending that to any month of the year?"

Her laughter stilled, and there it was—that look. The one when he first wanted to talk about their relationship; when he presented her with his heirloom pendant; when he shouted out that he loved her. It was a look that reminded him of a hungry animal eyeing a baited trap, and pausing to decide if it could grab dinner before the cage snapped shut and turned it into the dinner served.

He inclined his head, waiting. She visibly swallowed.

"Why do I get the feeling this conversation has nothing to do with Adam or my opinion of your looks?"

"Because it has nothing to do with any of that and everything to do with us." They had reached the ministry building. Eric sat on the bottom step leading to the offices and their future. He patted the space beside him. "Sit with me?"

Whitney sat, but didn't take his hand. She clasped hers together with a movement that suggested a subtle wringing.

"What if I modified any month of the year to just three months?" He claimed her left hand, and kissed the finger where his ring belonged. "Marry me? Three months, that's all I'm asking for."

"Marry you?" she whispered faintly. "For three months? Eric, I...I don't understand. Why?"

"Because then you can think of it as a trial marriage while I make progress in increments. Because I know that between losing your dad, your mother, and your friend, you've developed an aversion to making long range plans and if I hold out for the commitment I really want, I may never get it. And finally..."

"Yes?"

"Because I'm crazy in love with you. And I think you're more than a little crazy about me, too."

Nodding, nodding, looking as if she had just been handed an entire bakery instead of a cupcake, Eric thought he had her agreement—only for Whitney to shut her eyes as if doing some kind of hard thinking or mental math, before her bluer than blue gaze locked with his.

"What's the catch?"

"I want to get married today. Now. Before you have a chance to get cold feet and I end up with an indefinite string of maybes and we'll see's."

"And if it's not working out after three months?"

"You can have your walking papers, free to leave if you want, and never see me again. I can't hold you if you don't want to be held, and I won't fight you if you don't want me in the end. If you'd like that in writing we can have that notarized along with the wedding papers. Anything else?"

Just when it looked like she was going to throw herself into his arms with a resounding YES! Whitney stopped short, stalling on a footnote.

"Yes," she did say, only softly, her hand paused against his chest. "What about blood work? Don't we have to do that and whatever else people have to do before they can get married?"

"Not here." Pulling her up with him and not giving her a chance to think beyond the kiss he laid on her, Eric extended a hand toward the Ministry of Legal Affairs building. "And here we are. Shall we?"

When they emerged with the speed of a revolving door, Whitney tried to hide her disappointment that her cherished dream of a wedding had consisted of nothing more than appearing before some official called a Marriage Coordinator, their signatures on a declaration paper, and a license fee paid. It was a major downer after her earlier elation that Eric had given her the ultimate bucket list gift, no strings attached, and, MOST IMPORTANTLY: An exit plan he wouldn't question if/when the time came.

Now if this upward trend in her health took a dive and she needed to bail before their three months were up...? She would simply cite irreconcilable differences and take her papers on an early walk, Eric none the wiser. Win-win.

Amazing how ones reasoning skills could ramp up when you wanted something so bad you could taste it.

Only now that they were officially married, without so much as a kiss to seal the deal, she wished she had worked in some more contingencies. At least a temporary ring to wear. It wasn't like she was greedy—okay obviously she was, agreeing to something this risky because she so desperately wanted what she'd thought she couldn't have—but, dammit!

"That's it?" she asked, just to be sure.

"If that was it, I'd still be kissing my bride." He briefly pressed his lips to her temple. "I'll save the real one for the ceremony."

"You mean there's more?" *Please, let there be more.*

"Ah, *yuan-pao,* you know me better than anyone but apparently there's still more for you to learn."

He looked up then down the street, grumbled something about Adam being late, then suddenly covered her eyes.

"No peeking till I say so."

"What is it?" she asked excitedly as the sound of *clip-clop-clip-clop-rattle-rattle-rattle* drew nearer, nearer…

Then stopped.

Eric removed his hands and she blinked. And blinked again, unable to believe what had appeared before her eyes:

A white horse with gold and purple feather plumage sprouting from its crown, pulling an open, glossy white carriage that would put Cinderella's coach to shame. It had cans trailing from behind and ribbons and streamers and a pouf of white netting affixed on either side of the stepped up entrance. And there was Adam, transformed into a liveryman, extending a huge bouquet of tiger lilies and white orchids.

"M'lady." Eric bowed. "Your chariot awaits."

CHAPTER 15

"*How* did you do this?" Whitney asked as she waved back to the pedestrian well-wishers they passed along the way.

"How?" Eric snapped his fingers. "Magic."

Magic, Adam thought with a mental roll of his eyes. More like Eric enlisting the hotel's concierge for the matrimonial best of everything Antigua had to offer, and a jet-lagged brother running non-stop for the past few hours to ensure all was ready and set for the bride's arrival.

Giving Eric a thumbs-up to assure him it was a go, Adam settled back in the seat across from them and couldn't help but envy their happiness. Whitney beaming; Eric, oblivious to everything but her. Just to look at them was to want some of what they had. Life in the fast lane had gotten old. He wasn't getting any younger, either. His glory days of *GQ* photo spreads were trickling to an end, and what would he have then?

Anyone from the outside looking in would probably think he had more than his slice of the pie. Sexy cars. Sexy women. Sexy moves and clothes with an Adonis face and build that made those sexy women think of sex. Fantasy, pure fantasy. In reality, cars could be crashed, he could lose his perfect body and face in the second it would take to have a wreck, and those sexy women would evaporate the moment he needed them for the kind of loyalty, love and support that Eric believed he shared with Whitney.

"Adam," she called over the clip-clopping of horse hooves, the flap of reins by their dandy driver. "Love the outfit. Where did you get it?"

"This old thing?" he scoffed with a flash of his trademark smile and a dismissive wave at the Armani gold brocade vest. "It's from last year's collection. Not the sort of accessory anyone would want to sport on a daily basis but nice to have around when the need arises. Sort of like Jolene."

"Eric mentioned her. She's your girlfriend, isn't she?"

"Was," he corrected. "And if I have any sense, I'll keep it that way. We're…" How to say this? "We just don't have the stuff it takes to build a real future." He extended a hand toward the happy couple. "Unlike you and Eric."

Was it a trick of lighting or did Whitney's brilliant glow suddenly dim? Adam glanced at the sky. Some clouds were rolling in. When he looked back again she averted her gaze and buried her face in the crook of Eric's neck. But not before he glimpsed something troubled and evasive in her eyes and in her smile.

Whitney had secrets.

Whatever she was hiding, Adam could only hope the new Mrs. Townsend wasn't carrying some deadly ammunition that could blow a hole into the happily-ever-after his brother was expecting.

As the storybook-picture wedding chapel came into sight, heralded by the pealing of bells from its small tower, Whitney burrowed deeper beneath the protection of Eric's arm.

The stuff it takes to build a real future...like you and Eric. Adam's words had spread through her brain like a malignancy since he'd uttered them. She couldn't help but resent the innocent remark that threatened to spoil her reign as queen for a day.

And what of tomorrow? The day after that? Would she be dogged by thoughts of an uncertain future based on her lie of omission? *It's only for three months,* she reminded herself, *as long as you stay healthy.* And yet, who knew better than she how quickly those tides could turn, no matter how ferociously she prayed they would not? It was the reason she had fled the crowded clinic two weeks before in Jamaica, the smell of antiseptic and illness making her skin crawl and her feet race for the exit. It took half an hour to walk off her nerves and get the smell out of her nostrils before she forced herself to return—only to be told there were no more openings. They left the next day. Not only had she been reluctant to repeat the experience elsewhere, their field work had provided little opportunity to do so.

The horse stopped, Adam jumped out. Next came Eric, bouncing to the ground like a kid on a new pogo stick. He offered his hand, only to swing her out by the waist with a joyous laugh.

The formally dressed driver tipped his top hat. First to her, and then to an elegant, dark-skinned woman dressed in a chic royal blue sarong with a matching turban who introduced herself as Celeste.

Whitney couldn't help but notice the bride and groom were comparatively underdressed for the occasion.

Neither could she help noticing Adam's scrutiny, just before he bussed her cheek and whispered into her ear, "Eric's got a big heart. Don't break it, okay?"

Direct hit. She hadn't seen it coming. Whitney summoned a stiff nod and an equally stiff smile as memories of Marcia in Montserrat rolled in. Marcia, who truly, deeply, cared about Eric and was just waiting to pick up any pieces his new bride might leave behind should his heart be broken.

A swift, hard kick from her conscience coincided with a surge of anxiety that smacked-down what was left of her just-got-married high.

Eric offered his arm. "Shall we? The Marriage Officer's due to be here soon and that doesn't give you much time to change."

Eric had bought her a dress. One that would surely be as divine as the rest of the dream wedding he was giving her. Only in her dreams she wasn't shaking her head and stalling outside the chapel doors. They swished behind Adam, followed by Celeste, after it became apparent the bride wasn't going in and the groom was concerned.

"What's wrong?"

"Eric, I...I don't know if we should do this."

"Why not? Did I say something, do something to give you second thoughts?"

"No," she assured him, clasping his hand and wanting to bawl her head off while screaming at the top of her lungs. But more than anything, she wanted to tell him the truth. "The Truth isn't all that's unknowable," she heard herself say. Then earnestly, "Eric, the future holds no guarantees."

"I'm not asking for guarantees. I'm asking you to be my wife. For three months, no more, no less. Where we go from there, or not, that's completely up to you."

"No, it isn't!" *Stay calm*, she ordered herself. *Say what you have to say even if it means giving up the most important moment of your life.* "My—my friend, the one I told you about, said when she found out she was going to die it seemed to her like a blessing that she wouldn't be leaving behind a grieving husband. And—and I can understand how she'd feel that way. Life is so fragile, you know. It makes me afraid, Eric. I'm afraid of my own mortality."

"Aren't we all," he empathized. "Trust me, I completely get that. I also understand that you're a jittery bride I'm champing at the bit to get into her wedding dress."

"But Eric—"

"We're already legally married, Whitney." He tapped the envelope containing their marriage papers lightly against her nose. "And we made a deal. I'm holding you to it. If it makes you feel better, we can have the 'till death do we part' part deleted when we say our vows."

Yet again he had given her a "Get Out Of Jail Free" pass.

While her higher nature still hesitated, the not-so-higher moved in fast to selfishly grab that pass and run.

"Okay. As long as we keep the death part out of it."

"Then consider it done. Now let's get this party started."

As they neared the small changing room where Celeste, the dress-maker who'd be doubling as a witness waited, Eric imparted a final reassurance.

"Remember this and never forget it. If I had to choose between having one day, and one day only, with the woman who completes me or a lifetime with someone else, I wouldn't have to think twice about choosing you."

Whitney felt as if she were in a dream. A lucid dream in which a fairy godmother named Celeste fussed with her hair, touched up her makeup, and voilà, there was *The Dress*. A flowing pale gown the color of linen and made of raw silk with running streams of seed pearls. An empire waist suggested Renaissance; tattered scarf sleeves, vamp romance. The veil was equally unique. Netting only partially covered her face, like a femme fatale from a vintage film noir; it was attached to a garland of blood red roses and baby's breath. The exquisite ensemble's crowning glory was Eric's heirloom necklace, riding upon the bodice of a wedding dress that was equal measures of Tim Burton and Vogue.

Strains of *Ode to Joy* filtered in from the chapel proper. Celeste kissed her cheek. She said, "This man, he love you very much," and then Celeste was walking from the room and toward the aisle to stand as witness. Whitney cradled the bouquet in her arm and sent a prayer to heaven that God would be merciful, that one day, by some amazing grace she might sing a lullaby as she held a babe just so.

Feeling as if she had angel's wings upon her slippered feet, she floated toward the music and past ten marching pews, all the while gazing with adoration at the man who met her halfway, tucked her hand in the crook of his arm and murmured, "You are a vision."

"And you, a prince amongst men." Although, with his almond eyes doing a slow burn, his sleek black hair raked severely back from his chiseled face, and his magnificent frame cloaked in a grey linen morning suit that was anchored by a broad ruby tie, he could have been a raven who had assumed human form.

She felt both vulnerable and protected as he took her to be his wife with a voice that rang clear and strong.

"I do."

Eric slid onto her finger the band she had coveted in a display store in Jamaica, made of two hands with one cast in gold, the other platinum. The pearl held between them seemed to symbolize the balance of life, suspended by the joined forces of woman and man.

"And do you, Whitney Smith..." The officiant paused as Eric passed him a sheet of paper. "Agree to take this man to be your trusted friend and playmate, true companion, fellow road warrior, and faithful husband?"

"I do," she vowed, fully aware that the "till death do we part" part had been left out as promised while several other provisos had taken its place.

"By the power vested in me, I now pronounce you husband and wife. You may kiss your bride."

Eric lifted the veil. And as he did, she saw his eyes glitter with a foxlike intelligence. The brilliance of his mind was familiar; its covert workings, not so much. His lips were inclined to smile often, and while she'd seen many variations on the initial three, this was a smile that had yet to emerge. It was like he knew something she didn't.

And his kiss, it was different too. So gentle at first, only for his lips to slant and press harder, possessively, as if to imprint on her psyche, even more than her mouth, that she was now his, and he was hers, in more than name.

With her head reeling, Eric swept her off her feet and into his arms. They were halfway out of the chapel when she realized music accompanied their departure.

Heart and Soul.

Flower petals rained on them as they exited. It was a beautiful touch. She asked Adam and Celeste to join them for a celebration.

Adam had to fly to New York. Celeste had to close shop.

She threw the bouquet. Adam caught it. A hug and a wave later, she was back in the carriage with a ring on her finger and a supposedly temporary husband who was making her wish fiercely for some company on their wedding night.

Eric had her heart. But with a look, a kiss, he'd made it clear he wouldn't settle for less than her soul.

CHAPTER 16

"More champagne for my bride?"

"Yes, please." As Eric topped off her flute, Whitney eyed the rest of the bottle and wondered if there was enough courage in it for what remained of the night. Fortunately back-up was already chilling in an iced silver bucket, compliments of the private villa Eric had rented for a week.

"The way you say that, I'm given to wonder if you're actually nervous about going to bed with your husband."

Was she? Eric had sent the staff home early; she'd been hoping they would work late. But instead of blurting, "Of course I'm nervous!" Whitney managed to explain, "I've never had a husband before, Eric. Everything just feels different."

"Bad different?" He removed his cufflinks. She gave a little jump at the soft clatter of his jewelry hitting the glass table where an exquisite, untouched tiered cake with a tiger lily on top was parked. "Or, good different?"

"Yes. No. Both." She took another healthy sip from her flute. "I don't know."

"Whitney, look at me."

She did. Eric had left his chair, was kneeling on the floor, directly

116

in front of where she sat. Despite feeling a little ridiculous for her behavior, she knew something *was* different. Eric had expectations. Their relationship had shifted from her "we'll see's" and "maybe's" to a more profound kind of ground.

"I love you," he said simply, as if those three words were the only ones needed in an unsettled world to bridge whatever chasms might divide it. "We took vows today. Even if you decide later that you'd rather throw yourself into traffic than be married to me, tonight I need your assurance that you don't regret it already." He leaned in, but didn't try to kiss her. "I said I wouldn't ask, but now I'm asking anyway. Would you tell me what you haven't yet? What you know I've been waiting to hear?"

Whitney put down her glass. She touched his cheek. "How could you ever doubt it?"

"I don't." He pressed his lips into her palm. "I just need to hear you say it."

"I love you." The words that had been bottled up for so long came out in a whispered rush. And once released, they couldn't stop coming. "I love you, I love you. Love *you.*"

"That's exactly what I needed to hear. From my Whitney. My *yuan-pau.*" He extended his hand and she interlocked her fingers with his, squeezed tight. As if she had relayed the signal he was waiting for, Eric significantly concluded with, "But I especially needed to hear it from *my wife.*"

He rose from his knees, pulling her up with him, then chin-tilted her head to study her face. His own wore an expression that conveyed the same glittering intelligence that had slightly unnerved her earlier, but now it was infiltrated with a raw yearning that caused her to feel the same fight or flight instinct summoned by a dark stranger who had the courtesy to knock before barging in.

The dark stranger she had married kissed her. In all the kisses they had shared before, and there were too many to count, she had never quite felt that Eric had purposefully made it his mission to suck her into his orbit so completely that she had no means of escape; nor the desire for it.

That's when she realized. Eric had set a velvet trap: He had told her what he knew she wanted, needed, him to say before she would sign those papers and walk down that aisle.

It was the ultimate bait and switch: He had reeled her in on a three month agreement. And while she had been strategizing for an early exit if necessary, his sole purpose was to ensure that she never left.

Eric could taste the flavor of her shifting responses, he saw the way her gaze, her expressions kept changing with her private thoughts, her emotions. And he could certainly discern the effect it was all having on her physically.

The palms he swept over her back relayed that Whitney was actually trembling. So were the lips she kept partially closed, like gates that weren't completely shutting him out but neither were they providing full entrance.

It didn't take a genius to know that she was at least a little afraid. Of him, her new husband? He thought so, and that probably wasn't completely unwarranted. After all, throughout the entire business of getting married, he had known something that Whitney seemed to just now be grasping.

All of their previous interactions and intimacies, which had led to this day, fell into the category of: *Before*. Official papers, a ring, the vows they had taken in the presence of others were solid evidence of a new stage in their relationship that bore the distinct designation of: *After*.

It stood to reason that Whitney's anxiety was at least partially due to realizing she had made a legal commitment to a man she knew, but didn't fully know. And yet that was part of the mystery of marriage: That two people could grow and change together, that there was one person bearing witness to your strengths, your foibles, your transitions in life, and part of your pact was to hold each other accountable while being more supportive and compassionate than anyone else in the world when either of you failed.

If one learned more from their failures than their successes, he knew a lot about marriage. It was its own entity. It had its own persona. It was a big bang planet that could die at birth or be spun into the stratosphere by the people who created their own unique world, with their own unique language and culture. The best marriages were a creative enterprise with two highly invested team players who were better together than they were apart, yet understood the importance of allowing room for who they were individually...becoming.

He and Whitney had been like children playing. Now they had crossed a line. Marriage was for adults. Time to grow up.

Putting the kiss on pause that she wasn't wholeheartedly returning, Eric considered his best course of action to get this honeymoon night on the right track.

"I have another gift for you. But first, let's refill that flute." Yes, good idea. He didn't want to get her tanked but more Dom would hopefully get her easy again in the skin he dearly wanted to touch.

"Thank you, Eric."

Her relief was so palpable he wondered if maybe he should get her tanked. They could laugh years later about a wedding night when their greatest intimacy was him holding up her hair so it didn't join any miserable prayers over porcelain.

"Here's to you, Mrs. Townsend." He tapped the rim of his crystal to hers. "Here's to us."

Whitney looked from her glass with the last remains of her lipstick, to him, as if debating between an AA meeting and throwing her lot in with a wine wielding Bacchus.

"There's no rush," he assured her. "We can dance, we can drink, we can order out for pizza if you'd prefer that over lobster, and spend the rest of the night eating cake." All but the top tier. That they would save for their first anniversary. "What I'm trying to say is that as much as I'd love to slip you out of that dress and into nothing for a proper commemoration of quite the day, I am completely okay with just hanging out tonight."

"Really?" At his nod, she asked, "What about tomorrow?"

"Maybe I'll get lucky and you'll make out with me while we watch a movie."

Now she was smiling. "And the day after?"

"My patience will be completely worn out. Even ten pairs of Nikes hitting ground at full speed won't stand a chance of you outrunning me." He reached around her back, slipped his hand beneath the scooped fabric, and with an adroit move between thumb and forefinger, unhooked her bra. He knew what bra she was wearing and had every intention of continuing to undo it for as long as the elastic held up. "So, what might I grant my wife on our wedding night? More Dom? Pizza? Cake?" A pause and he hopefully added, "Me?"

"I think we need to get naked."

"Do you now?" He inclined his head, appearing to consider. "Why?"

"Honestly, Eric, nothing has felt familiar today and I could use some familiar ground. I'm thinking once we're back in bed, where we have spent an awful lot of time, things will just feel more normal."

He softly laughed at her naiveté, at his own before Whitney had turned everything he thought he knew about life and love on its head. She had taught him more in six weeks than he had learned in three decades. His wife—yes, *his wife*—was a gifted teacher. Hopefully she would deem her husband not too shabby himself.

"We can get as naked as we were yesterday, and all the days before," he told her. "But it won't be the same."

"No?"

"No." He kissed the wedding ring he had put on her finger, and then led his willing bride towards the bedchamber door. "It'll be better."

As Whitney came slowly awake, stretching with a voluptuous abandon, her first thought was that her new husband was not one for making false promises.

Reaching over to touch him, her palm connected with a still-warm mattress where he no longer lay. A dusky pink light filtering in from plantation blinds called it early dawn, and further assured her that Eric was not in bed.

Perhaps he was in the bathroom. Hopefully he wasn't elsewhere taking an emergency call. But then she noticed the French doors leading outside to the veranda were open. A breeze fluttered the flowing curtains, tendrils of sheer fabric that reminded her of the wedding dress that Eric had asked for the honors of removing, before requesting she do the same for him. There was no urgency to get each other's clothes off; it was more an unhurried event that almost seemed ceremonial, even ritualistic. The lights had been dimmed but there were no candles, there was no music, only softly spoken words in an atmosphere that felt like an alchemy of magic and reality; of fantasy and substance; of solemnity and delight.

Eric had been right. It was different. And it was better.

She felt alone without him sharing the mattress with her. Getting up, she saw her wedding dress that Eric had carefully draped over a nearby chair made of carved teak. The matching chair beside it tended his tailored suit.

Again she thought of the difference in their act of disrobement; the difference in their lovemaking which followed. He handled her differently. She responded differently. It was as if their bodies were talking a slightly different language that she didn't yet have the ability to interpret. And oddly, they didn't engage in a lot of fore-play, unless she counted their extended divestment of wedding clothes. Neither did they see how many new positions they could check off the Mystic Master's copulation list. No, it was nothing like that.

They had pulled down the sheets together—her on one side, Eric on the other. For long moments they just stood there, looking across at each other. There was some serious dialog going on between their eyes but neither said a word. Then Eric had slightly smiled, and this smile was different, too; it was a smile that said they could relax now, that they were a team with a plan. He slightly bowed, extended a hand to the bed, and she felt good, warm, somehow just right as she accepted his invitation and opened her arms to likewise invite him to join her.

The way he traced the length of her arms, her torso and legs, without pausing to investigate the prime treasure in between, it was if he was touching her for the first time...or rather, touching her like this for the first time. It was a touch that felt reverent, protective, and unmistakably territorial.

She wanted him to mark that territory; wanted to mark him as belonging to her, only to her, as he did. A fine trade-off that didn't bear negotiation: She'd bent her knees, dropped them open like the spread of butterfly wings, and whispered, "Now."

His accommodation was immediate. No teasing, no wooing, not even a kiss. It was a face-to-face, eye-to-eye purposeful act of physical joining completed in a single movement that was less thrust, more a slow, deliberate pressing until he could go no further and she was full of him.

She touched his face. Her wedding ring, so much more than a beautiful new bauble, rested against his cheek as he began to rock her.

Her breath caught in the same moment his did. They shared a rippling pleasure that was hardly earth-shattering, yet in its quietness was somehow even more intense. Like they had shared a secret, made a pact.

Whitney thought of how they had fallen asleep. Her head resting peacefully on his chest, his arms protectively around her while he stroked her hair. The last thing she remembered was the kiss he pressed to her forehead, his whispered, "Sweet dreams, Mrs. Townsend."

Eric knew why he couldn't sleep, why he had left the bed with his new wife still sleeping in it. It was the reason why he was working off his frustration with lap after lap in the heated pool that their honeymoon suite opened out to.

Their wedding had been perfect. Their wedding night had been perfect, too. Almost. They had established a landmark point from which all their future interactions would radiate. Whitney, whether consciously or not, had colluded with him on the new path they were on when they pulled down the sheets in tandem and she said, "Now."

He had worn "the uniform" as he had begun to think of the condoms they used as a precaution, even if they were almost always tossed away empty. And for the most part he was fine with that. His greatest pleasure was in bringing Whitney—*his wife*, god, he loved the sound of that—as much pleasure as he possibly could. And he certainly had more than his personal share, able to enjoy multiple climaxes with each one building on the other because they weren't predicated on spreading or spilling his seed.

Clearly, Whitney wasn't ready to have a baby, and agreed, it was too soon. Given their level of activity, she'd been prudent to visit that clinic in Jamaica two weeks ago. She hadn't said anything about it, and he hadn't mentioned it either since that would reveal him for the spymaster he was, digging into the tote where she kept all the personal things that would overly crowd her purse.

Maybe that's where she was keeping her pills. Or maybe they were in her tote. Or the luggage that he wasn't about to investigate either. As for why she had opted not to mention or wish to discuss the additional birth control, he could only presume that it gave her a needed sense of independence and control over her own body, her own future, that their nearly non-stop togetherness had to some degree usurped.

So, he had his secret. Whitney had hers. Made them even enough. Especially since, between the two, his was the greater infraction on the trust upon which their marriage had to be built.

He took another lap under the dusky pink sky that heralded dawn. And he wondered if Whitney might awaken because she sensed he was no longer there.

He wondered if she would find the wrapped box he'd left beside the chair where he had so carefully placed her wedding dress. Inside the box was an old silk kimono, the gift he'd never gotten around to giving her en lieu of a honeymoon teddy.

As if his thoughts had summoned her, Whitney emerged from the room where they had made some kind of history. As she approached, she fanned out the elegant box-like sleeves with her arms spread, until she stood by the pool where his heart nearly stopped when she undid the obi belt just above her waist, laid it aside, and opened the kimono to display all that he had ever coveted as her lover, and even more now that she was his wife.

"I missed you," she said.

"You wear it well," said he.

"The kimono or the missing you part?"

"Both. Shall I get out, or should you get in?"

She removed the kimono, placed it on safe dry ground with the obi belt, and dove into the deep end where she had found him treading water.

He went after her, swam to catch the water goddess he had seen emerge like a pagan Aphrodite out of the river where she had kissed a shell and sent it sailing to the moon after singing "Twinkle, Twinkle" to the stars.

He'd been in the deep end ever since but he was no longer treading water. Yesterday had seen to that.

Catching her by the foot, she managed to slip free, so he quickly caught her by the waist with one hand, speared his other through her hair, and tangled his legs with hers as their mouths met and they emerged from the deep beneath into a rising morning sun.

A parrot squawked from an over-reaching palm that waved its blessing over two naked bodies that were all but one. His lips, his hands, they were all over her; and hers, all over him. This was familiar; they had been here many times before. But how much things could change in only day. You could be well and happy on one, in a burn unit the next, with three of your best friends dead. Or, you could be a single guy running for a taxi and nearly missing a plane, then winding up next to the woman who would bind you to her and render you forever changed before you even knew her name.

He longed to be further bound. It was the one blemish on an

otherwise perfect wedding night. For once, just once, he wanted, *needed,* to have nothing between them.

As he kissed her with the urgency that was in him, and she wrapped her legs around his hips, the scientist he was shook hands with the satyr who wasn't ruled by ethical considerations and was only too happy to invite a conversation:

You did your research and you know it only takes a week for birth control pills to kick in. It's been two weeks. What are you waiting for?

I'm waiting for her to tell me so I can shuck the goddam condoms and not admit to my intrusion.

But that's just the thing, isn't it? You want an intrusion. You want to do something you haven't before and you want to do it with...your wife. Yeah, you like the sound of that, don't you?

A wife deserves absolute honesty.

Not if that honesty lands you in a heap load of shit. Forget all that crybaby wha-wha-wha sorry I did this, did you possibly do that, please forgive me, and since it should be safe, can I please—

That's enough. We will not have that conversation.

Then what will you have? Better to ask for forgiveness later than permission now if you want to stamp your seal along with those papers. You did put a ring on it—and yes, last night was great, no argument there. But if it wasn't lacking something, then why were you up before dawn, swimming laps in a pool? Like, the pool she just happens to be in now, with her legs strapped across your engines and too far gone to notice if one of those raincoats aren't conveniently in the water with you?

You're not a good guy.

Nobody ever said you had to be perfect to be one. Go for it.

Whitney thought he looked like a particular actor in The Devil's Advocate. While he didn't see the resemblance himself, he had a keen appreciation for the gray areas that could lure a man from what he knew to be right from wrong—especially when his own higher nature wasn't heeding heaven's call.

The path he chose was as primal as any man's could get: to enter the sacred chamber of the woman he would die for, kill for, and mark as his.

He was partially in when his conscience whispered, *Wait.*

He was nearly half-way when every sensory trigger in his body began to shout *This is amazing, why did you wait so long!?*

Almost there. *Wait, wait!!*

And then it was done.

Eric closed his eyes to absorb the pure ecstasy of being encased by her velvety texture. To finally know how it felt to be completely linked with absolutely nothing between them, to fully penetrate his lover and wife, no condom for once to imply squatter's rights.

You got what you wanted, now take it and leave. It's not too late.

As he began to withdraw velvety walls clenched tight and started milking away at his good intentions while nature dictated he thrust instead of depart.

It took every ounce of discipline and training accumulated over more than a decade to make a split-second decision.

A swift retreat. A mind bending release.

"Sorry," he gasped, "Sorry."

"For what?" she gasped back as he bobbed between her thighs.

If Whitney was still too forgone to figure that out, the satyr was getting a curtain call before he bowed out.

"For not bringing you breakfast in bed."

"I'd rather have you for breakfast."

Oh, but you just did. Apparently, even if she'd had the wherewithal to realize his crime of omission, she wasn't aware of the close call, or that his rare release was so violent there had to be enough tadpoles swimming around to fill a nursery.

Of course it could also be that she wasn't worried, given her extra precautions.

He dearly hoped that Whitney would bring the subject up soon. Meanwhile, he would be responsible. He would wear the damn condoms. But only for so long. Because there was going to come a point, and in the near future, where he would come clean and suffer any consequences if it meant he could feel her, all the way up to her baby palace, with nothing between them again.

126

CHAPTER 17

Dear friend,
Big news!!! I'm married to Eric. Things were great before but, I don't even know how to describe what it's like now. It's as if we've formed our own little secret society that nobody else can join. And there's this sense of…stability? Calm? It feels like being on a high wire, a mile up in the sky, and it's thrilling but not scary because there's this great big net you know is waiting, and if you fall, you'll still be safe. A lot like parasailing, only…
Better.
Eric wants to take me to Portland to see a little houseboat he owns—who knew?—and from there we'll go to San Francisco so I can meet his family over Thanksgiving (only a few weeks away, gulp!). Actually, I spoke with his parents and Grandmother Ming on the phone. I was nervous at first but they were all just wonderful and made me feel genuinely welcome and accepted, even sight

unseen. For Eric to make me a part of his family…
I'm not sure he could ever realize just how much
that means.

And yet I am fully cognizant that that which is
given can swiftly be taken away. Not to worry,
there are safeguards in place in the event of an
emergency.

We decided to extend our stay here in Antigua,
where our old routines have picked up some new
ones—such as making the bed together and reading
the paper while sipping our tea. Eric making
breakfast. Me burning dinner. It's…domestic.
Sweet.

I'm so content that I would just as soon not
attend the play we have tickets for tonight. In
truth, I would rather stay home, even if the
villa is a bit too grand for my personal tastes
and a bungalow sounds cozier. So does a little
houseboat.

Well, it will probably do us good to get out.
Hopefully Eric won't want to dance the night away
after the play. I woke up a wee bit tired this
morning. Nothing I'm concerned about since even
Wonder Woman would be exhausted after what's been
quite the honeymoon!

Guess that about wraps it up. Maybe I'll take a
little nap while Eric's running a few errands in
town.

Love, the Ecstatic Mrs. T

~

She sent the letter. Two days later, she followed it with another, detailing her joy and only that since she had to believe everything was all right, that she was well. But after three scribbled postcards, Whitney could no longer ignore the fact that all wasn't right because well she was not.

They had gone to another play and she had fallen asleep.

He had made her favorite breakfast of a conch omelet and fried plantains that she could hardly get down.

When Eric wanted to take her parasailing she'd told him her favorite new sport had lost its appeal after reading about someone whose parachute had collapsed and they'd fallen to their death in shark-infested waters.

She hadn't read any such article, but death was very much on Whitney's mind as she lifted a pen. It shook. Her hands were unsteady and her stomach gave another lurch while she tried to summon the strength to write what she feared would be her last missive.

My dear friend and confidant,
I'm trying very hard not to cry. Something is
wrong; terribly wrong.
Eric's been pampering me for the past few days,
ever since he decided I must be coming down with
a bug of some sort that's to blame for my
lethargy. I'm going along with his reasoning and
taking it easy but no matter how much ling-chih
or his other herbals I consume, no matter how
much sleep I get, the fatigue won't go away. It's
a struggle to wake up and once I'm awake, all I
want to do is sleep.
I'm trying so hard not to freak but the questions
keep coming and won't go away. How could this
happen to me? To us? Was three months so much to
hope for? Dammit, we deserve those three months
and more. So. Much. More.
My fear has taken on a life of its own. Eric
knows something isn't right. He got a call and
was put on alert that he may be needed somewhere
in South America. Before, I would have insisted

on going along, but instead I told him that I
should hold down the fort in his absence. He said
he was worried about me, wanted to take me to a
doctor, that he would start looking for backup in
the event he got called in.

I told him it was silly to see a doctor for
nothing more than a virus I probably picked up on
the street (oh my god, my stomach still drops
when I think of him saying "doctor"). I told him
that if he got the call, he had to see to his
responsibilities and I would feel even worse if
he didn't because of me. Of course that just
seemed like more evidence that I'm supportive in
a way that Amy wasn't—so just chalk up another
lie to go with all the rest.

Until I met Eric, I don't think I told more than
three little lies in my whole life, unless I
count all the lies I probably told myself. Ambi-
tious girl that I am, I just seem to have gotten
better and better at that because, boy, have I
come up with some real whoppers.

When Eric asked me to marry him, he handed me the
exit plan. I was greedy enough to agree while I
told myself that maybe I wouldn't need it. Then I
fed myself all that crap about citing irreconcilable differences and cutting it off sooner if the
worst happened. We have no irreconcilable differences. Eric knew I would never want to leave. I
can make up whatever excuse I want, but he won't
buy it.

And if I tell him the truth?

He deserves it—deserved it from the very beginning. But I was selfish. I was cowardly. And that
much hasn't changed. I cannot bear the thought of
subjecting him to watching me die. It's a

horrible thing to witness, and no. No. I can't do
that to him. And honestly—wow, Whitney, honesty,
what a concept!—I can't do it to myself. I cringe
to imagine him seeing me the way I did Mama
towards the end. Withered to nothing, bald,
clawed hands mindlessly trying to yank out the
morphine drip while I silently, guiltily, prayed
she would just die and remove us both from the
pain, the awfulness of it all.
I pray now. I pray for a miracle. And I pray for
the strength to do what is right after doing so
much that was selfish and wrong.
Must go. So tired. Need a nap while Eric's off
shopping. Hope he doesn't cook another big
dinner. Even my sexual appetite seems to have
disappeared.
He gives the best hugs. The best everything.
Lucky—Me

"Whitney? Whitney where are you?" Eric called with increasing urgency as he searched the villa he'd reluctantly left, minus Whitney, days before.

He'd known he shouldn't go despite her insistence. He'd known she wasn't feeling well, so tired, no appetite, and why on earth had she been so dead set against seeing a doctor? If for nothing else to put his own mind at ease.

Easy his mind was not.

For the first time in his career he'd left in the middle of a crisis situation to tend to personal business—a wife who wasn't answering the phone and had him no longer just worried, but worried sick.

Where *was* she? Eric stared dumbly at the open closet. Empty. Except for her wedding dress and the kimono.

"What's going on?" he whispered. Then, as the reality of her disappearance clicked, "What the *hell* is going on?"

His voice splintered the silence before fading into the nothingness of dead air. There was no lilting laughter to be heard, no words of comfort, just this awful churn of his breathing, the hard thumping of his heartbeat echoing between his ears as he raced from room to room, seeking some clue.

Then his breath was sucked right out of him; even his heart seemed to cease beating. There had to be something wrong with his eyes, making his vision zoom in and out on what looked like an engraved invitation to *A Nightmare On Elm Street.*

On the carved teak entry table he'd rushed past in his hurry to make sure Whitney didn't lay unconscious on the bed, or worse, he saw the necklace.

The feeling left his fingertips. They were amazingly steady as he lifted the pendant made of onyx and alabaster with two small rubies, dangling on a chain that was no longer around her neck. He laid it down with the care reserved for a delicate figurine easily shattered. Next he picked up the symbol of his eternal fidelity to a woman who had discarded it.

He felt as still and lifeless as the gold and platinum hands holding a pearl between them. Eric stared at the pearl, shaped like the world that had suddenly tilted on its axis.

Fearing he might drop the ring, he placed it on the envelope that contained their marriage documents. And then he picked up another envelope, one with his name on it.

Ripping open the seal, he read the contents. Or at least he tried to read the swirling words, filling his vision like so much spilled black ink.

My dearest Eric,
You deserve so much better than this. You have
given me everything I ever wanted in life: Love.
Laughter. Friendship beyond measure.
And what have I given you in return?
Lies.

My life was, and is, far more complicated than I led you to believe. I tried to pretend those complexities didn't exist, but pretending does not make it so. I mislead you into believing I was someone I am not. I married you under false pretenses. And Eric, no marriage built on hidden agendas can possibly last. Three months, perhaps, but not for a lifetime. And a lifetime is what you were really after. For me to continue this charade is to mock all that is vital and necessary for the very thing you most want.

You are a good, good man, Eric Townsend. You deserve a happy, wonderful life and someone who can share it fully. For this reason I urge you to immediately have the marriage annulled on grounds of desertion.

I won't be back, Eric. And please, don't waste your time trying to find me. The airline has assured me that my destination is privileged information they won't give out—and even if they did, from the very beginning I made sure that you don't know where I'm really from, or who I even am, so you have very little chance of finding me. But should you manage to do so, it would be disastrous for us both. I've already brought you so much pain, don't be a glutton for punishment.

I hope that one day you may be able to forgive me for the unforgivable. If the Fates are kind, we'll meet again in another lifetime. Till then, carpe the hell out of the diem as you explore your way along the path you'll have to chart without me. Indeed, Eric, certain truths aren't meant to be known.

Just as some names are better left undescribed.
Love always, Anonymous

CHAPTER 18

hitney felt sick. Sick in her heart. Sick to her stomach.
Acid churned around what little she'd made herself get
down for breakfast today. Or was it yesterday that she'd last eaten?
Since returning to her apartment in Mobile, her time had been spent
alternately sleeping, weeping, and staring at the walls of her perpetu-
ally darkened bedroom.

She didn't want to go outside, didn't even want to open the
curtains to see the sunshine. Those things of nature had once given
her joy, but there was no joy to be had in her anymore.

Life held no meaning beyond the memories that wouldn't go away.
They beat at her relentlessly, whether waking or asleep. Her heart was
broken. All of her was broken. She wondered if she'd had a nervous
breakdown. At least she didn't think sane people crawled on all fours
in a dark hallway to heave into a toilet without the vaguest idea as to
the time of day, day of week, or week of the year. Had New Year's Eve
passed? Had Christmas?

Surely Thanksgiving had come and gone, Eric returning home
without the wife he had planned to bring. She had done that to him.
She had deceived him, hurt him beyond imagining, and humiliated his
sense of good judgement in those he could trust. *Betrayal.* Let her

count the ways. The guilt eating her up was carnivorous and she deserved every last *chomp.*

But she had done the right thing. Just look at her now. She couldn't bear the thought of Eric seeing her like this—a ghost of her former self.

Though who that self was, Whitney was no more certain of that than she was of the time.

If only she could turn back the hands of the clock and make it stop, she'd be forever young and vibrant, the great adventuress Eric had admired, adored. Turn the clock back a little further and she'd be alone but self-sufficient, capable of dealing with the nightmare she was trapped in now.

How she longed to be the old Whitney again. Not this mewling lump of nothingness without a spine, whimpering, "Eric, Eric. Please forgive me. I need you to hold me, to love me, to make this nightmare go away."

She had his number. She even had Grandmother Ming's number. If she called, he would come. How desperate she was to cling to his strength while she wasted away. Mind, body, spirit, they were slipping from her fast. Yes, she must be losing her mind, actually tempted to plug her phone back in, and undo the last good deed she had done.

The temptation was so great that she hooked a hand over the sink and pulled herself up. For a moment she was so dizzy she feared she might pass out. Leaning against the porcelain for support, she waited until the dizziness passed. Her head cleared, slightly. Not much but enough to know she had no right to make that call without confronting the image Eric would see should she make it.

She fumbled for the light switch. Her eyes stung as if torched by fire after being cocooned in a dark, dank cave.

Slowly, ever so slowly, Whitney raised her eyelids, letting her eyes adjust to the light above the mirror.

One glance and she shut her eyes. Tight.

Is this what she had become? How proudly she had once asserted she was becoming who she wanted to be and getting there by whatever means felt right.

Oh, she had become something all right. A ghoul, according to the mirror. But could it be the mirror had lied? Surely she didn't look that bad.

Whitney forced herself to risk another look.

The mirror hadn't lied. Her cheeks were sunken, dark circles rimmed her eyes despite the sleep she couldn't get enough of. Her sun kissed skin was a memory of the past. Like her and Eric. Never, never could she let him see her this way. Pasty complexion the color of chalk, her hair a rat's nest of matted tangles, lips cracked.

She touched them and tried to imagine Eric wanting to do the same. All she could imagine was revulsion. She disgusted herself. Her breath tasted foul. Sniffing, she decided the rest of her smelled no better.

Had she actually come to this? Dying was one thing but to die with such little dignity was less than pitiful.

She had to snap herself out of this stupor and scrape together a smidgeon of self-respect.

The bite of cold water from the faucet had the effect of a bracing slap. *Slap. Slap.* She soaked her face with handfuls of it, faster and faster, until it streamed down her throat, drenching the slip she had on. And how long had she been wearing this stinking, stained slip she never wanted to wear or see again?

Peeling it off like a reptilian second skin, she weakly flung it into the bathroom trashcan. This was the slip she had worn beneath a smart shirtdress Eric had bought her, and even that seemed a betrayal, running away with the clothes that had come compliments of him. She hadn't even bothered folding her things, just threw what she could get her hands on into her luggage...except for what she dared not take: Wedding gown. Kimono. Ring. Necklace. Legal papers.

The flight was a hazy memory. Neither did she quite remember getting home. All she knew was that somehow she had arrived and fallen into the bed she'd hardly left since...whenever it had been. And for however long that was, she hadn't cared enough to change out of the slip or put on clean linens.

Suddenly feeling as if she were the embodiment of a neglected nursing home, Whitney filled the tub and congratulated herself on caring enough about her person to pour half a box of bath salts into the rushing water. A small victory yet it felt hugely significant to do something for herself beyond wallow in self-pity and ignore the fact her hair had the consistency of starch.

She scrubbed herself clean from her head to her toes but avoided more than a cursory swish between her thighs. The water would simply have to do because to actually touch herself there would be to invite the image of Eric beside her, inside her. Holding her, loving her, filling her with joy, filling her up with him—

No. No, she couldn't let herself remember. To do so was to start unraveling the slender thread of sanity she had managed to salvage.

She finished her bath, watched the sheen of filth and despair she had discarded go down the drain.

And now...what? What did she do next? Change the sheets and crawl back into the bed she had consigned herself to like some vampire in a coffin? She should put on clothes. Open the curtains to at least see if it was day or night. She could do that much, right?

It was daytime. But what day, what month and year? Not that it mattered, but she was a little curious to know. Curiosity, oh that was good. A sign she wasn't completely comatose despite all evidence to the contrary.

Scattered crackers and a half-eaten bowl of what might have been cereal were on her night table. Assorted other discards littered the floor.

Her legs were wobbly but she made it to the living room. Her luggage stood by the door where she'd left it. She didn't have the strength to lift even the smaller suitcase Eric had bought her in Saint Croix, nor the heart to carry the contents to her bedroom.

She stared at the door she hadn't stepped past in...however long she had been back. Suddenly, more than anything, she wanted to get out of here, get on a bus, a plane, a train, any mode of transportation that would take her far, far away from the walls that were pressing in and the luggage that linked her to another life that belonged to someone she had created.

Though she didn't trust her legs to make it down the street, she thought she might be capable of driving. Not far, just to the nearest convenience store.

It felt amazingly good to get in her Honda Accord, twist the key and crank the engine. Not exactly a Jeep careening through a rain forest but—

"Stop it," she snapped. "Just keep your eyes on the road and your mind on the present. Here. Now. You can't go back and you can't afford to remember. Cut it out of your brain, you're not dead yet, Whitney. Make the most of what time you've got left or forget the store and head for the nearest pawn shop. Better to buy a gun and get it over with than sink back into that hellhole you're crawling out of, hand over fist."

Hand over fist, the way she'd spent her money. Did she still have that five grand in her savings, in case she lingered on?

She was thinking about practical matters. That was good, too; at least she wasn't completely stark raving mad. Her hands, a little steadier on the steering wheel, belonged to someone she hadn't seen for a while—the girl who had been her mother's caretaker, then had taken care of herself long enough to know she could do whatever needed to be done next.

For now she would settle for just getting to the convenience store where she could buy bread and fresh milk to replace the mold and curdles from a can of Carnation she had tossed, with a heave, before deciding on her destination.

Destinations were like fresh air. Destinations had purpose, no matter how small. Just like the wreaths hanging on modest front doors, the Christmas trees decked out behind the windows she passed, indicating that the holidays weren't over yet.

"Look on the bright side," she told herself. "At least you don't have to worry about buying presents."

Her mirthless laughter had a hollow ring to it, like a paper doll some child had put away, tired of animating a pretend playmate.

Such a child she had been. What fun while it lasted. Laugh enough for a lifetime and love with the heart of a fool.

Dr. Clark had given her good advice and she couldn't regret following it. She could only regret the damage she had done as a result. But not enough regret to blow her brains out. Yet.

Walking into the nearest 7-11, buying a carton of milk, and picking up a newspaper seemed a far better option.

December 23, that was the date. Which meant she'd been holed up for a little over a month. A month of madness. Whitney shuddered and her stomach gave a queasy lurch. Only hours ago she'd been crawling around on all fours, having spiraled down so deep that her personal hygiene was nonexistent. Of course she might have had the presence of mind to wash off earlier if her period had—

Her period. When was her last period?

Her heart stopped. And then it raced faster than the dart of her mind as she combed it for a time frame that settled on a little over two weeks before their wedding. November 1, that was their wedding day. And now it was December 23. Which meant...

"No. No, it can't be." Her knees buckled and she dropped the milk carton to grab hold of a shelf. White liquid pooled around her feet but all she could see was the newspaper splayed on the ground, the date staring up at her.

"Ma'am? Ma'am, are you all right?"

Whitney couldn't find her voice to reply. The best she could do was nod, mumble an apology and get out of the store with the halting gait of a tin soldier minus his oilcan.

She made it to the car, slumped into the seat. Resting her head on the steering wheel, she took several deep breaths and tried to calm herself. Only the harder she tried to stay calm the more frantic she became to assure herself there was an explanation she could live with because she couldn't bear to think that she might have committed a heinous crime against nature.

A nervous breakdown, severe depression; that could throw her cycle out of whack. Couldn't it? And even if not, leukemia was a disease of the blood, an insidious stalker that just might rob her of a menstrual flow. That was a possibility, wasn't it?

Her stomach gave another lurch and she gagged on the bile rising up in her throat. Suddenly she felt sicker than ever. Too ill to drive back to her apartment, much less the drugstore. But she had to. First, the drugstore.

Head swirling in a dense fog, she grabbed the first pregnancy test kit she saw—conveniently parked by a display of condoms. Miracle of miracles she made it back safely into her assigned parking spot. And then she was at her apartment door, keys in her shaking hand.

"I don't want to go in, I don't want to go in," she chanted, dreading the potential results far more than the squalor to which she was returning.

A white Camaro zipped into the space next to her Honda. That would be her neighbor, Carl. He drove even faster than he talked once he got started, a chatterbox who set her teeth on edge.

She was so close to the edge right now that she'd surely start howling if he said so much as "Hello." Just as his car door opened, Whitney shut the apartment door behind her.

Leaning against it, she slid down. And sat there, just sat there by her unpacked luggage, head between her knees. She was panting, almost hyperventilating. She had to take some deep breaths and get a grip.

She took what grip she had and the pregnancy test kit to the hallway bathroom. Her insides were so tied up it was almost impossible to pee onto the strip. So innocuous looking, just this small flimsy gauge that would tell her, was she or wasn't she?

After what seemed forever to get her bladder to cooperate, it did.

Then forever wasn't long enough.

The results confirmed the worst: Whitney Smith was a monster. It wasn't enough to break Eric's heart. His baby was in her belly, a child in the making who was innocent of any wrongdoing and didn't deserve the fate she would share.

The thought filled her with self-loathing. The pregnancy wasn't intentional but that wouldn't make her any less guilty of a total lack of moral responsibility—

Unless she could hang on long enough for the baby to survive.

Premature infants were born every day and pulled through, thanks to the miracles of modern medicine and the doctors who practiced it.

Dr. Clark. She had to call him. Explain her condition. It didn't matter if he thought her a horrible person for it, all that mattered was doing whatever it took to keep breathing until her unborn child was capable of picking up where she left off.

That's right, she had to take charge again. Do what was necessary, responsible. The woman Eric had fallen in love with had lived for the day with no thought to the future or the repercussions of her actions. That wildcat had put an innocent life in this position, but thank heavens for the old Whitney, she knew what to do.

Greeting her old self like a long lost friend she could depend on in a time of need, Whitney went directly to the phone, plugged it in and made her call.

"This is Whitney Smith," she said without pause. "I need to speak to Dr. Clark. Immediately, please."

CHAPTER 19

"Where the hell have you been, child?"

Dr. Clark's bark of greeting triggered a wince at his shout and a protective hug of her stomach at the reference to *child*.

"I need your help, Dr. Clark. I need to see you—"

"A day late and a dollar short, young lady. Do you realize I've been calling every damn day and keeping the post office in business with all the damn letters I sent and you never bothered to open? Now where the hell have you been?"

What could she tell him? *Oh, no place worth mentioning, just hanging out by active volcanos, high diving off cliffs, having a whirlwind affair and getting an education in the intimate arts. Falling in love, getting married, telling myself I was in remission when I was really in denial, getting pregnant, running away, and having a nervous breakdown.*

"Let's just say that I checked out of reality for a while and now I'm back with a very big problem. How soon can I see you?"

"Now's not soon enough to suit me. Get yourself over here lickety-split and we'll discuss your problem after we draw some blood. We need another test, Whitney, and we need it now. We needed it months ago."

The urgency in his voice made her grip the phone tighter. "Why?"

"I'll tell you after the test."

"If you want me over there now, you'll tell me now."

After a thick silence, he cautioned, "I don't want you to get your hopes up."

Even as they sparked to life, she answered, "Of course not."

Palms sweating, knees shaking, she hardly breathed lest she miss a single syllable of the words that came out in a rush of excitement tempered by a heavy note of warning.

"There's a chance your initial tests were incorrectly diagnosed. No way to tell until we take another sample. You have to be prepared since the results could be the same but I do have cause to believe otherwise."

"You mean…I—I…Dr. Clark, are you sure?"

"I won't be sure about anything until—"

"I'm on my way."

An hour later she was in Dr. Clark's office. Feeling like a prisoner on death row praying for a stay of execution, she tried to follow what he was saying. The last time she sat here she couldn't remember his name; now she was anxiously awaiting the results of the new blood test he'd immediately taken, and expressed to the lab.

"A few weeks after you took off, I was at one of these gala things. You know, a banquet, boring speakers and beepers going off all over the place since there were a lot of doctors around. Anyway, me and my better half got put at a table with a fine young man I taught awhile back in med school. Turns out he was upset that night and it wasn't because his wife was making eyes at me."

Dr. Clark slapped his thigh and chortled. A little too heartily. Whitney knew he was trying to take her mind off the life-or-death balance that hung on the ring of a phone.

Her heart hammered, her muscles twitched. Nonetheless she forced a stiff smile and wagged a trembling finger at him.

"Now Dr. Clark, tell the truth. She wanted to get rid of her husband so she could make a play for the handsomest doctor in town."

"You're a flirt, Whitney. And a very brave young woman. The truth is, I nearly choked on my overdone filet mignon when Cam—that's Dr. Cameron Lark, as in Dr. C. Lark—started fretting about a certain patient of his. Seems she'd been diagnosed with low thyroid, a pretty bad case of it but nothing that couldn't be fixed with the right meds, lower stress levels, a better diet, rest and exercise and all that other good stuff that makes for healthy living. Odd thing was, she was living healthy already. Even odder, she collapsed and wound up in the hospital a week after her initial blood tests came back. Which would you rather know first, the day those tests were done or the results of the second testing?"

"Dear Lord," Whitney whispered. Something wet was on her cheeks. Hope seized her and wouldn't let go though she tried to break its hold. She couldn't hope too much, not yet, because if the phone rang and the news was bad then she'd be back in the ranks of the living dead and once she got out of this horrid, horrid place she couldn't bear to go there again.

"That's right. The two of you were tested on the same day. As for the results of that second test…Needless to say, Dr. *C. Lark* was beside himself when his patient, *Whitney Smith*, expired from acute myelogenous leukemia. She went fast, there was nothing he could've done to save her, but it really did upset him to lose a patient like that. Of course, he wasn't the only one upset. I tore out of that shebang and wanted somebody's head. After I got ahold of you and made sure my suspicions were confirmed."

He stared at the phone as if by staring he could make it ring. Whitney laid hands on her concaved stomach. She wanted to demand assurances that Dr. Clark didn't yet have to give. As for wanting somebody's head, if she had been put through all this for nothing then she was in the market for an ax.

"How could something like this happen? I mean, if there was a mix-up and our tests got switched."

"Plain and simple? Human error. The lab could transpose the

results. Or the transcriptionist could accidentally do the same. With two identical names and two similar ones, even a careful recorder might have made a mistake."

"And you think that's the case here," she prompted, wanting that much assurance at least.

"I think there's a very good possibility. I think that possibility is increased if someone was distracted because they were having a bad day, had a fight at home before work, or was maybe under the weather. I'd like to lay blame on someone if there is blame to be had, but the fact of the matter is, we're all capable of making mistakes so I hope you'll keep that in mind before getting sue crazy like everybody else, and that said, I think this damn phone better ring before I stick my neck out further than I already have."

He slapped the desk and barked, "Ring!"

As if obeying the orders of a higher command, the phone did ring. Dr. Clark grabbed it up, said urgently, "Tell me what you've got, Susan."

Whitney's gaze froze on Dr. Clark. Her life depended on this call. The life growing inside her depended on this call.

Though the conversation didn't take more than a minute it seemed like hours, days, weeks before Dr. Clark hung up and shouted, "Glory be and hallelujah! Congratulations, Whitney! Negative. Not a trace, you're clean as a whistle. Well, except for some thyroid issue we still need to address."

Whitney didn't remember falling to her knees but the next thing she knew Dr. Clark was helping her up and patting her back while she sobbed, "Thank you, thank you, dear Father in heaven, thank you."

"There, there now. It's going to be all right, child. Everything's going to be all right."

Laughing and crying for joy all at once, she blew her nose on the handkerchief Dr. Clark pulled from his pocket.

A baby on the way. A baby! A baby! She'd gotten her life back and a baby to go with it. A sweet little bundle of love she would hold and rock and kiss and never, ever desert the way her father had deserted her.

The way she had deserted Eric.

Her laughter trickled to a halt; her smile faded. She turned somber eyes on Dr. Clark.

"What's wrong, Whitney?" he asked kindly. "Now that we've got this crisis out of the way, maybe you want to talk about that big problem you mentioned earlier."

"I'm pregnant, Dr. Clark," she answered bluntly. "I'm not sure how it happened but it did and thrilled as I am to be expecting, I'm appalled to know I conceived when I could have killed my own child if the test had turned out differently."

"Only one way I know of for something like that to happen and it takes two to do it." Dr. Clark pulled at his chin and had the good grace not to stand in judgment. Not of her, anyway. "I don't mean to pry, but I can't help but wonder who got you in this condition, Whitney. After all, raising a child is a tremendous responsibility and any man who would shirk his duty toward his own child isn't much of a man."

"He's very much a man, Dr. Clark," she asserted, quick to rush to Eric's defense. "And he would never shirk his duties."

"Then why isn't he here with you?"

"Because he doesn't know where I am."

"And why is that?"

Though she wasn't proud to admit it, there was no way to dress up the truth and it was high time she started telling it. Not only to Dr. Clark but to herself.

"I was afraid to tell him I was dying because I knew he would have stood by me until the end. I couldn't bring myself to put him through that. Or to let him see me unable to take care of my own basic needs, to be reduced to what Mama became. So I ran away."

"Ran away?" Dr. Clark shook his head at her. "Whitney, that's not like you. I've never known you to run away from anything in your life. Well, except to run away to wherever you ran away to, before you came back."

Whitney snorted in self-derision. "You're right," she had to agree. "Running from reality isn't like me at all. Much less to be deceitful or to endanger the life of an unborn child. But I did and all I can say is, I acted out of character. Eric didn't. Unfortunately, that means I know him but he doesn't really know me. And how could he when I don't even recognize myself?"

She stroked her belly and silently wished their child to take after Eric. But no matter how their child turned out, she couldn't give it less than a happy, stable home.

Dr. Clark squeezed her left hand. "Give him a chance and don't underestimate yourself. From what you say, this Eric would make a good husband and father. I'm sure he'll do the right thing by you."

It was an assurance meant to comfort but it left Whitney uneasy.

"Yes, of course he would," she softly replied. "But Dr. Clark, I won't have any man who stays with me out of duty because he got trapped into a relationship with an imposter."

CHAPTER 20

*L*ast-minute Christmas shopping should be a drag. *Au contraire*
—what a delight!

Au contraire. Eric spoke French. German, Italian, Chinese,
and no telling what else. Her?

All she knew was English. And the universal language of the heart.
How it did speak now, alternating between disturbing whispers and
joyous shouts.

Ignoring the whispers of uncertainty and niggling fears, Whitney
gave a soft whoop of jubilation upon finding a tiny silver brush, then a
darling pale green diaper stacker embroidered with yellow daisies, on
a clearance table at TJ Maxx.

Whether boy or girl the diaper holder would be perfect for itsy-
bitsy diapers when the time came. She had time, precious time, and
never, ever would she take it, or life, for granted again. As for love,
while she'd never taken it for granted, there was a price for loving
with the heart of a fool and it wasn't hers alone to pay.

A baby didn't leave room for making hasty decisions or using poor
judgment. She needed to call Eric, and soon, but she was still too
vulnerable, still more of a mess than not. She needed to be on firmer
ground before making contact.

The reasons why were many but they all coalesced into the simple fact that he loved a woman she had made up as she went along. A woman with nothing to lose who had been in the process of "becoming" and what a load of crap that was now.

The real Whitney Smith, the one who had existed for 27 years before a false alarm sent her racing into a reckless adventure, was now knee-deep in the consequences of her recklessness. She no longer had the right, or the inclination, to partake of the communion cup from which she and Eric had once guzzled.

Perched on her couch, Whitney hummed "Away in a Manger" along with the stereo. After a sip of steaming hot cocoa, she sat it on her mother's Duncan Phyfe coffee table and put the finishing touches on the small tinsel Christmas tree she kept stored for holidays. She'd always longed for a big fir dripping with bows and ornaments and candy canes and filling the air with that heavenly scent of evergreen but the apartment was small and she simply couldn't justify such an expenditure when there was no one around to enjoy it but her.

"Maybe next Christmas," she told the baby. "After all, it won't be just me anymore. You'll be here and..." Her gaze drifted to the pile of mail she'd picked up at the post office after leaving Dr. Clark's office yesterday. She hadn't sorted through it yet, hadn't even taken off the thick rubber band holding the stack together. Just looking at it made her heart pound, her palms sweat. Her other life was in there and seeing Eric again, only a snapshot away.

"Well," she said shakily. "You have your presents and Mommy has hers. Should we save them all for Christmas morning or open one apiece tonight and unwrap the rest tomorrow?"

"Joy to the World" played in the background and Whitney wondered how Mickey was spending his own Christmas Eve. He would be grateful for a gift of shoes. Why hadn't she thought of that before now? Because while everyone else was sending cards and presents, she'd been on the threshold of insanity and wallowing in the muck of misery in surroundings that would make a pigsty look fastidious.

That had been only yesterday.

Today she was going to live. She was going to have a child and be the best mother ever, even if she had to raise it alone. That would take a lot of wisdom and strength.

Was it wise to open a letter, even just one? Her gaze darted to the old upright piano she had closed so she couldn't see the keys after a wisp of *Heart and Soul* had whispered through her mind and brought her immediately to tears.

With trembling hands she lifted the mail from the end of the coffee table and placed it in her lap, close to the child her body housed.

"Okay, baby, that's your daddy snuggled up against you. His face is in lots of pictures and his name's on lots and lots of pages. I hope you get closer than this and he holds you one day, but...we'll have to see what the future brings. For now, it's just you and me, kid. And since the kid in me can't wait, let's each open a present tonight. You first."

Closing her eyes, Whitney picked a gift beneath the tree, pretending she didn't know what she'd wrapped less than an hour ago. After carefully keeping the paper intact so she might press it between the pages of a baby book, she exclaimed, "A rattle!"

Shaking it in the air like a maraca in an island band, she had a flash of dancing feet, a strong arm coming around her and bending her back; a passionate kiss.

The smile left her face. She laid the rattle down. Folded her hands over her stomach to again press the letters and postcards to the fruit their origins had spawned.

For a while she continued to debate. Quickly she pulled free a letter. She knew by the stationery where they had been staying, what pictures were enclosed. Sliding a nail under the seal, she decisively took out the contents to confront whatever emotions might emerge—

And almost as immediately grabbed the tape she'd wrapped the presents with. Consigning the re-sealed envelope with the rest into the seagrass tote, up it all went onto the upper ledge of her closet, pushed as far from reach as possible. The tapestry luggage she had taken to Dominica, filled with the wardrobe Eric had bought her and would soon no longer fit, went under the bed. As did the smaller, exquisite leather piece from their shopping spree in Saint Croix.

"I shouldn't have opened that letter," she whispered, feeling very fragile. Her heart was fragile. And unruly. Whitney knew she couldn't let it mess with the head she had to keep firmly on her shoulders. There was a baby to consider now and it was up to her to protect them both from the stranger inside who shared Eric's last name.

CHAPTER 21

a muted celebration trailed behind Adam from the New Year's Eve party going on in Grandmother Ming's living room. The reason for the hushed revelry was slouched in a chair on the darkened back porch that Adam approached, having volunteered as family emissary.

"Eric?" he called softly. "Hey, bro, why don't you come join us? It's almost midnight and you shouldn't be out here alone."

"You're right about that." There was a slight slur to his voice, compliments of the amber liquid he swilled in the glass he raised in the moonlight. "I shouldn't be alone. I should be with my wife."

Adam dropped to a crouch beside the brother who had always been the logical one, the strong one, the brave big brother he'd always looked up to. Man, was he worried about him. Everyone was. Eric, usually so vital in their midst, had been remote, his level of distress evident in his long silences, the amount of time he devoted in private to the phone—and it sure wasn't for the usual purpose of work. Given the state he was in, it was probably for the best that Eric had cancelled his lecture tour. The appearance in Cambridge a few weeks back had apparently been too challenging to even consider repeating.

"You know, Eric, when we were in Antigua, in the carriage, I made a comment about your future and Whitney got this look that told me something wasn't quite right. I remember thinking, `she has secrets.'" He'd also told her not to break his brother's heart. But she had. The number she'd done on Eric made Adam want to get in her face. "I probably should have said something to you. I'm sorry that I didn't."

"Wouldn't have made any difference. She told me I don't know how many times, in how many different ways, and I didn't listen. Even on the chapel steps, what did she say? `I'm afraid of my own mortality.' And what was my answer to that?" Nearly knocking the glass over he put aside, Eric pulled out the wedding ring that was always as close as his pocket. "`If it'll make you feel better we can take out the till-death-do-we-part part.' That made her so happy. God, how could I have been such an idiot?"

"Listen. You have to quit beating yourself up. If you can't do it for you, do it for me, for the rest of the family."

Eric heard Adam's entreaty, and yet he didn't. Ever since he'd started putting the pieces together, his mind had been on constant replay: The story about the friend who'd died young, the private letter that started with, "My dear friend." Whitney's red flag about blood tests, then her refusal to see a doctor. All the we'll sees and maybes, even refusing to accept his family heirloom as more than a loan.

The whole picture had coalesced in a moment as crystalline as when he realized he was falling into the kind of love that you never got out of, the kind that stole your breath so completely that you couldn't imagine living without the person who filled up all the empty spaces you didn't even know you were missing.

Now it was like he couldn't breathe. The simple process of just getting through a day was akin to being submerged under water and held down by the fist of god. He couldn't work. He couldn't sleep. He couldn't think beyond the hospitals still left to call, the next lead to trace, another investigator to hire. For all the good any of that had done him thus far. He'd begun to wonder if Whitney Smith was really her name.

"Eric, look at me." Adam gripped his shoulders, gave him a small shake. "I know you don't want to hear this. But there comes a point where you have to think about self-preservation. If you can't find her, slowly killing yourself is not going to bring her back. You need to be prepared to accept that."

"No," he snapped. Tempering his voice, he made himself say with feigned calm, "No. She has to be somewhere. And I will find her."

"But what if you do and she's...?"

Adam left the question hanging, the question that hovered like an invasive black plague, stalking the hope he clung to.

"I can forgive her anything as long as she's alive. But Adam, if she cheated us out of sharing what time she had left, if she didn't trust me to love her to the very end and be there for her when she needed me the most, I'll never forgive her for that. Never."

A sympathetic nod, and Adam glanced at his watch. "Understood. But it is now 11:55 p.m. and if I don't have you joining the rest of the family in the next two minutes, the highest chain of command will be here to see to it for me."

With a force of will he wasn't feeling, Eric stood on unsteady feet. Even as messed up and drunk as he was, he knew he didn't want Grandmother Ming coming after him.

CHAPTER 22

*B*y mid-January, Whitney had more dilemmas than solutions. She was somewhat more emotionally stable, if she didn't count the hormones that had her bouncing all over the place, but she was still in survivor mode. Funeral homes didn't give advance purchase refunds. Neither did lawyers whose fees were non-refundable. With her finances in jeopardy, her self-esteem shaky at best, all she had left was her pride and that wasn't in very good shape either.

The job market was tight. Maybe Winn-Dixie would call, even though the HR person had suggested she was overqualified. If that fell through, she did have an application in at Burger King. The late shift paid extra and she could support herself until something better came along.

There were other options. Such as legal grounds for a lawsuit for the personal suffering the misdiagnosis had put her through. A part of her wanted blood but Dr. Clark would be implicated and she couldn't do that to him. Besides, if she hadn't taken it upon herself to grab the report off his desk and refuse to see Dr. Goldberg, the mistake would have been caught. She would have been put on Synthroid—instead of the motherlode of *ling-chih* and herbal supplements that clearly had helped—and told to work on the same life style adjustments that had gotten her temporarily healthy before the pregnancy had sent her into a reverse tailspin. But even if she took that low road, no telling how much time it would take and she needed a game changer *now.*

Next option: Go to the library and appeal to Mr. Andrews' sense of humanity. Her old position was surely filled but they often needed part-time help with cataloging, re-shelving, things like that. However, considering Mr. Andrews' lack of humanity and her lack of professionalism in leaving, chances were slim to none of getting rehired for even maid duty.

The third and final option was the most tempting. It was the option she contemplated yet again as her hand hovered over the phone.

The lines were all rehearsed in her head. *Hi, Eric. It's me, Whitney. I am so, so beyond sorry for hurting you and running off the way I did, but you see, I thought I was dying. Since then I found out that I had something very treatable. Don't worry, I'm not asking you to honor a marriage to someone you don't really even know, but I'm afraid I need your help because....*

That's as far as she'd gotten with her speech. She kept trying to say it aloud but the words always got clogged in her throat. She hated what she had done to Eric. Hated the absolute vulnerability of her situation. Hated for him to ever wonder if she had only come crawling back because she needed his financial support.

Her hand was shaking. The lump in her throat felt like a baseball. And the yearning that was in her was a constant physical ache that threatened the tenuous control she still struggled to maintain.

Whitney turned away from the phone. She went to the dresser drawer where a champagne cork shared hallowed space with a reminder of her priorities: a rattle, a silver brush, a diaper stacker and a skein of pastel-hued yarn, destined to be a blanket.

She had to find a job, get at least a toehold. Anything that elevated her above destitute. Then she would contact him. It had to be soon, before she started to show. There was a critical truth they both deserved to know: Could Eric fall in love all over again with a very different woman from the one he had married? Of course she was morally obligated to tell him about the pregnancy no matter that outcome, but even she would not stoop to entrapment by using their baby as a bargaining chip.

~

She didn't get a call from Winn-Dixie. The job at Burger King lasted less than a week. The smell of burgers on the grill had been more than her heightened sense of smell and sensitive stomach could take. After gagging into a bag containing someone's order of a Whopper and fries, the manager had taken her aside and tactfully suggested she apply at McDonald's.

Now it was the beginning of February. By all estimations, she was three months pregnant. Soon there would be no insurance, no place to live. Add trapped and desperate to destitute, and here she was, sitting on the bottom step of the Mobile Public Library.

The grand, old structure had never looked so enticing. Or so formidable. Still gathering her courage, Whitney wondered how many times had she climbed these palatial stairs as a child, then later, as an eager assistant with a master's degree in Library Science? She'd only been twenty-three, plowing straight through from undergrad to graduate degree, then applying the same workhorse mentality to her profession.

All that overtime had netted her a big promotion and the added responsibility that came with the title of Children's Librarian. At twenty-five, she had been extremely young to assume such a demanding position. It had been such an honor that she had worked even harder—so hard that her body had finally rebelled against the long hours, fast-food diet, stress and more stress, and lack of downtime.

It had taken an in-her-face wake-up call to stop and smell the roses.

Whitney sniffed the small bouquet she'd brought as a peace offering. As she had bought them, it occurred to her that Mr. Andrews might not have been so unapproachable before had she thought of him as a person with his own needs, instead of a dictator who set the standard of the time she put in. Could it be he hadn't expected her to match him hour for hour, that maybe he simply didn't want to go home? Too bad she had seen him as the enemy rather than a human being she might have more in common with than she had thought.

Of course she saw a lot of things differently now. Life was too short, too precious, to hold grudges, to blithely ignore its beauty and nature's riches. It was too short to beat herself up for past mistakes. So she got off her duff, and marched up the stairs, flowers in hand. When she reached the top landing, she ran smack into Mr. Andrews.

Noticing the small brown bag he held, she said, "Mr. Andrews, I was just coming to see you. But it looks like you're off to lunch. Mind if I join you?"

His stunned expression reminded her of the moment she'd quit. Whitney didn't laugh now. He was brown-bagging it and probably planned to eat alone on a park bench. That's how he usually took his lunches in nice weather and she felt a little ashamed that she'd never asked to join him before.

He pushed up his glasses and glanced at the flowers suspiciously, as if he thought she might have a trick daisy amongst the blooms to squirt him with.

"If you came to gloat, Ms. Smith, you may not. If you came to bring me flowers, you may."

From the way he said it, she knew he didn't believe for a second she was here to bring him flowers. As for gloating, it bothered her greatly that he thought her capable of smiling on whatever his misfortune might be.

"These are for you, Mr. Andrews. Along with my apologies for leaving you in the lurch the way I did. It was very unprofessional of me. I can't excuse my actions, but if you can spare me the time, I'd like to explain why—which is what I should have done before I left."

He didn't immediately take the flowers, but his expression said he wanted to.

"You left because of me, Ms. Smith. And it seems you set a trend.

Your assistants were quite loyal and followed your lead. They liked working for you, but refused to answer to a slave driver like me. Or should I say, 'whip master?' Either way, we're still searching for replacements, the children's department is a shambles and my position as branch manager is shaky. Happy?"

"No," she whispered, those damnable tears springing to her eyes with embarrassing ease. "I'm so sorry, Mr. Andrews. I never meant to do you harm. The truth is, I didn't quit because of you, I quit because of a serious personal problem."

"How serious?" He seemed genuinely concerned.

"Very serious."

"Then why didn't you tell me?"

"Because it was easier to walk away than explain something I couldn't bring myself to talk about—especially to someone who I thought wouldn't care."

His small flinch assured her that Mr. Andrews most definitely had the capacity to care; he just had a hard time showing it. He cleared his throat and asked awkwardly, "Would you tell me now?"

"Only if you take the flowers and call me Whitney."

He took the flowers and shared his lunch. As they sat together on a park bench, Whitney wasn't sure who was the more amazed. Mr. Andrews as she related her story—minus her pregnancy and affair with Eric—or her, since the man she had once detested proved to be a truly sympathetic soul.

Apparently inspired by her frankness, Mr. Andrews admitted, "I considered you a rival, Whitney. The more you worked, the harder I had to so you wouldn't outshine me. I thought you had designs on my job and because of that, I wasn't very pleasant. Not that I was ever on anyone's party list, but with you, I showed my worst colors." He ducked his head. "I hope you can forgive me for that."

Whitney touched his hand. He looked up, and she saw his isolation, his longing to belong, his loneliness.

"There's nothing to forgive, Mr. Andrews. If I'd made more of an effort to get to know you, I would have realized you not only belonged at the top of my party list, but that we could've made a good team."

He raised a brow; the sides of his lips followed suit.

"We still could, Whitney. That is, if you're interested in a certain position I'm racing against the clock to get filled. I believe you more than meet the requirements: A team player who can whip the children's section back into shape and dispel the doubts that have arisen about my ability to oversee the library."

"Mr. Andrews?" She offered her hand.

They shook on it and parted with a brief hug and big grins on their faces. They had high hopes even if it wasn't yet a sure deal. As branch manager, Mr. Andrews could hire and fire, but he still had to go through the appropriate channels.

True to his word, he spoke with the library's director who gave the go-ahead to get her back ASAP. She was rehired with full benefits, and was to start Monday.

After profuse thanks to Mr. Andrews, who called with the news Saturday morning, Whitney hung up the phone with a huge sigh of relief.

The insurance was almost as important as the job itself, considering the baby she should have mentioned but was afraid would complicate matters. Once she had the department back on track, she would tell Mr. Andrews.

Strange that she didn't dread that revelation half as much as the call she had to make to Eric. She'd sworn to do it as soon as she was beyond the desperate stage and had a job to depend on, instead of just him.

Do it, she ordered herself.

Whitney picked up the receiver. Her palms pumped sweat. Her breath was barely a wheeze.

She punched three numbers. Stopped.

Look, if you call him now, you won't be able to concentrate on your job and Whitney, you can't afford to screw up. Wait a week, then call him.

She continued dialing. She had to call him now, she'd waited too long as it was and she was dying to hear his voice, to see him. Soon she'd be showing more than her slightly rounded tummy, so there was no time to lose.

Ring. Ring. Did he still have her wedding ring? Or did he decide to get rid of it after the way she'd left him, no explanations, not even a kiss goodbye? Had Marcia already offered to help him pick up his broken pieces?

"Hello, you've reached Eric Townsend. Please leave a message, and I'll return your call. If this is regarding the reward offered for any information leading to the whereabouts of Whitney Smith-Townsend, please state your name, where you can be reached, and..."

The plea in his voice ripped the ground from beneath her feet.

Whitney bowed her head in sorrow, in shame. How could she have done this to him? To hear him sound so weary, frayed, hollow...

Beeep. Her cue to respond.

"Eric," she began tremulously. "This is—this is Whitney." She could feel her vocal cords moving, but she couldn't hear anything beyond the roar in her ears.

"This is Whitney," she repeated. "I'm very, truly sorry about everything and—and there's so much to say, only I have no idea how to say any of it. Except..." *I love you beyond words, I miss you every second, and I'm so afraid you won't feel the same way once you know who I really am.* "We need to talk, Eric, and after we talk you can decide if and when you want to see me. You might not want to. I'm not...me. I mean, I'm not the me you know."

Did that make sense? She had to be honest with him, honest with herself. In truth she couldn't yet handle a face-to-face meeting, not when she could hardly form a coherent thought or put together an intelligent sentence.

"What I mean is," she tried to explain again, "I think it's a good idea for us to get reacquainted on the phone—maybe a chat or two—and then take it from there." Now what was her number? That's right, area code 251, the rest came by rote. Time to sign off, try to come up with something warm but cautious, hopeful but not too.

"I know I've caused you tremendous pain and Eric, I'm deeply sorry for that. I think of you often..." *Constantly, except for when I'm thinking of the baby, but the baby's part of you.* "And, well, take good care. I hope to hear from you soon."

Whitney replaced the receiver. Softly. With trembling hands, she stroked her slightly rounded abdomen and whispered, "I tried, baby, I swear I did. I tried to tell your daddy where to find us and I will, but we have to be very careful going forward. First we'll talk, that's what we'll do. A conversation or two and in a couple of weeks, I'll be settled back into work and be ready to risk—"

The sudden ring of the phone stopped her cold. Palms still sweating, they were closer to drenched in the three rings it took to gather the strength to haltingly answer, "Hello?"

"Whitney? Is that you?"

That depends, Mr. Andrews. Just which Whitney did you want to talk to? The good Whitney, the bad Whitney, or the Whitney who thinks she's back on track only to fall apart at the sound of Eric's voice and was too cautious, too cowardly, to tell him where I am when he's offering money to strangers to help find me?

"Yes, Mr. Andrews, it's me."

A pause, then Mr. Andrews continued, "Sorry to call you at home again, but I forgot to mention Storytime is scheduled for Monday. I've been pinch-hitting but if I have to deal with those antsy little rug rats one more time, I'll pull out what's left of my hair. Besides, I'm sure the, uh, tykes will be as glad to have you back as I am."

"Thanks," she said, "I'll come up with something special over the weekend."

"Good! Then I'll see you first thing Monday morning."

"Nine a.m. sharp," she promised.

The expected goodbye on the other end didn't come. After a small silence, Mr. Andrews asked quietly, "Are you all right?"

"Of course," she lied. Making sure he bought it, she added, "You just caught me in the middle of planning some activities for next week. Behind as I am, I wanted to get a head start."

"Sounds just like you. But could you do me a favor and not burn too much of the midnight oil? You know I don't need you showing me up from the get-go," he kidded, their inside joke.

Whitney managed a companionable laugh.

Managing to get through the rest of the day was another matter. Important as it was to get some plan of action together for work, her concentration was zero. Her gaze kept wandering to the phone that wasn't ringing while her mind refused to budge past the person who wasn't calling.

Was he in Europe for the lecture tour he'd so wanted to take her on, so he could show her Paris, Rome, Munich and beyond? Or could he be as close as his houseboat in Portland, or maybe San Francisco, seeking some wisdom or comfort from his dear Grandmother Ming?

Whitney had her number; Adam's too. Eric had wanted to make sure she had access to his family should anything happen to him.

Had it? By Sunday, she was pacing the floor and several times came close to calling a sweet, old lady who had every reason to hate her guts after the grief she'd dished out to number one grandson. So why didn't she call to make sure Eric was all right, even if he wasn't picking up his messages?

Cowardice. Shame. A possibly not so irrational fear that something may have happened to Eric on an emergency call and she would be the one responsible.

Monday morning finally dawned, clear and bright. Whitney could not say the same for herself. She had slept horribly, awakened by a vivid nightmare: Eric called in to tread a volatile mountain, his mind preoccupied with a runaway bride he was on a manhunt to find, then *boom*, returned to the earth he so loved, scattered into a million pieces.

The nightmare had given her true sympathy for Amy. Eric had been candid early on about his role in their divorce, how Amy had wanted a baby but he had not been on board, only for his near-death event to put the final nail into their marital coffin because Amy could no longer live with their unshared priorities in life.

It was a struggle for Whitney to get her own priorities straight on this very important, first day back morning. A lot was riding on her ability to stay focused, to prove herself deserving of this second chance at the library. Putting on make-up helped, even if it did take longer than usual to disguise the fact she looked like hell after a night that left her more exhausted than rested.

Clothing was another challenge. She had managed to go from a scarecrow to barely fitting into her clothes in six weeks, and she knew it wasn't owed to her adjusted thyroid. Fortunately she was still able to wear her best suit—a nicely tailored navy jacket and pencil skirt that was just a wee bit tight, complemented by a white silk blouse that wouldn't impress Eric's fashion sense, any more than her mother's cameo brooch at the top. After doing her hair into a French twist and slipping into dark dress pumps, Whitney surveyed her image from top to bottom in the full-length mirror anchored on the bathroom door.

In her mind's eye she saw another mirror, Eric's hands lifting over her head to drape a part of his family's heritage around her neck.

She touched her mother's brooch, a world apart from the exquisite yin-yang pendant it had taken everything in her to leave behind.

Stop it, she scolded herself. *Stop it right now before you ruin your make-up along with the day before it even gets started. You can't change anything that's happened, but you can read to the children and prove to yourself that despite all the uncertainties in life, you are still a darn good children's librarian. And that much, come payday, you can take to the bank.*

Glancing at her watch, the one she'd rediscovered in the cutlery drawer, she saw it was already 8:20 a.m. She was due at nine and wanted to show up at least ten minutes early. Not only that, work would take her mind off Eric, so the sooner she got there, the better. And, who knew, maybe there would be a message waiting when she got back.

After sending up a prayer that such would be the case, Whitney grabbed her purse, along with a sack containing a can of ginger ale and soda crackers in case she became queasy. Fortunately, her stomach felt fine this morning.

A single step out of her ground-floor apartment and her stomach bottomed out.

A car was parked in the slot next to hers. It wasn't Carl's Camaro which had a compulsive tendency to peel in and out even faster than he talked. Nor was the man emerging from a BMW an irritating neighbor coming home after a night on the prowl.

Eric's gaze locked with hers.

Whitney dropped her purse, the sack, the rest of her couldn't move. At first his feet seemed to be moving through quicksand, only to break free and into a full run. Just as suddenly, his hands were on her, cupping her face, stroking her arms, gathering her to him.

"Thank God," he was saying in a ragged voice of disbelief, "Thank God, *yuan-pao*. It really is you."

CHAPTER 23

*H*is hands were actually on her, assuring him that Whitney, his Whitney, was alive. And for that, he could forgive her anything, no matter what her answers might be to the questions that could wait. Right now he just had to get her alone, take this reunion and his desperation to hold her, into the privacy of the apartment he still couldn't believe she had emerged from.

The front door was still open and he walked her backwards, booting the door shut behind them. Pressing her to the wall he asked no questions and let his hungry, urgent kiss do the talking...

In what was a fairly one-sided conversation.

Her hesitation to embrace him and kiss him just as needfully was an echo of how he had run to her while she stayed rooted in place on the sidewalk, her face immobilized by an expression of shock. Something wasn't right with Whitney's response. This wasn't how he had envisioned it at all.

In the endless days since her disappearance, the endless hours that had passed since receiving her message in Ecuador, running with the critical landline number that pointed to South Alabama, and having her physical address tracked down by the time his plane landed, he had imagined that she was unwell. But it had never occurred to him that she would appear perfectly healthy—nor had he anticipated his wild child bride, the one that had stripped off a kimono before diving nude into a pool and strapping her legs around his waist, would transform into a buttoned down schoolmarm who was actually *checking her watch?*

Maybe he did need some immediate answers after all.

"Excuse me, but, am I making you late for an appointment?"

"Eric, I...I'm so sorry. I don't even know where to start."

"Let's start with you telling me whether or not you're sick."

"I was. I thought. It turned out to be treatable, not fatal." Her pleading yet guarded gaze flicked down to her watch again. "It's complicated. I'll tell you everything...after work. I know this sounds horrible—it is horrible—but I can't be late, not this morning. Please try to understand."

Was he hearing right? Had Whitney just informed him that she was more concerned about being late for work than explaining what the hell was going on? He had never dropped acid but the moment was so surreal, he wondered if this was how a bad LSD trip would feel.

Eric shook his head, trying to clear it, get some semblance of equilibrium back.

Apparently taking his head shaking as a "no"—which he wanted to unequivocally deliver anyway—she rushed to add, "If I'd known you were coming, I would have welcomed you better than this. But Eric, I have obligations and responsibilities that have to be seen to. If I'd had any idea you planned to be here today...but, I thought you would call first and—"

"Enough!" His palm hit the wall. He'd never slammed a wall before but the release felt so cathartic he was tempted to hit it again, only harder. But he didn't. He let his palm continue to rest a good distance from Whitney's startled face, listened to her sharp intake of breath as he cut to the chase.

"If anyone understands the prioritization of work and duty, I do. But it is truly unfathomable to me that you would anticipate a courtesy call, particularly given the circumstances of your last departure.

Equally disconcerting is your sudden preoccupation with the time when we should be making up for the months—*months*, Whitney— that will most definitely bear discussion once we have some essentials out of the way. Starting with a call you need to make. To work. An emergency just came up. I don't know what you do for a living, and frankly, at the moment, I don't give a damn. Whether you're teaching school or you're Mayor of the city, I'm sure your colleagues will understand that they will simply have to do without you today. I, however, have absolutely no intention of letting you out of my sight."

Her mouth slightly trembled and it looked like her eyes were starting to well up. Good. Some sign of emotion. He wanted to kiss her like the inner mandate it was, but the hell if he was going to invite another response that had the substance of wood.

The phone rang. Whitney moved to answer it but he caught her, pressed her back against the wall before she could escape.

"You aren't actually going to answer that, are you?"

"I have to," she said, again glancing at her watch, then back at him, her eyes reminding him of Blue Willow dish plates suddenly dropped and about to smash on the floor. "Oh no, it's probably—"

He raised his hands, let her go, watched her mad dash to the phone that was parked on a nearby vintage console.

"Hello? Mr. Andrews? Mr. Andrews, an emergency came up and... Yes, yes I'm okay....Yes, I know Storytime is scheduled at ten....Oh, the director just walked in? Of course I'll be there. I'm on my way."

As she hung up, Eric could only stare in disbelief at the woman whose floral sundresses had turned into a dour business suit with an unattractive cameo brooch; at the primly contained hair that had always swished in a ponytail or blown free in the Caribbean wind. He found himself wishing she would slap him. Maybe that would knock out this sudden crazy urge to grab her and shake her and demand, *"Who are you and what the hell have you done with my wife?"*

Whitney was glancing frantically around the room, her eyes lighting on him with each pass, as if seeing a ghost from her past and not knowing what to do with him.

It hurt to have her look at him in such a way, so he did some glancing around himself:

An old upright piano. An afghan and doilies on the serviceable furniture. Needlepoint and craft fair decorations on the wall. Heaps of books, some kind of knitting project, even a crystal candy dish with peppermints on an old fashioned coffee table.

"My purse, where's my purse?"

"Probably outside the door where you dropped it."

She patted the up-do hair he wanted to get his hands in, scatter the pins on the floor so he could spear his fingers through the length he'd bound around his wrists…in what seemed a lifetime ago.

As he watched her make a cursory check of the state of her clothes, his mind flashed back to the first time he'd seen her with none, only the moon and stars to share his bravo company.

"You look very nice," he assured her quietly when more than anything he wanted to roar. His gaze settled on the mess he had made of her lipstick. "Beautiful."

"Thank you for being kind."

"I don't feel kind." He took a step forward only for her to take a step back. It was not the dance he wanted, nor the one he intended to have before this day was through. "I actually feel a little sick myself right now with the choices you've decided to make."

Her eyes did some more darting. This time from him to the knitting project on the coffee table. A skein of pastel yarn gave him pause. He walked to the table, picked up what appeared to be a small blanket in the works, made with softer than soft yarn and equally soft colors of yellow and green and pink and blue…

"It's a blanket for a friend's shower," she blurted.

He just barely caught himself from snapping, *And we both know how giving you are when it comes to friends and dying wishes.*

Eric carefully returned her knitting to the table. He needed to get himself in check before making this disaster even worse. Maybe it was best if they took a little breather before getting back into the ring. The one in his pocket belonged on her bare finger and getting ugly with Whitney was not going to move them closer in that direction.

Rather than the ring, he took out his car keys and jangled them as a reminder of when she had taken him on the ride of his life where he had shouted his love in a rain forest jungle.

"Since you're determined to go to work, would you rather drive us there, or give me directions instead?"

"Eric, it's my first day back at the library."

So. She worked at a library. The book distribution business indeed.

"And your point is?"

"I don't think I can concentrate with you there."

"I'd be more worried than I already am if you could. Save your breath arguing. I'll only tail you if you don't take me with you. You know, second verse same as the first: Dominica. A charter to Montserrat you were determined to hitch a ride on while I went to work and you pulled soup kitchen duty?" That wasn't all she had done. The kids. The storytelling. Now it was starting to make sense. "And just as you promised you would stay out of my way while I tended to business, I'll do the same for you."

"But Eric, I—"

He held up a hand to silence her when it was her mouth he longed to cover and ravage until she gave up every secret she'd kept from him. "It's the best I can do and a stretch at that. Now we can extend this conversation as long as you like, but the outcome will be the same —the only difference being, just how late do you want to be?"

They arrived at the Mobile Public Library on Government Street at 9:55 AM. Whitney was grateful Eric had driven since she didn't trust herself behind the wheel, given the tremor of her hands that hadn't stopped shaking since he had arrived, looking slightly gaunt in his khaki slacks and chambray shirt, but no less heartbreakingly handsome. The moment he touched her every nerve end, every muscle, every internal organ including her stomach had responded like a revved up hotrod in Park with the accelerator gunned to the floor.

How she was going to get through the day with Eric in any kind of proximity, she had no idea. Of course leaving him behind to possibly poke around in her apartment hadn't been an option either—especially after nearly having a full blown panic attack when he picked up the baby blanket in progress.

The small composure she'd gathered on their mostly silent drive to the library fled the moment Mr. Andrews urgently waved her to the front desk.

"The kids are going nuts in there while most of the moms are taking a break in the paperback section. Not only that, Mr. Richards wanted to welcome you back personally and he's cooling his heels in my office. You deal with the kids and I'll deal with him until…"

His attention shifted from her to Eric, standing so close behind her she could feel his body heat. Suddenly, Mr. Andrews looked at her funny. He seemed to be scrutinizing her face—especially around her mouth.

"I hope you don't mind, but I brought a guest with me," she ad-libbed while belatedly wondering why she had neglected to inspect any evidence of smeared lipstick.

"Uh, of course I don't mind. Everyone's welcome at our library." Mr. Andrews appeared to be doing some ad-libbing himself as Eric moved closer and offered a gentleman's grip.

"Eric Townsend. Whitney's husband and the reason for her delay. My apologies."

Mr. Andrews shook hands with the gusto of a dead fish. Whitney gave him credit for that much, considering he looked so stunned that smelling salts seemed more in order than her hastily improvised, "Now that we have the introductions taken care of, I'd better go to see to the children."

CHAPTER 24

his was usually the favorite part of her job, where she always shined, enticing the kids with illustrations and props while playing the actress who could assume the characters' voices in the tales she was reading out loud.

Not today. Her stomach churned and her voice trembled. She held the storybook no better than she did the children's attention as they fidgeted in a large semi-circle around her reading chair. In the midst of it all Whitney silently prayed Eric wasn't within hearing distance, privy to her failure.

Finally, the once-upon-a-time favorite part of her job was over—only for her lackluster performance to receive an honest evaluation from the kids who were discerning enough to mention, "Gee Miz Smith, you didn't do too good today."

Like she needed them to tell her. God, what an ordeal.

A tug at her skirt and Whitney looked down to see a little girl with big doe eyes and bright red braids flashing a shy, toothless grin.

"Hi, my name's Mary and I don't care what everybody else said, I liked your story. Could you read me another one?"

A flash of Montserrat, of Mickey and all his blokes begging for "just one more" in a big tent under threat from a smoking volcano filled her mind and filled her heart, reminding her of what Storytime was really all about.

"Mary, I would love to read you a story. Do you have a favorite one picked out?"

"Sure do." She extended a Dr. Seuss selection that stirred an image of Pierre's seen-better-days cab, the book was that well-loved from its handling.

"Well what do you know, this is one of my favorites, too!"

Whitney made a mental note to order another copy as she pulled a little chair next to hers and did a much better job with "Oh, the Places You'll Go!" than she had with her botched production of "Bo, The Rascal Cat."

Mary's mother joined them and when they thanked her at the end, Whitney knew it was really she who owed them the thanks.

"I hope you come back, Mary. We'll have another Storytime next week. And you'll be my favorite listener."

"Can't wait!" she chirped. "I just love to get read to."

As they departed and Whitney went about the business of getting everything back in order, she considered what books said about their readers. She had read widely, all her life, as a means of escape. But even as an adult her favorites included "Oh, the Places You'll Go!" along with "The Secret Garden."

Dark garden...Moon grotto.

The immediate clutch between her thighs made her feel as if she belonged anywhere but in the children's section of the library. Oh, the places she had gone, indeed. Venturing into secret gardens where desires were explored outside the confines of a life that was predictable, but safe.

"That was nice." Eric's voice, behind her. So were his fingertips, skirting the side of her exposed neck, before lightly brushing her shoulder and just as quickly withdrawing the touch she craved. "Reminds me of another time you made someone else's day."

She was afraid to face him, afraid she might act on instinct and

173

plaster herself against him. As for the other time he was referring to, she didn't want to ask since the present was difficult enough without bringing up the past. Even his earlier jangle of car keys had made her feel like she'd been shoved into a time travel machine and transported back to a rain forest jungle where "safe" and "predictable" weren't part of their equation.

"Turn," he whispered. "Turn to me."

Her body responded on such immediate call she could have been Pavlov's dog. Legs pivoting, torso floating in what felt like slow-motion, until she faced him, apprentice to sorcerer, utterly riveted by his amber-flecked gaze, the slightly almond shaped eyes, sculpted cheekbones, dangerously kissable lips.

There was a fluttering in her chest, in the deepest chambers of her inner residence, demanding she acknowledge there was someone else inside that was so insane for this man, so crazy to pick up their wanton affair, that she was ready to grab him and run without bothering to inform Mr. Andrews he needed to find a new librarian because, yet again, he was shit outta luck with her.

Her. The other Whitney. The one that had landed two consenting adults, along with an *oops!* baby into this mess.

The reality check allowed the rational librarian to shrug, breathlessly say, "Just doing my job," and go about picking up the picture books the unsupervised kids had left scattered all around.

What a metaphor for the other woman Eric had fallen for.

"Here, I'll help."

Their hands paused over the same book. He moved before she did, catching her by the wrist, pressing his lips to its interior. The familiarity of his touch was a slow warm trickle through her veins while her pulse shot up so fast for a second she thought she might pass out.

The clearing of a throat and light tap to her shoulder had Whitney jerking her wrist away.

Mr. Andrews. Making a valiant effort to be cordial as he explained Mr. Richards, the director, had left for a meeting but had invited them all to lunch.

The polite summons included Eric.

"I appreciate the offer," he responded, "But business is better conducted without outside company."

"Outside company, are you kidding?" The words were out before Whitney could stop them. "After all, what's a library without the people who write the books? Since Eric's got one on our shelves—checked out when I looked last Friday—I think he more than qualifies to join us for lunch."

"We've got your book?" Mr. Andrews' voice rose with bookish excitement. "Fiction or nonfiction?"

"Non-fiction." Eric gave her immediate superior a self-effacing smile. "My work's important to me—as Whitney's is to her—and it pleases me greatly that you'd have a copy of my text in such a fine facility."

As Eric gestured to the surroundings that were vast enough and had an undeniable charm, Whitney knew the grand old dame was very much in need of a facelift. She also knew any vanity Mr. Andrews had was invested in the library he oversaw.

"It is a fine library, isn't it?" he replied with the sort of sigh a Romeo had on reserve for his Juliet.

Eric's arm came around her with a natural elegance, reminding Whitney of an exquisite shawl draped over the shoulders of a queen, make it of hearts. Only for hers to break a little when he said:

"Indeed your library is fine. But just as a room without books is like a body without soul, a room filled with books doesn't count for much without the souls who love them. I'm sure you consider yourself fortunate to have Whitney bring out the best this library has to offer."

"Of course, I told her so myself just the other day." An approving smile at Whitney, and Mr. Andrews turned the conversation back to Eric. "Now about this book of yours. What's the title?"

"Nothing you're likely to recognize. It's a scientific text called *Volcanology: A Retrospective Analysis of—*"

"'*Earth and Man.*' No wonder your name sounded familiar. I'm the one who checked that book out! Not the sort of thing I usually read, but I caught a *National Geographic* special on PBS about volcanos and it was so interesting, especially an interview they did with a scientist who was nearly killed in an eruption and…say! It was you they were interviewing! Well, I'll be darned." He gripped Eric's hand and pumped it enthusiastically. "Dr. Townsend, it is a privilege to officially meet you."

The look Eric slid her was apologetic. She could see his slight grimace even as he smiled for the benefit of her boss. Eric, such a class act.

"Then it's settled," the self that wanted to be classy, too, decreed. "Eric will join us for lunch."

"Absolutely!" echoed Mr. Andrews.

Two hours later, Mr. Andrews and the director of the entire library system, Mr. Richards, were now Bill and Al to Eric. They were so clearly enthralled with his company that Whitney felt like a fourth wheel at her own "welcome back" lunch. It was just as well since she was a freaking wreck from trying to appear professional while Eric lightly stroked her right knee beneath the table.

"So tell me, how did the two of you meet?" Al—that was still Mr. Richards to her—directed the question to Eric.

"Oh, Whitney's much better at telling stories than me," he demurred, seemingly unaware his compliment stung like a fresh cut switch—only for his smile to openly reveal the sly, cunning fox whose intelligence was seductive and boy did he know how to wield it. "Go ahead, darling. You tell them how we met."

Darling. He'd never called her that before. Then again, what a relief he hadn't said "kitten" or "*yuan-pau.*"

Throat dry, Whitney took a sip of her iced tea and fiercely wished for champagne.

"We met on a plane. And, well, one thing led to another and…" Trailing off, she clamped her knees tight as Eric's light stroke turned to knowing fingers that slightly inched up.

"Oh, *come now*," he interjected. "It was one of those whirlwind romances that suck the air out of your lungs and the oxygen from your brain." His meaningful eye-lock dared her to dispute him.

She managed a tight smile and a corroborative nod. "Yes," she agreed while wanting to put her fork into more than the West Indies salad on her plate. "It was like you read about."

By day's end, Eric was concerned about how far Whitney's health concerns might still extend. She looked ready to drop.

"You're sure you're okay?" he asked as he opened the passenger-side door.

"I'm fine. It's just been a really long, hard day."

"No argument there." Quick to beat her to the seatbelt, he strapped his mystery wife in. Not only did it get his hand on her hip, along with a little gasp from her lips, it felt symbolically significant to harness her in from chest to lap, right next to him, for the duration of their drive.

Eric got behind the wheel, intent on steering more than the car.

"I'll make dinner," he told her as they glided under a tunnel of ancient oaks dripping moss. Beautiful, like nature's cocoon. If he could wrap Whitney up just as tightly he would. "Where's the nearest grocery to your place?"

"Winn-Dixie's the closest, but Eric, you shouldn't have to cook after—"

"I insist. You're tired and we're not eating out." Absolutely not. Enough public exposure. "Any requests?"

"Surprise me."

"Careful, there might be a tracking device on the menu."

Her typically free laughter was strained and his grin didn't reach his eyes. Yes, there was *that* between them. Just add his new trust issues to the dirty laundry list of things they had to sort out.

They drove in silence other than her directives, until he cut the engine. "Want to come in with me?"

"If you don't mind, I'd rather rest out here instead."

"I figured as much. Just don't go anywhere."

Whitney responded by scooching down in her seat with a yawn and hitting the lock on her door.

Eric tapped the control panel to lock the remaining three and didn't pretend it was a joke before heading into the store. Of course he knew she'd still be there when he got back but he needed to hear the *click-click-click* of her containment, and he wanted her to hear it too, 'cause *Lucy, you got some splainin to do!*

Despite her obvious exhaustion, they were due a come to Jesus meeting that should have taken precedence over work that morning. It wasn't like he was an out of line boyfriend wanting attention, or like they'd had a little spat he thought more important to clear up than respecting her professional obligations. Oh no, this was something entirely different that came with gargantuan, life-altering proportions.

From where he stood, it was Whitney who had disrespected the sanctity of their marriage, and it was Whitney who had disregarded the utter devastation her past actions had caused when she chose work over the man that had been in a perpetual state of panic while he searched for her. And no, he didn't give a rats ass that it was her first day back on the job.

Still, that didn't stop him from adding a few nice touches to the cart to help temper the coming storm. And it didn't stop him from quietly shutting his driver's side door and hungrily studying her, head rested against the passenger window, lips slightly parted for that cute little sweet snore. Her body slumped into seat leather, he noticed yet again that she had gained some weight, but proportionately so given the strain of her blouse, as opposed to the twenty pounds he had dropped in her absence.

Well. He wasn't good at waiting, they both knew it. Good thing she was getting a nap. It was going to be a long night.

"And here we have napa cabbage, mushrooms, sprouts, chicken breasts, a lemon, sesame seeds..." Several other items landed on the counter, followed by a box of lavender bath salts, which he placed in her hands.

"Thank you, Eric. What did I do to deserve this?"

"The same thing you did to deserve these." A paper bag folded at the top opened and out came a bouquet of bright colors.

The flowers weren't tiger lilies with a raffia bow but the scent was just as sweet and the stargazers among the chrysanthemums could have been wild blooms surrounding her in paradise.

If it was Eric's intent to disarm her with more than a smile, it was working. The nap in his car had done wonders, too. A bath to wash away the day's remains might even make her feel human.

As if reading her mind he suggested, "Why don't you put that Calgon to good use while I throw dinner together?" Producing two jalapeños, he added, "I'll be sure to make the stir-fry nice and hot, just the way you like it."

"But, I..." Her voice trailed off as he looked at her. Of course, Eric had never just looked at her. She had forgotten how it felt to be a secret keeper while enduring his scrutiny. "Maybe just half a hot pepper," she hedged. "I'd rather not have it too spicy."

"But you always picked the spiciest dish on the menu. The hotter the better. Why the switch?"

"I—I've had some digestive issues."

"Does it have to do with the no longer fatal medical condition we still need to discuss?"

If only he knew. "I'd rather discuss that later, Eric."

"Then later it will be."

His ready agreement wasn't expected. It made her wonder if maybe, just maybe, he would let her off the hook for the night since he hadn't attempted the grilling she had braced herself for as soon as the front door shut to her apartment.

From a final bag he pulled out a six-pack of Dixie Beer—no surprise since he always liked to sample regional offerings—followed by a pretty black bottle of Freixenet sparkling cava.

"The champagne selection was pretty limited," he apologized, "But I thought we could still enjoy this. Would you like a glass to keep you company since I believe it's a bit precipitate for me to be joining you again in the tub?"

Whitney longingly eyed his offer. A rare single glass wouldn't hurt the baby but she had been extra vigilant after taking such poor care of herself in those horrible weeks of insanity when she didn't know she was pregnant. Besides, Eric would soon realize that his party girl was no longer partying.

"Thank you for the offer but I'm afraid I have to decline due to the same digestive issues. The doctor put me on a fairly strict diet."

The flick of his gaze from her breasts to her hips was by no means critical—quite the opposite—but it did bring into silent question just what kind of diet the doctor had put her on.

"It turns out I have a thyroid issue."

"I see. Would this be in addition to the digestive issue?"

Knowing Eric would research any conditions she might cite, and knowing Dr. Clark hadn't put any restrictions on her diet due to the thyroid, Whitney tiptoed with care.

"There seem to be two different issues. When the doctor explained it the medical terminology was over my head. The important thing is that I now have a proper diagnosis and I've been following doctor's orders." In hopes of spinning this landmine in the right direction, she added, "Of course the really great news is that he also determined that I'm otherwise healthy and I'm not going to die."

It was impossible to decipher Eric's expression. There seemed to be some kind of see-saw between mental calculation and clashing emotions. Strong emotions she sensed he was struggling to contain. It reminded her of that startling moment when his palm connected with her wall. She knew Eric would sever his own hand before ever raising it to strike her, but she also knew that beneath his rational, superbly controlled surface lurked some vast waters that, if plunged into deeply enough, could be brooding, even a little dark.

"You're right," he said quietly. "There could be no better news in the world than that. I wish I had been there when you got it." He put the pretty black bottle of sparkling wine into the refrigerator. "We'll save that for after your diet isn't so strict. Would you like one of these to sip in the tub instead?"

He handed her a ginger ale without waiting for an answer. Whitney took it, along with the lavender bath salts, and made a quick exit. As she swiped up her knitting and hid it from sight en route to the tub, she wondered how long it would be before Eric figured out that one plus one made three.

CHAPTER 25

*W*hen she emerged from the hallway bathroom in a terry cloth robe, Whitney made a beeline to her bedroom. The first thing she noticed was the vintage embroidered kimono and obi belt laid out on her bed. The silk was slightly wrinkled but never more beautiful, this honeymoon present from Eric in Antigua.

Had he actually been carrying it with him on his travels since she had left it behind with his ring and necklace, her wedding dress, their marriage license?

She had tried not to envision what his response had been when he found her leavings because she knew it was awful. Eric, however, wasn't the ostrich she was; he confronted, examined, wanted to know how things worked and sought solutions.

Unlike herself, he had *not* avoided imagining what had driven her away and what she was returning to, of that she was certain.

Whitney made herself glance around the bedroom. Forced herself to remember what this room had looked like—what *she* had looked and even smelled like—before a newspaper had her racing, still half insane, for a pregnancy test kit.

Only for everything, within hours, to completely change.

There could be no better news in the world than that. I wish I had been there when you got it.

Whitney cringed. He hadn't been there that day and never in a million years would she want Eric to witness the depths she had proved capable of sinking. But she had crawled out of that dark, dark hole, calling on the dependable Whitney she had once been and more than ever still needed to be.

Maybe he could learn to love her, too?

It was with that question in mind that she considered her newest dilemma: Put on the kimono that a very different version of herself had once worn? Or make a "take me or leave me the way I really am" statement by joining him in the boring lounge pants and oversized top she typically schlepped around in to get comfortable? Another option was one of her granny gowns…but, not an option.

She longingly traced the kimono's embroidered pattern of a yin-yang symbol rising like a moon above fuchsia peonies embedded against pure, raw silk.

This was no cavalier gesture. It was a dare, a challenge, that Eric had wrapped up with a temptation bow.

To emerge wearing the kimono was to say "Come into my bed where you laid this. I will open my arms and open my thighs just as I did on our wedding night. By giving my body to you, to touch and enter and claim, you will have the proof that I'm trying to fix what I have broken and sex will help us heal."

Was she ready to do that? Of course that hellcat Eric had fallen in love with was already panting at the idea of opening her arms and thighs—especially the thighs—but there was more to Whitney Smith than he knew and she wasn't so sure he'd find the other side of the package so attractive.

She and Eric had some troubled history now, all of it of her making. And the big, sloppy mess she'd made needed to be cleaned up before they got naked. Right? After all, you didn't roll around in a mud pen and then climb under the sheets without getting them all dirty, too. And, okay, even if part of her really wanted to show him her different, new body, see how he would react—*who cares about the sheets?*—another part felt shy, self-protective, not ready to expose herself so quickly. Just imagining that level of vulnerability, of his body covering hers, pushing inside until he could almost touch the tiny human he had put into her womb...

Reckless anticipation had her nether realms reaching; moist palms and a nervous stomach weren't so quick to agree.

It was an impossible decision but she made her choice.

Only to immediately regret it when she saw Eric had transformed the small dining area into a romantic, intimate setting. An old candelabra she had picked up at a garage sale was lit with tapered candles. It graced the middle of her mother's small claw foot dining table, now dressed in the white linen that only came out for holidays. Eric must have found it in the mahogany buffet—along with her mother's best wheat pattern china and goblets that didn't clink like real crystal when you toasted. With iced tea, of course.

Rounding it all out was a single stargazer lily fronting a gold melamine bowl filled with a blend of stir fried ingredients that smelled heavenly even ten paces away.

Eric inclined his head and, other than a slight downward turn of his mouth, made no comment regarding her inelegant choice of dinner wear.

Still, she knew.

"M'lady." He gave a slight bow, pulled out a chair. "I await the pleasure of your company."

The Dixie beer wasn't all that great, but it had more sparkle so far than Eric's subdued dining companion.

"More water?" he asked when that was well and truly the last question on his mind.

"Thank you, but no." Whitney gave him a small smile then focused on moving the stir fry around on her plate.

This was not the same woman who ate with gusto; who had passed a finger through another candle's flame, put her finger to his lips and murmured, "Maybe I like playing with fire."

Even while he had warned her about the consequences of curiosity that first night, her naiveté had enchanted his senses. This new side of Whitney certainly had him curious now, but in no way did he find her wearing the equivalent of a fire extinguisher to the table enchanting.

The kimono had been symbolic: her chance to meet him halfway by acknowledging the last time she'd worn it. Never mind that he had toted it here, there, everywhere since she had Dear Johned him in Antigua.

The other evidence of their history—and future—resided on his person or in the luggage he had propped beside her couch.

The vintage coffee table fronting it still had a candy dish but, interestingly, her knitting project was no longer there. Hmm. Well, she'd always been tidy, so maybe that wasn't so strange.

She glanced at the watch she had worn since his arrival despite eschewing any such reminders of time during their cohabitation. He had it down to the day: 61 together. As for the 82 apart, time for some answers.

"I notice you keep checking your watch. You never did that before."

"Time's the last thing you want to think about when you're afraid you don't have much."

"I wish I'd known."

Seconds ticked by. He wanted her to look at him. Not at the plate, not at the damn watch.

"Is it bedtime yet?" he casually asked.

That got her attention where he wanted it. "No, not yet. But I do need to get up by my usual time—about 7 a.m.—to be at the library by nine."

"Sorry I made you late today." Then deciding at least one of them needed to be honest, he amended, "Actually, I'm not in the least bit sorry. But I do understand you don't want a repeat of what happened this morning, so why don't we address at least one of our problems before calling it a night?"

Her gaze darted in the direction of her bedroom, then uncertainly back to him. It reminded Eric of his jittery bride on their wedding night. Only now he couldn't ply her with celebratory drink—yet another switcheroo in this puzzle she was presenting.

He had always loved puzzles. And this one was about to get at least a right corner put into place.

"Why did you leave me like that?"

"Because…" She laid down her linen napkin and met his probing gaze. "I left the way I did because I thought I was dying, Eric. Because I thought it was the right thing to do."

"Anything else?"

"Yes," she admitted. "Death is ugly. It's horrible. I lived it. I watched my mother die and I couldn't put you through that, too. Or put myself through watching you watch me. I know you have every reason to doubt anything I say, but I swear that much is true."

"I believe you."

He pushed aside his plate, then Whitney's, clearing the space between them on the table. It was a small table and wouldn't take much pounding—which was unfortunate since he would very much like to swipe everything off and pick up where they'd left off in the pool. For now, however, a small table would serve his higher purposes.

Eric extended both hands, palms up. Whitney laid her own upon his. So trusting. He didn't want to abuse that trust, but Jesus had just called a meeting.

"When did you find out?"

She closed her eyes.

"When?" he repeated. "Tell me when you got the good news and open your eyes while you tell me."

As if peeling up blinds that were bound by Velcro, she whispered, "December 23rd. It was a Wednesday."

He could feel a muscle working in his cheek while he waited for her to fill the pregnant silence.

"When I came back I…I wasn't in good shape, Eric. It took me awhile to get myself back together while I was trying to figure things out. I don't know how anyone handles a situation like that with any kind of grace, but I probably handled it as poorly as anyone can. I think. Maybe. Maybe not. I don't know."

"You don't know," he repeated, and tried to find some compassion in his heart that wasn't showing up on demand. "And while you were trying to figure all that out, did you consider there was another person who, also on that day, was fearing the worst had happened? Someone who would readily swallow poison in exchange for your life?"

Whitney dropped her gaze. He caught her hands and held them firmly, as he did her feet to the fire.

"Look at me."

Slowly she obeyed and he saw all that she was feeling: Misery. Guilt. Shame. So undiluted and raw he almost took pity but...another day. He was taking no prisoners tonight.

"Now. There must be a reason you chose to keep this very important information to yourself for...let's see. Wednesday, December 23rd to Saturday, February 6th..." He stretched the seconds out, as if counting each day on a mental finger, allowing her to feel a tiny fraction of his own excruciating wait. "Huh. 42 days. I'm sure you would never intentionally subject me to 42 days in absolute hell, so there must have been a very good reason to justify your silence while your *husband* was half out of his mind, trying to find you."

He listened to her shallow breathing, saw the first tear trickle down her cheek, past her chin, drop. Whitney could cry him a river but she wasn't getting a handkerchief yet, not even a free hand to wipe away her own snot.

Leaning slightly closer, he tightened his grip and prompted, "Well? Let's hear it. What was your reason for waiting 42 days before deciding to contact me?"

"I..."

Swallow. Blink. Blink. To her credit she did not look away and he gave her points for that. God knew she could use them.

"Go on."

"I blew all my money."

"Excuse me?"

"I said I blew all my money. I had a nice savings account—maybe not a lot to you, but it was a lot to me—thirty-three grand and some change. I took care of my responsibilities, made sure I had enough to come back to die on. I just hadn't counted on living and not having enough left over to pay the rent."

This was about *money?* He was speechless.

"And I, well, right before you met me I had quit my job in a very unprofessional way so I didn't think I could go back. So I looked all over trying to get work before I contacted you..."

This was about *employment?* He could only stare.

"I tried. I tried to call you sooner, but I couldn't bring myself to come groveling and ask you for a handout. I had to find a way to stand on my own two feet again first..."

This was about *pride?* At least that much didn't surprise him.

"And there was something else. Something important."

Drum roll. He inclined his head, waiting...waiting...

"I realized the woman you fell in love with and wanted to marry was a very different version of who I was before you met me. I was making myself up as I went along so it was an imposter, not me, you were with that whole time. And I didn't want you to find out that I was a fraud who had acted completely out of character because then you might not want me anymore. After all, you're worldly and successful and could have any woman you want—and now you see where I live, how I make my living, what a little piece of the world I live in. So there you have it. I didn't call because I felt like the real me couldn't compete with the fake one you fell for."

Fear.

Eric let go of her hands. Extended his napkin. He waited while Whitney composed herself.

"I appreciate your honesty, Whitney. I'm sure that wasn't easy to confess."

"It was terrible." She sniffled.

He didn't care. The courtroom of emotional integrity was now in session and he was holding her accountable. Whitney lacked experience, not emotional intelligence. *When the student is ready, the teacher will appear.* Ready or not, here he came.

"I'll tell you what's terrible. What's terrible is having your opinions decided for you, predicated on your lover's insecurity and absolute bullshit. You seem to think I don't know who you are, when the truth is actually the opposite. 'See me as I've never seen myself before.' Do you remember those words? Was it a fraud riding my hips and giving me something precious that she'd never given another man? Was it a fake who sang 'Twinkle-Twinkle' to the stars while she had no idea I was watching, and took possession of my heart? Oh, no."

Now he leaned forward, finger pointed straight at her.

"No, you don't get off that easy. I may need to learn some new things about Whitney Smith, but it seems there's even more that Whitney *Townsend* needs to learn about herself."

He watched her tight swallow, let it sink in. But when she started to push back her chair he held up a hand.

"We're not through yet. We need to talk about money. It's something married people actually talk about, Whitney. They talk about budgets. They talk about bills. They talk about goals and dreams and who pissed them off at work. It's where the tires hit the pavement—and yes, they talk about car repairs, too. Now apparently your relationship with money, and the security it brings, touched a nerve that's associated with your ingrained fear of dependence. Especially on a man. Thanks, Dad. I'm trying to put myself in your shoes and yes, I can understand pride. I've got more than a little of it myself. But for you to so cling to it, to believe you would be debasing yourself by bringing me into your inner circle of confidence…"

Deep breath. Better make it two.

"Well. Let's just say that I'm glad to not be sitting in your disingenuous chair. Having the man who loves me more than anything ask: Was it worth it? Was holding on to your precious independence, your precious pride, *for 42 more days* while surely knowing I was twisting in the wind without you—was it worth it? And looking back over the landscape of it all, was keeping your silence worth it? Because I'm asking you now: Do you think you might have been just a little bit selfish, no matter the cards you thought you'd been dealt?"

Eric leaned in closer, closer. Close enough to whisper into her ear, "Maybe even a little bit...*cruel?*"

He heard her gasp. Felt her flinch. Settling back into his chair, he took some satisfaction in her stricken expression. He had made his point. Drawn an indelible line in the sand. No, he didn't think Whitney would ever consider so royally disrespecting him and their marriage, or undermining their relationship as she had, ever again.

As far as he was concerned, this conversation was over. The horrific blight on their past, addressed. Holding on to what could not be changed would be anathema to their future, and that future meant far more to him than grinding them down with a grudge. Time to move on.

But. He had one more line to draw, a responsibility he was giving to her, that was not unlike the night she had given up her virginity and made him a virgin all over again.

"I'll be sleeping on your couch tonight," he informed her. "And every night going forward—until you put on that kimono. Until then, consider us roommates, and if you like, even girlfriend and boyfriend. Without benefits. I won't settle for your crumbs, Whitney. We made vows that you reneged on and I kept. If it makes you feel any more secure, we can stick to the original three months of our agreement. Two weeks down. Ten to go. But they don't start until we pick up where we left off—with my ring on your finger and the two of us behind a bedchamber door."

CHAPTER 26

*W*hitney stared up at her popcorn textured bedroom ceiling and wondered if Eric was asleep on the couch. She needed to pee. But she would have to skirt the edge of the living room to reach the bathroom and she did not want him to hear her tinkle-tinkle-little-star over the hum of a fan on its last legs.

She had always known she was out of her league with him, even while pretending to be someone she wasn't…though, according to Eric, that was pure bullshit. And he said it with such authority, it was hard not to think he just might be right.

The man she had married, with her own ignorant caveats in place, clearly understood what marriage was supposed to be all about. That same man had accused her of cruelty.

She was aware that she'd made selfish choices, but when he whispered *cruel* it felt like an invisible fist landed in her solar plexus. Cruelty suggested callous indifference. Anguish visited upon someone else. A lack of humanity, compassion, moral conscience.

If he had called her a bitch it wouldn't have carried nearly the loaded weight of that one word: *Cruel.* And for Eric, who so delighted in indulging her, to fillet her in a single swipe with the equivalent of a stiletto slipped from his boot…

191

Whitney shivered. With one word he had told her the depth to which she had plunged her own knife into him. And continued to plunge it day after day after day. Just so she could hang onto her precious pride. Her precious independence. Her insecurities and lack of self-knowledge.

Was it true? No one had ever spoken to her like that. No one had told her before to take a good look at herself and do some serious self-examination, to consider how her behaviors impacted others, particularly those who cared for her the most.

Just remembering Eric's pointed finger made her squirm.

So did needing to pee.

For some reason he had gone unexpectedly light on her for all the days prior to December 23. He seemed to understand, or at least accept, the sort of scarring that had come with her mother's death. What had upset him the most were the 42 days she had remained MIA. Those 42 days were the sticking point because she had withheld critical information.

And boy, he didn't even know the half of it yet.

They had never talked about having children. She only knew that one of the reasons he and Amy got divorced was because she wanted a child and he didn't—and his profession had played significantly into that.

It seemed that she and Amy had more and more in common.

A sound came from the living room. Eric's voice. The bedside clock called it just after midnight. He was talking, trying to keep his voice hushed. She had seen him take enough calls at odd hours to know there was an emergency somewhere on the planet and his expertise put him at the tippy-top of consultants.

As his voice drifted through the thin walls between them she heard the opening, soft shutting of the front door.

Whitney seized the moment. She didn't bother to grab a robe to put over her granny gown before racing to the bathroom. Even with the *rrr-rrr-rrr* of the tired fan, her anxiety was putting the kibosh on letting her bladder loose. She turned on the faucet in hopes of getting more than a trickle started.

Once she was done, hands washed, she breathed a sigh of relief. Eric's calls could easily take twenty minutes, sometimes hours. Even with her delayed ability to get the job done, surely he was still outside.

A soft rap at the bathroom door was followed by, "Whitney? Are you okay in there? Did dinner upset your stomach?"

Oh. Shit. Well, thank goodness she hadn't needed to take a number two. She was calling management tomorrow to get the bath fan replaced.

"I'm fine!" Whitney glanced in the mirror. She wished she had on some lipstick. Mascara, too. Not to mention a handy compact to powder the blush she could see spreading from her cheeks to the scooped white cotton with a pink bow at her neck.

She could feel his presence on the other side of the door, waiting for her to open it.

Oh, stop it! You're being ridiculous. How many times has he seen you naked, and you're worried about him seeing you in a gown that belongs in a convent?

She opened the door. And there he was. Chest bare, a pair of black boxers riding his hips, and wearing that smile that could charm the pants off a nun.

"I'm sorry if I woke you."

"No, no. I thought you were asleep on the couch. Sorry if I woke you."

"No such luck. Haven't slept a wink. And considering what I'm seeing now, don't expect I will." He twirled a front strand of her errant hair. Let go. "God, you're beautiful."

"Eric, I..."

She didn't have any idea what she was going to say, but before she could say anything else he fingered the pink ribbon at her bodice.

"Nice gown."

The rising tent in his boxers that she could sense closing the distance, verified by a furtive glance, confirmed his appreciation was sincere.

"I know you need your sleep so I won't keep you up. Like you, I do have some work I need to get done tomorrow"—he pretended to check a non-existent watch on his wrist—"Make that today. I can work here or find a local café if that makes it easier for you."

Would it? It would be easier to concentrate at work, and she didn't think Eric would go snooping through her closet or check out the luggage under her bed where she'd stashed the baby blanket. But he did love to sniff her bras—*even her washer-bound panties!*—so she couldn't discount the possibility he might be tempted to get familiar with her private quarters, including the lingerie drawers that had some evidence she still needed to hide.

Just for a little while. Eric had a right to know that he was going to be a father, no matter her uncertainty about his reception to the news. But it was her news to deliver and she had a right to decide on its timing—which sure wasn't now.

"Why don't you come with me again," she ventured, "You could work in another area of the library, meet me for lunch, maybe drive around town to investigate until I get off. Then we can grab some drive-thru at Colonel Dixie for dinner, make camp in front of the TV, and you can drink your beer while I wish those digestive issues weren't keeping me from joining you. How does that sound for a plan?"

"I said it before and I'll say it again: Lady, I like the way you think. Wait. Note to transcriptionist: I love the way you think."

And with that he kissed her forehead. Left her standing at the bathroom door and headed for the couch.

As she reluctantly went her separate way, Eric called to her, "Sweet dreams, Mrs. Townsend."

"Sweet dreams, Dr. Townsend," she said back.

Whitney left her bedroom door open a crack. Just in case he decided the kimono wasn't a prerequisite to a little snuggling.

He didn't avail himself of her discreet invitation. But just as she was finally falling asleep, she thought she heard Eric's deep sigh, followed by a murmured, "I miss you, *yuan-pao.*"

~

From a discreet distance Eric watched Whitney, hungrily. His need to have her back was like a living, breathing, carnivorous thing that wanted to gobble her up with more than his eyes.

He had to be careful with that. Eighty-two accumulated days of internalized panic, despair, and craving for any kind of physical contact didn't dissipate overnight.

God, what the woman was teaching him. He wasn't the good traveler he'd always believed himself to be. He wanted fixed plans and more than an ETA for ring to finger, kimono to floor. The patience Whitney was forcing him to master was like training for the Olympics Decathlon.

How long was this going to take? A day, a week, a month?

The whole money thing was a bigger bugaboo than he'd ever expected. Whitney associated money with the scarcity of it, while he'd always considered it a tool to responsibly manage and enjoy. The ability to be charitable was important to him; she was loathe to be considered anyone's charity case.

How could she ever think he would consider her as such? She was his wife, his lover, and it gave him joy to provide her with the security she hadn't had growing up.

What part of that didn't she get?

Of course it wasn't Whitney's fault that she hadn't had any role models in the marriage department growing up. She hadn't even had any siblings to look out for, or who would look out for her, while they learned the art of negotiation over chores and trading Halloween candy.

Patience. He had to remember that he was ten years older. Had to remember this wasn't his first rodeo and Whitney had been on a steep learning curve ever since they met. To see where she'd actually come from left him amazed that she'd had the balls to jettison herself out of the stale confines of an apartment that felt like a mausoleum dedicated to preserving her mother's belongings—like the vintage china and linens that looked brand new because they'd been stored in a dark cabinet to await something important to justify their use.

Last night had plenty justified it.

Oh. Hell. Yes.

If the journey of a thousand miles began with one step, per the ever wise Lao Tzu, then they were well on their way.

He was frankly fascinated by all the new layers he had to pull back to get to the Whitney he knew. Should he take her to Portland? He could see how she liked his floating crib, lay out the bait for a change of residence. Unfortunately, with this work schedule of hers—

Whitney glanced in his direction. Even with a good fifty feet between them the connection of their eyes was so electric that anyone intruding on their line of vision ran the risk of getting zapped.

That did it. He was stepping on the gas. Patience surely had its virtues, but Whitney had not married a patient man.

CHAPTER 27

"*L*et's watch this," Eric suggested as he picked out a movie from the small stack beside the TV in her living room. "Nobody puts Baby in the corner."

Dirty Dancing was one of her all-time favorites, but how many times would she have to hear *Baby* while Eric fulfilled his promise of dinner, a movie, and dancing when all she wanted to do was collapse?

He had already moved her coffee table, transferred the blanket he had slept with from couch to floor, and had their Colonel Dixie takeout spread like an irresistible picnic in front of the tube. It was perfect. It was romantic. It was only 7:30 and she was ready to crash. Between the emotional upheaval, readjusting to work, pregnancy's demand for sleep, and the constant energy buzz that Eric's proximity created...

Whitney tried to stifle her yawn only for Eric to put aside the movie. Just on top of the television, where they both stood, as he placed palms on her shoulders.

The fissure of sensation was immediate. He hadn't tried to kiss her again since he'd appeared out of nowhere and back walked her into the apartment where his palm, that felt so gentle now, had connected with a wall. His touching of her since had been so limited that her imagination, along with her hormones, went wild when she thought of him fingering more than a ribbon on her gown.

"Are you sure you're okay?"

"Of course." What a lie. Had she become pathological? "The last couple of days have been really intense and I think it's just caught up with me. I'm sorry, Eric, but I'm beat."

"Don't apologize, I know the feeling. I haven't slept well since our last night together in Antigua. I'm not saying that to make you feel bad, I just want you to know that I commiserate." He casually plucked a pin from her hair, followed by another. "I remember the first night we slept together and how it was the best sleep I'd had in years. I never told you, but that's when I knew we would get married."

"What?"

"Uh-huh. Just like that, I knew. The same way I knew the exact moment I was falling in love with you. That happened the next night, in Montserrat. It was really amazing, suddenly being aware of this stunning emotion that was unlike anything I'd ever experienced before. I felt like I'd gotten hit with a bat and all I could see were stars."

Several more pins gone, her French twist was all but tumbling down, as were any defenses that went by the name of prudence.

How did he do it? Honesty was always his first weapon of choice to advance any hidden-in-plain-sight agendas. It was how he had convinced her to marry him on the courthouse steps in Antigua before giving her the wedding she had secretly dreamed of with a princess bride dress, a Cinderella coach, even the ring she had so wanted in the jewelry store window in Jamaica but refused to try on...

Wait. How had Eric known those details? Was he that much of a mind reader...or had he read one of her letters? She knew the exact letter she had written to herself, when they were in Jamaica, and she even knew the day because she went to that awful clinic intending to get some birth control pills and—

And why was she only now putting it all together?

"There," he pronounced, threading his fingers through her unbound hair and admiring his handiwork.

Whitney caught his hands, stared directly into his eyes.

"Did you read any of my letters?"

For once she had the satisfaction of seeing Eric completely blind-sided. The shoe was on the other foot for a change and given his slight flush, he wasn't comfortable with the fit.

"One," he admitted. "It was inexcusable and I felt terribly for giving in to my curiosity. Actually, it was more than curiosity. You were evasive and it bothered me. There was a little insecurity at play on my end, too. I wasn't proud of any of it, and I knew I should tell you, but I also knew I wouldn't. At first, anyway."

Something in her said she should leave this alone, forgive him for his one infraction of her trust after the motherlode of disservices she had done him. But...no.

"What do you mean by, 'at first'? Was there a reason you thought you might reconsider telling me?"

"There was." He nodded to the couch. "Maybe we should sit down to discuss this."

"No." She let go of his hands, crossed her arms over her chest. It felt self-protective to cover the heart that was suddenly beating too fast and not for the usual reasons. "No, we will discuss this before I decide whether or not I want to sit down with you at all."

"All right," he sighed. "The letter I read indicated you were worried about getting pregnant so you were going to a clinic to be on the safe side. At the time I wasn't sure why you didn't want to tell me about getting on the pill, but after my invasion of your privacy, I didn't want to ask. Shortly after that, something happened when you put on the kimono and dropped it by the pool. Do you remember that particular morning?"

How could she forget? Their lovemaking had always been phenomenal, but after that special, "better" first wedding night, the morning after had tripped into something even beyond that. It was like the kimono was a sorcerer's robe and the wedding ring, their vows, endorphin potions that had mysteriously transformed her overnight. She'd felt almost delirious when—

"I couldn't tell if you were too far gone to notice I wasn't wearing the usual protection. My other thought was that maybe you weren't concerned because you were taking extra precautions yourself—along with the whole bedchamber thing that made the condoms mostly secondary anyway. But this time was different. I cheated. It was a close call. And I knew that I desperately wanted to have that experience again, with nothing between us and me not intervening with nature—and if that meant I had to confess to knowing about the clinic, it was only a matter of time before I'd take whatever consequences you deemed fair to make it happen. Of course I was hopeful that you would come forward about the pills first and spare me a confession…along with any subsequent consequences."

Oh. Oh. There were consequences all right. She stared at him mutely while a thousand thoughts and emotions swirled through the hormonal maelstrom of the body Eric had impregnated, and now she knew exactly when.

In the face of her silence he hastened to add, "And also of course I never would have done such a thing if I thought there was even a remote possibility of getting you pregnant. Even knowing you should be ninety-nine percent safe, I did find my better judgement before it was too late, so I hope that counts for something."

Did it? She supposed, but it wasn't the reassurance she needed. *Of course I never would have done such a thing if I thought there was even a remote possibility of getting you pregnant.* She really wished he hadn't said that.

"Whitney? I wish you would say something."

Well, Eric, the fact of the matter is I am pregnant thanks to your little lapse of complete judgement. We know that doesn't happen very often, now don't we? Just so you know, I died a thousand deaths in a few hours' time when I first found out, but after I wasn't a monster anymore, I was ecstatic. So what do you think of that, Mr. Globetrotter? Here's what I think: You'll step up to the plate, because that's who you are. Unfortunately, we still have a BIG problem. Amy asked for one baby. Selfish me wants more. I want it all— the house, kids as in plural, you mowing the lawn instead of living out of a suitcase and moonwalking on lava. So, I'm already wondering, how long will it be before you get antsy? Before a frazzled wife and a baby crying at two a.m. aren't as exciting as all the other thrills you could be missing with the ring of a phone?

His cell phone went off. Eric grimaced.

"Go ahead," she told him, giving him his own Get Out of Jail Free pass. "I've got my job, you've got yours. Take the call."

He looked from her to the satchel with his laptop, the ringing phone it also contained.

"They can leave a message. I'll call back. This is more important."

His pointed glance at the front door was not lost on her, or its implications about where his priorities were placed while as of yesterday morning she was still getting hers straight.

Touché.

"Considering how important your calls usually are, I appreciate that, Eric. And, as you said to me last night, I do appreciate your honesty. Such confessions couldn't be easy for you either."

"Actually, being able to confess my failures to you is a relief from continuing to keep it all to myself. I try to be a good man, Whitney. And you make me want to be the best one I can be. But I do fail. We all do. And if I don't kiss you right now that's a failure that's all on me."

His mouth came down and obliterated any thought beyond the connection of their lips, the immediate hunger he relayed and just as equally summoned. The feel of a knowing, masculine hand plowing through her hair, then anchoring her neck was familiar yet new all over again, as was the way his other arm cinched her waist and pulled her flush against him.

He was hard. Hard for her. A very small voice told her they needed to get their accumulated baggage sorted out and relegated to a non-recycle bin first, but there was a wildcat inside that she suddenly didn't have the will or the want to restrain. Maybe she would regret it later, but nothing could dilute the thrill of this moment unless she let it, and *that* was not going to happen.

The practical librarian was no match for the unleashed tigress that came out with a roar—she was the woman who understood that life was full of tradeoffs, and when it came to survival of the fittest, nice girls didn't always win.

She grabbed a handful of Eric's shirt, gripped the front of his belt, and down she pulled him to the floor. So much for Colonel Dixie. Salvador Dali was going to have one hell of a picnic.

Eric's back to the blanket, she straddled his still fully clothed torso, brought his hands over her breasts. *Oh god.*

"Take off my blouse. Take off all the rest."

When he answered with only a hot gaze riveted to her achingly sensitive breasts, filling his palms to overflowing, she lightly whipped her hair across his face before taunting him with a sultry whisper.

"So what are you waiting for? You know you want me. Now come and get me. *Baby.*"

Eric wasn't sure what switch got flipped but he wasn't about to bring up the kimono as a stipulation to doing Whitney's bidding. Drawing a line in the sand was one thing; being stupid was another.

Still, he hadn't gone through sheer hell to finally get her back only to do a rush job and hope she didn't have regrets once the heat of the moment gave way to more practical concerns. Like work in the morning and watching the clock.

Fortunately, he had seen to one practical concern at the grocery store, just in case.

The anticipation was such, the moment so longed for, he could feel a fine tremor snake through his veins and pulse through the fingertips he stroked from her neck and down to the first button of her blouse. One. Two. Three. He finished the rest and reminded himself there would be another time when buttons could go flying. His palms were only too happy to connect with soft shoulder skin, and slowly drop prim white silk to the floor.

Her bra was utilitarian white, not the pretty pink number he had first seen under Bungalow #1's covers, but boy oh boy, did he suddenly have a thing for modest white cotton that didn't plunge in the front and required an amazing amount of dexterity to release four hooks from the back.

Savoring his unrestricted access to warm flesh and sweet curving spine, he took an inordinate amount of time to slide off the straps. As soon as her breasts tumbled free, Eric was aware of two things, no three. Her breasts were much fuller and areolas darker than he remembered—but it had been a long time. *Too long.* There was also a glow about her face and skin that shimmered from the inside out, more radiant than he remembered, even at their wedding when she was an absolute vision.

But, again, long time, and this was really the first he had seen her more like the Whitney he knew than the stressed out, overly cautious alter-ego whose exhaustion had bowed to his third observation:

Their sexual chemistry, the primal alchemy no amount of science could explain, that had been so fundamental to their origins, had emerged intact despite the hits they had taken.

As he gazed at her breasts, then raised his eyes to meet hers, still bluer than the Caribbean Sea but somehow more Mona Lisa mysterious, Eric knew one more thing:

Rome was not won in a day, or in a single night's sating of pent up need. Tomorrow they would still have issues to address, and that was fine.

Their foundation was solid.

CHAPTER 28

"My, you seem chipper this morning, Whitney. Married life must agree with you."

"Indeed it does, Mr. Andrews." Oh yes, being thoroughly primed and treasured by the most amazing lover in the world was definitely good for a woman's soul. Not to mention all the body parts that had been succinctly reminded of how much they had missed him. Her legs were still wobbly, her nipples pleasantly sore, inner thighs feeling like she had been to workout boot camp, and it was a good thing she was prudently dressed for the library so all the little love suckles from her neck on down didn't show.

As for her hair, it hardly qualified for professional presentation unless that profession involved spending a lot of time on your knees and back. The latter of which had been planted on the kitchen countertop not five minutes before she had raced out the door to drive solo to work.

"And where might your husband be? I was hoping he would join you again today. It's nice having him around."

"I couldn't agree more, Mr. Andrews. However, Eric had some catching up to do with his own work that was better conducted outside of the library. I'll be sure to give him your best when I get home."

"Please do."

Mr. Andrews cleared his throat, pushed up his glasses. Some slight, nervous fidgeting managed to intrude on her blissful mood, reminding her that she was, after all, an employee of the county with a certain reputation to maintain. She should have checked her lipstick before waltzing in on a Dirty Dancing high.

"Is there anything else you want to talk to me about?"

"Well...yes." A little more fidgeting brought her closer to the earth and her responsibilities in it. "I have to say it came as a surprise to find out you were married—to a very fine scholar and gentleman I might add—and I'm certainly glad for you both. But when you agreed to come back it never occurred to me that you might have a husband, especially one who works and lives elsewhere. Portland, I believe. Should I have any concerns that your new husband might expect this to be a temporary position and you could be leaving us again?"

"Did he say anything to you to indicate as much?"

Mr. Andrews adamantly shook his head. "Nothing of the kind. It's just something that occurred to me as a possibility, and I wanted to be sure there aren't some complications that could crop up. I'm only being careful and looking ahead."

Being careful and looking ahead. "Of course I understand." What an understatement. "Eric and I have a lot of details to iron out Mr. Andrews, but I can tell you that while he does have a residence out of state, he travels extensively. The road is more his home than Portland. That's not the kind of lifestyle that works for me, so no need to worry."

"But if he's gone all the time and you stay here, what kind of marriage is that?" Mr. Andrews momentarily clamped a hand over his mouth. "My apologies. It's not my place to ask such a personal question."

But ask he had and if that much was apparent to Mr. Andrews, who to her knowledge had never been married, her concerns for their future were legitimate.

"No offense taken," she assured him. "In your position I would be asking, too. As I said, Eric and I are still figuring a lot of things out, but I won't leave you in the lurch again. Promise."

As Whitney made her way to the children's section, she felt like she'd cha-cha'd through a door only to have a bucket of cold water land on her head after a smokin' hot night. Not that the flames were completely doused. Despite the double-slap reminder they could have some seriously big trouble in little China ahead, she still felt like a simmering nympho ready to go back at it again.

Was that normal? Not that anything had been "normal" about their relationship from the very start.

She wished for some kind of epiphany, a magic bullet "ah-hah!" moment that would obliterate her confusion and shine a light on a perfect path that would lead them to a fairy tale ending, just not by the Brothers Grimm.

"I *told* you that Charlie had a playdate today—that you could have him Saturday instead."

"But I took the day off! I thought you said I could have him today *and* Saturday."

"You heard wrong. Now lower your voice before someone hears. How did you find us, anyway?"

"Like I care if anyone hears that you're keeping me from my kid?" Male voice louder now. "As for how I found you—I followed your car when I went to pick him up at the house I'm still paying for. What do you think, I'm some kind of stalker?"

"Mommy? Daddy? Please don't fight…"

Whimpers. Voices hushing. Fading, taking the dispute elsewhere.

Whitney shook her head. The library being a public facility, outbursts and confrontations occasionally occurred. She'd even had to call the police a few times. But this one hit a little too close to the bone.

It was terrible to see a child put in the middle like that, tugged between two parents who must have thought they were in love once, bought a home, started a family, only for something to go terribly wrong and tear it all apart.

She and Eric had to determine if they could get their priorities aligned for the long haul. Not everyone was cut out to be a parent and even good parents weren't always perfect. She'd seen so many extremes: Too indulgent, too lenient, too hovering, too impatient…

Children took a lot of patience. Eric was not patient by nature. He'd even told her early on that he considered it a personal character flaw and he hoped she would be patient with him when he…failed.

I try to be a good man, Whitney. And you make me want to be the best one I can be. But I do fail. We all do. And if I don't kiss you right now that's a failure that's all on me.

Well, he certainly hadn't failed in that department.

Did he love her? Oh, yes. Was he a good man? The best. An amazing lover? What an understatement. Was he cut out to be a father? She thought so, fiercely hoped so. But did he even want to be a father?

She wasn't calling Amy to get the answer on that one.

Theirs was a different relationship—and yet, what did it say about their relationship when she didn't have an answer herself? She'd never even seen him interact with a child.

Still, that did not lesson her moral responsibility to tell Eric she was carrying *his* child. She just wished that responsibility was occurring under conditions that were closer to normal.

Normal would be so nice. Normal, like going to a birthday party instead of zip lining through jungles with Tarzan in Trinidad and Tobago—though that had been crazy fun.

Could Eric even do normal?

Kids and normal…hmm. When she had reached out to Daisy, a previous assistant, asking her to come back, Daisy had invited her to a birthday party. Cooper was turning five. He was very rambunctious. A bunch of his little buddies were coming to his party on Saturday. As for Daisy, she had been quickly expedited by Mr. Andrews to return to work the following week.

"Whitney." Speak of the devil. "Seems we have a situation with some parents having a shouting match in front of the library and a bawling kid while the cops are trying to break things up. Think you could come out and read the poor kid a book or something while things get settled…hopefully outside of court?"

"On my way."

Swiping up several picture books, Whitney made tracks to lend what assistance she could. One thing she did know: She and Eric would *never* put a child they shared into the same position, no matter any disparity of priorities.

As for those priorities, forget Amy. She would take Eric to the birthday party on Saturday with hyped up kids on a sugar rush and see how he dealt with her idea of a real future together.

Even if he passed with limping colors, she would put on the kimono. She would deliver the news. The chips would fall from there.

Eric was doing his best falsetto with The Ronettes singing "Be My Baby" when he pulled into a spot marked VISITOR. He waited for "She's Like The Wind" and "Hungry Eyes" to finish before getting out of the car, where he left the *Dirty Dancing* soundtrack for the romantic weekend getaway he had planned.

Still humming, he made his way to Whitney's front door and pulled out his new key. That's right, Whitney had officially given him a key to her apartment and he liked to think it had more than a little to do with him having the key to her heart. They hadn't quite made it back to the "L" word stage last night, but there was plenty of physical evidence to support it.

Just as he opened the door Whitney's neighbor zoomed into the parking spot next to hers. For a moment Eric was tempted to tap on his window and say, "Hey buddy, that's my wife's spot next to yours, slow it down, okay?"

Instead he shut the door, left his boots by the entry, and told himself the days were numbered that Whitney would even want to live here. And why should she when he could provide her with so many alternatives to this tidy but dreary place? Even if Whitney was satisfied with it, he wasn't. And some of that had to do with feeling like he was revisiting the scene of the crime whenever he looked at the front door or the phone she had raced to answer for a summons to work.

That still stung. He'd get over it. A change of address would help. They could talk about it after she gave the signal he was still waiting for, and it wasn't an "oh baby, take me now" divestiture of clothes.

Just as he was about to set up his laptop and give Marcia a call to confirm he wouldn't be making it back to Ecuador, Whitney's phone rang. He considered answering it but didn't want to encroach on any further communications, be they in her purse, closet, drawers, or even a phone in plain sight.

Still, he couldn't help but listen to the voice leaving a message after Whitney's greeting, followed by a beep.

"Hi Whitney, it's Janet from Dr. Clark's office. Just a reminder about your 4:30 appointment on Friday. See you then."

Eric stared at the phone. Its silence only seemed to accentuate the pulse in his ears—not quite a roar but he recognized the internal sound of alarm. His bowels didn't turn to water as they had upon finding her letter and wedding ring, but there was enough residual damage for a déjà vu moment.

Whitney was being treated for some digestive and thyroid conditions. Maybe that's what this was about. God, he hoped so. And he wished to god he didn't have this awful sense of near paranoia that something else might be wrong. Shit, he hated this. Hated suspecting she might be keeping something critical from him again. Hated the immediate impulse to race to the library to make sure she was still there and demand to know why she had a doctor's appointment and hadn't thought it might bear mention given the sensitivity of this particular subject between them.

Get a grip, he told himself. A few deep breaths and he felt a little calmer. Some cold water splashed on his face from the kitchen faucet helped. So did remembering how he'd hoisted her onto the countertop and having her for breakfast shortly before she'd left for work. He'd had the satisfaction of noticing she didn't check her watch.

Returning to the living room, he lifted the blanket that he had folded after picking up quite the picnic. Eric buried his nose in the blanket she had given him to sleep with that first troubled night after their little come to Jesus meeting. Inhaling deeply, he could still smell her unique scent on the fabric, he could smell their sex. His body responded and he recognized a difference in this arousal—it was both desperate and primal. It reminded him of the times he had masturbated while he fantasized she was still with him; then choking back tears after he came. And it was always a full coming, none of his little meditative tricks to up the anticipatory ante. He'd needed that absolute release while he relived in vivid detail the moment he nearly lost it inside her.

He wished he had. He wished she'd never gone to the clinic and he'd braced her against the side of the pool to thrust up as high as he could go before ejaculating with the force of a loaded inseminator shot straight into her womb. Her baby palace.

It was an instinct that had whispered to him in the pool, and in her absence had escalated to an internal mandate: Procreate. Plant your seed inside this one woman and create a permanent bond that not even time or death can sever.

Last night, he'd lied. While he would never take Whitney against her will to comingle his DNA with hers, if she spread her arms and opened her legs and didn't tell him to stop, he would knock her up in a heartbeat. They could figure out their shit later.

Driving home from work, Whitney wondered what would greet her when she arrived: Another picnic? More of Eric's fantastic cooking? Possibly something along the lines of a snack to pick up where they'd left off that morning? As tempting as all that sounded, what she needed more than anything was a really big, warm hug after she told him about the awful fight at the library. One that only got uglier after she went to help with an inconsolable child.

Pleased to see his BMW in the Visitor section of parking, she could feel her heart speed up as she eagerly opened her apartment door, saw his boots beside the entry—*aw, thanks Grandmother Ming for teaching him that. I like it, and so does this cheap carpet*—and kicked off her black pumps to join his brown leather.

Even though he was immediately visible she called, "Oh honey, I'm home!"

Eric looked up from his laptop parked on the coffee table, in front of the couch where he sat. He smiled, though it was hardly what she'd call disarming, charming, or easy. It was an unusually strained smile for him, and his voice had a tight quality to it too when he responded, "Hey, kitten. How was work?"

"Not the best."

"In what way?"

"There was a bad scene between some parents who seem to be in a custody battle over their little boy. The police got involved and I tried to comfort him, but there's not much you can say to make things better when a child has to watch his father get in the back of a police car."

"I'm sorry to hear about that. Sounds terrible."

"It was."

Eric seemed preoccupied, listening but not really. He didn't get up to give her the hug she needed, and she didn't want to have to ask for what he should have offered.

She could feel him watching her as she walked over to the little adjoining dining area to deposit her purse on the empty table. Her mother's finery was still laid out on the nearby buffet. Everything was in its place, but something was out of synch.

"Mr. Andrews asked about you today," she chattered to fill up the answering silence. "He said he liked having you around. I told him that was ditto for me."

Eric nodded.

"Hey, I had an idea," she blabbered on, "Why don't I show you some of the local sights this weekend? We could go to Dauphin Island, or better yet, take a drive over the bay to Fairhope—it's a really pretty, artsy little town—and we could even go to Gulf Shores. I want to take you to Lambert's, Home of the Throwed Rolls!" Just thinking of their big slabs of bacon and fried okra with the huge yeasty rolls literally thrown across the restaurant to waving customers usually made her hungry. But one bite right now and she might choke.

"Sounds nice." Eric rose from the couch, slowly approached. He stopped mere inches away, tucked a stray tendril of hair behind her ear instead of going for the bobby pins. "Even nicer would be packing a bag and getting away for the whole weekend. Actually, I'd like to start the weekend as early as possible. Let's plan on me picking you up from work when you get off at five on Friday and we'll hit the road from there."

"But we were invited to a birthday party this Saturday morning. One of my assistants is having a big celebration for her five year old. You know, pin-the-tail-on-the-donkey, even a bouncy house, cake and ice cream..." Why was Eric shaking his head? "We don't have to stay the whole time," she rushed to add. "It starts at ten a.m. and we could be in Fairhope by noon."

"We'll take a raincheck on the birthday party. What I have in mind for the weekend doesn't include pin-the-tail-on-the-donkey." He glanced in the direction of her phone, where she could see the answering machine light blinking. "By the way, looks like you have a message."

"I'm sure it's nothing important." Certainly not as important as her getting Eric to that birthday party. He wasn't even leaving it open to discussion! "I'll pick the message up later. So, getting back to—"

"I think you should pick it up now."

His eyes narrowed as he studied her, making her feel very uneasy about this entire exchange.

Since she couldn't dig in her heels without appearing to have something to hide, Whitney briskly strode to the phone to tap the message button—only for her stomach to hit the floor upon hearing, "Hi Whitney, it's Janet from Dr. Clark's office. Just a reminder about your 4:30 appointment on Friday. See you then."

OH! SHIT! *How could she have forgotten about the ultrasound on Friday??*

As she wondered wildly if Eric had somehow unveiled further information, she felt both his palms on her shoulders, insistently turning her to face him.

"I heard the message come in. Are you keeping something from me?"

"No!" The frantic denial was out before she could rethink it. But what was there to rethink? Unless she was ready to skip from arguing about a birthday party he didn't want to go to and the real reason she wanted him there.

Struggling to keep her voice, as well as her insides calm, Whitney tried again. "What I mean is, it's just a follow-up appointment. Nothing serious. I should have called today and rescheduled."

"What if I said I'd feel better if you kept the appointment and let me come with you?"

"I'd say…let's split the difference." This wasn't even up for debate. Eric had every right to be a part of this—and she had a vested interest in having him present. Even if he wasn't keen on the party, or fatherhood in general, maybe once he heard the first heart beat that would change his thinking. "I'll call to reschedule for next week. And yes, of course you can come with me. Okay?"

"Okay."

Whew. That was close. At least she'd bought the weekend to pull out the big guns.

His expression visibly softening, he cupped her face and confessed, "When I heard the message, it took me back to a really dark place. I was afraid you were hiding something from me again, something bad."

"No, no," she promised. "I'm not hiding anything bad."

The relief he poured into a melting kiss was almost enough for Whitney to tell him she had news, wonderful news. If she knew that he would think it wonderful too, she would tell Eric now, even if the timing was rotten.

The needfulness she felt in him, provoked by the dark place she had created in this beautiful man, made her want to reassure him of how much she loved him, no matter their differences. And there was something else she needed to do for herself—salve a small portion of her guilt.

Whitney tugged at his belt leather, got it undone. Unzipped his fly. Lowered his pants.

She got down on her knees.

It was forgiveness she asked for and penance she gave with her lips around his straining desire for a woman who had neglected his needs while she put hers first. Did he understand what this was really about? Did he realize she wanted him to see her remorse in full technicolor, 3-D view as she laid it at the altar of his virility, and sought absolution with a carnal prayer?

Wanting him to see more than smoke in her eyes, Whitney looked up as she fellated him, but his head was tilted back, breathing ragged. As she made the most exquisite love she was capable of making this way, she palmed the taut orchid bags that were responsible for fertilizing a hidden grotto whose walls were weeping, raining into a dark garden slick.

His hands were on her head, guiding her rhythm—until he suddenly whispered, "Stop."

In his slitted gaze she saw something raw in Eric, something deep and naked that was like looking into a hidden vault where he had stored all the damage he'd suffered. Whatever answer he saw in her eyes seemed to hit some tipping point that ripped any intimate civility aside as he hoarsely commanded, "Get up" while he hoisted her to her feet.

In moments he was sweeping her purse off of Mama's good table and had her back planted flat on it.

He hiked her skirt up to her waist, yanked down her hose, her soaking wet panties, threw them somewhere out of sight.

"Open." His gaze was on the crux of her thighs where she could feel his palms urging her to obey his repeated demand to, "Open. Open for me."

She spread her legs and only momentarily felt his fingers test her readiness. And that was it. In he went.

This was not the elegant lover she knew, angling her to get in as deep as he could while gripping her hips and urgently thrusting, then grinding his pubis over hers and making her water for more.

Eric had never taken her like this. He was a man possessed. Hungry. Desperate. Demanding. She was completely aware he wasn't wearing a condom and not for a moment did she care. What difference did it make now? Other than knowing he had to be fully cognizant of what he was doing and the repercussions it could have if he didn't pull out—or even, possibly, if he did.

It almost felt like a punishment for driving him beyond his threshold of reason and control and she felt every bit deserving of the consequences. Indeed, if this was Eric's way of getting his pound of flesh, she wanted to pay...and pay some more.

She didn't care if her mother's table collapsed it was shaking so hard—only for Eric to suddenly pull her off, bend her over, and administer a smart slap to her buttocks.

"Say you want this."

"I want this." She gasped as his palm went *smack* again.

"Say you want me." His breathing was ragged, hot on her neck.

"I do. I want you."

Eric plunged back into her and began to ride her like some outlaw racing for his life even as he flipped off the posse hot on his tracks. *Smack.*

"Say you deserve this," he gnashed out.

"Yes, *yes.* Absolutely—" Instead of another *smack* he leveraged her forward so she had to brace her forearms against the table where she and Mama had shared many a meal. If her mother wasn't dead already, what was happening right now would surely kill her on sight.

The wayward daughter, however, wanted the comeuppance Eric was dishing out. He was rough, but not so much that she was worried about him hurting their baby, as he cupped her inner thighs and spread them wider, gaining a deeper access.

"Do it," she begged. "Whatever you think I deserve, just go ahead and do it."

She stared down at the tiger oak grain of the table while Eric pounded into her from behind. She had a flash of seeing her purse with all its various hues on that fateful day in Dr. Clark's office when a lab report that carried the equivalent of a death certificate sent her on a crazed quest to gloriously embrace life before it was too late—only to land her...here.

Here, where she felt Eric push all the way up, suddenly stop. He held the position, didn't move. She continued to stare down at the table while he gyrated a finger over her cleft until she sucked in her breath and shattered into a million orgasmic pieces, all of them coalescing into the chant of his name.

Just as she was sure he would finish by not sparing the rod he had planted against her cervix, Eric muttered a profanity. He abruptly withdrew. She heard his quick, jerking movements, the sound of slick flesh rasping through palm, and soon she felt the hot spurt of his semen shower her buttocks, the small of her back.

His palms followed suit and he spread the profuseness of his release over the sides of her hips until his fingertips met around her belly. There, he stroked her gently until what had been wet was sticky, and what had been sticky became dry.

She was still bent over and staring at the table when she felt him tug down her skirt. He leaned down and whispered in her ear, "My apologies, *yuan-pau*. I'm not quite sure what came over me."

She didn't want him to apologize. She wanted him to be inside her again, screwing her senseless and with purpose. That's how it had felt, like a deliberate ravishment that was intended to end differently than it ended up turning out.

"It's okay," she whispered instead. "You didn't hurt me."

"I'd never hurt you. Not deliberately, not ever." Hands around her waist, he urged her up and around, until she was anchored in his arms.

Eric's expression was hard to read. Despite his words, he didn't look the least bit sorry, but he did appear disconcerted.

"I think it's best if I continue to sleep on the couch until I have a little more control over my actions. I honestly don't trust myself in bed with you right now." His palms slowly slid down, gripped her hips. With an aggressive jerk that brought them flush he warned, "And Whitney, neither should you."

CHAPTER 29

*E*ric was not pleased with himself. He'd come *thisclose* to
deliberately trying to ensure Whitney would be bound to
him in more than name. At least he had given her fair warning.

Fortunately, as Friday rolled in and she rolled out of her parking
space to head for work, he had more than a tenuous grip on the
demons that had been set loose with the message from Dr. Clark's
office.

She had rescheduled for the following Wednesday. He was
welcome to join her. Dr. Clark would like to meet him.

That had helped tone down his anxiety and frankly barbaric
instincts. Good god, what was he, Neanderthal Man? Apparently that
apple was capable of rolling farther than his Earth and Man retrospective.

While he suspected the extension of time between appointments
was a test—to see if he would continue to prioritize their relationship
over the more dangerous on site aspects of his work—interestingly,
that didn't bother him. He had no intentions of flying off anywhere
unless Whitney came with him anyway.

What did bother him was how she seemed to cling to her
surroundings, like the familiar afforded her some kind of safety, when

he wanted his proximity to provide all the security she needed, no matter where life took them. That would preferably be far, far away from this damn apartment that was closing in on him by the day.

He had some packing to do. They hadn't further discussed the weekend since he'd practically nailed her into "Mama's table," but he was whisking her away the second she stepped out of the library's doors and taking her to the historic Grand Hotel. They were booked for two nights in a honeymoon suite overlooking Mobile Bay, less than an hour's drive from the Florida border.

A change of scenery at this point wasn't just advisable, it was essential. He would turn off his cell phone. Leave his laptop behind. Bring the kimono, along with wedding ring, heirloom necklace, and wedding papers—everything but the wedding dress that was smashed into his luggage. Not only was it horribly wrinkled, he didn't think it would still fit her, especially in the bodice.

Oh. Her breasts. Who knew a thyroid condition could elevate a gorgeous set of knockers into a Renoir work of art?

"Down, boy," he muttered. "Save it for later."

He had only ventured into Whitney's bedroom that first night to lay out the kimono...and then again yesterday...and the day before. Just to lie on her bed, touch her sheets, bury his nose into her pillows. But he hadn't checked out her drawers or even her small walk-in closet.

That's where he found the kimono. It was loose and the obi belt adjustable. That would still fit. He hung up her wedding dress in its place. There was no sign of the outfits he'd bought her on their Saint Croix shopping spree. She'd really liked those outfits and he couldn't imagine that she had heartlessly dumped them at the nearest Goodwill. But he wasn't going to snoop to see if she had relocated his gifts into her chest of drawers.

No, sir.

Neither was he going to pull down the tote on her upper shelf to find out if all the letters and postcards she had sent were hidden— along with the one he still didn't regret reading despite his otherwise pleadings. *Shhh.*

219

As much as he wished they would never have secrets between them, he truly doubted that even the best marriages were without them. Sometimes secrets might even serve a kind purpose. Like keeping it to himself that Whitney's present wardrobe was not only limited, it was really frumpy and not in a good way.

Never mind packing a few outfits, he'd buy her some new clothes over the weekend. He just needed to bring a few essentials.

But look as he may in all the obvious places, he couldn't find an overnight bag...

Wait. There was one place he hadn't thought to look.

Bending low, he flipped up the dust ruffle, and looked under her bed. Sure enough—jackpot! There was that ever so familiar piece of tapestry luggage she had carted from Bungalow #1 to here, there, and yon; next to that was the smaller leather piece he had bought her in Saint Croix. Eric chuckled, remembering how she'd had him juggling their assorted luggage in the hotel lobby while she marched to the checkout desk...

But then he thought of her extending the credit card that had contributed to her financial despair and her subsequent decision not to call him.

His chuckling stopped. He wondered how long it would be before it ceased to hurt—knowing she had kept critical information from him. That she had excluded him from her suffering. Deceived him with her silence. It didn't get more serious than life and death, and Whitney had not trusted him with the knowledge she carried.

Eric swallowed what felt like nails going down his throat. He had to get past this. It wasn't fair to Whitney or their future to dwell on past slights and hurtful mistakes that couldn't be undone. He had to trust that Whitney would never betray him like that again. That she in turn would trust him to respect her confidences and treat her as the person most essential to all that he valued in life. Trust and respect were a major part of the foundation on which their marriage had to be built.

And *that* was what had stopped him from finishing what he had started without a condom in sight.

The fact that Whitney hadn't protested his lack of protection while he went at her like a madman made him want to deserve her trust that he would make a timely departure. Even more, he wanted to be deserving of the moment when they came together in a mutual purpose and shared in the joy of her discovery.

That meant he'd better get a move on to pick up some more lamb-skins on the way to the library.

Upon opening her piece of tapestry luggage he quickly realized where her wardrobe had gone. The various articles of clothing were all thrown in and his mind went where he didn't want it to go: The day Whitney wrote the letter, grabbed her luggage, and ran away. That's how the contents looked—as if she had thrown everything from a closet and drawers into a suitcase without taking the time to fold and properly pack. The impact of seeing the state she must have been in was like a visceral punch to the gut.

He quickly zipped the luggage back up, returned it under the bed. Good, out of sight, out of mind. He didn't need any more demons unleashed to bang her through the walls of the Grand Hotel and straight into Mobile Bay. Hopefully the other piece was empty so he could finish this bit of packing duty and get the hell out before he suffocated on stale air and nightmares past.

Eric laid the bound leather suitcase that begged for travel decals to adorn it on the bed they had yet to share. He tripped one latch, then the other. Lifted the top and...

Blinked. He blinked again to make sure his eyes were working right.

His fingers felt oddly detached as he lifted the skein of pastel yarn and knitting needles that had disappeared from her coffee table. Then one by one, he touched the remaining items:

A small package of disposable diapers. A diaper stacker to put them in. A tiny silver brush. A pair of crocheted botties.

And a rattle that shook in his hand.

Friday downtown traffic was nerve-wracking as usual and Whitney took a long Zen moment before getting out of her car. Ever since whatever had happened Wednesday night, Eric had behaved like a dog on a leash and muzzled for good measure. While she was sure his restraint was for her benefit, she would much rather have Eric all over her than providing some honorable kind of protection from what she really didn't want to be protected from:

The man who wasn't always in perfect control of his emotions and liked to pound his chest. He and that hellcat—the one she had given up on keeping in check—had a lot in common. They got on famously, in fact. But Whitney the nester and mother-to-be still had to be practical. She had to be prepared.

And she was going to tell him about the baby.

He was right; getting away for the entire weekend would be good for them. Forget Cooper's birthday party. She would suggest they run with his idea of hitting the road tonight. As for packing, she'd take the kimono and maybe not much else. It seemed that the Good Whitney wasn't immune to corruption; she'd found herself wondering how she could use their ravenous attraction as a lure to keep Mr. Globetrotter closer to home. No, she wouldn't use the baby as a bargaining chip. But that hadn't stopped her from considering the mutual benefits of using herself as bait.

Just the idea got her all hot and bothered. But she was slightly nervous, too, as she shut the front door behind her. The room was dark. The curtains Eric liked to keep open were closed, sealing out the meager light of early dusk. She had seen his Beemer in the Visitor spot, so she called, "Eric?"

"In here." His voice came from her bedroom. It, too, was cast in shadows, giving an ominous edge to his summons. "Come. I'm waiting for you."

A prickling sensation at the nape of her neck increased with each step forward—then escalated like mercury plunged into a vat of boiling water as her paces were accompanied by the sound of *Tap... rattle...Tap...rattle...Tap...rattle...*

Tap.

Her bedside light flicked on. The near darkness broke like a crystal vase shattered on concrete with the stony expression Eric wore. He sat on the edge of her bed, his eyes raking from her startled face and down to the belly she instinctively covered as he continued to tap the baby's rattle into the palm of his hand.

Beside him on the mattress was her open piece of luggage where she had hidden all of her baby treasures, now exposed and looking so vulnerable and small next to the man responsible for their purchase.

"Did you have something to tell me?" His voice was low, too quiet, and each soft strike of the rattle seemed like a judge's gavel pronouncing her guilty, guilty, guilty.

"Eric, I..."

"Yes?"

His gaze shifted to hers again, pinning her in place and making her feel like a wayward soldier, caught in the midst of a treasonous act and facing a firing squad of one.

"I was going to tell you."

"When?" *Tap...rattle...Tap...rattle...*"WHEN?"

His raised voice shattered the charged air along with a final *TAP* before he gently laid the rattle into the luggage and rose like a smoldering volcano that was ready to blow. Each step he took forward, she took one back, feeling as if the floor was encrusted earth that might cave beneath her weight, and if only it would. She wanted to be swallowed up into a dark hole, wanted to be anywhere but trapped between the bedroom wall she had backed into and Eric's firmly planted hands on sheetrock, ensuring she couldn't duck and run.

"Going somewhere?" He laughed shortly, no humor at all. "I don't think so, not this time. Now let's start with you telling me, when did you find out?"

She took a serrated breath and willed herself to pass out, just faint so it would all go away.

"When?" he repeated.

"December 23rd." She could hear her voice shake; could feel her legs tremble. No, she didn't think she could run even if he let her. "It was the same day I found out about the misdiagnosis. But I...I took the pregnancy test first, that's why I called the doctor, thinking I was a monster, that I was going to die with your baby, my baby, inside me."

"Our baby," he corrected. Eric swallowed tightly and she felt like a monster all over again when he barked, "*Our* baby, goddammit!"

And then he started shaking his head at her, just shaking it with a look of disbelief, like he'd gotten hit by a car and was watching himself bleed all over the pavement, and she was the driver.

"Just when I think you can't amaze me more, you do." He didn't say it the way he had when she'd told him she was a virgin. He said it like she was a cynic. "I can't pretend to grasp how horrific that must have been—or how wonderful when everything changed in a day. But I can try to imagine our positions being reversed, and for the life of me I still cannot fathom your ability to so coldly exclude me from the two most significant experiences any human can have: Life. And death. You discarded me like I was rubbish kicked to the curb when you left. I've wrestled with that but I forgave you because I realized in some misguided way, you were trying to do something noble. Then we have those 42 days that don't bear rehashing because we've covered that history, and I forgave you for that, too. But now. *Now* we have a new development. Not only did you find out the reason you ran away to begin with was no longer a reason to keep me expelled from your life..." He shook his head at her again.

"Well." Eric snorted. "You had the joy to offset the pain and you kept them both to yourself. I asked you if you thought you might have been selfish by not coming to me in your time of need. And now I have to ask you, just what kind of regard do you hold me in by secreting something like this from me?"

He lightly touched the base of her throat where she couldn't swallow and her pulse thrummed madly. Ever so lightly he traced his fingertips down, over her breasts, past her waist, and stopped at her slightly rounded belly.

Where he laid his hand she felt a slight fluttering. And she knew. It wasn't her nerve-laden stomach doing flip-flops. She was feeling the baby move for the first time. She didn't think Eric could feel it, the sensation was so fragile and light, but the moment was so stirring that tears sprang to her eyes.

"Save your tears," he said gruffly, still stroking her stomach. "They don't move me right now. I've been devoted to you from the beginning and how ironic that after everything you've dished out, it would take you conceiving our child to beg the question: do you even have the capacity to be half as devoted to me?"

His eyes searched hers and she tried to say something to explain, to put this right, to make this awful moment that wasn't supposed to happen like this, transform into something...better?

Her mouth moved but nothing came out. She seemed to be paralyzed against the wall as she felt his hand retreat, watched him turn his back, swipe up his keys on the nightstand—where she just then saw her wedding ring, the necklace, the envelope containing their marriage papers.

He was almost out the bedroom door when she finally called, "Eric!"

He stopped, turned. His eyes were unreadable, as if he were hiding something important from her too now and wasn't sure if he should trust her with the truth they might relay.

"Yes?"

"Are you...are you happy about the baby?"

"What do you think?" His hooded gaze shifted as he raised an eyebrow, tilted his head.

"I—I'm not sure. I hope you are."

"For Chrissakes, Whitney, don't you know me at all?" He raised his hands in a gesture that could have been disgust or surrender, maybe both. "I'm fucking *thrilled*."

Eric grabbed his overnight satchel on the way out, left his briefcase and cell phone behind. As soon as Whitney's front door closed behind him, he punched air.

Yes. YES!! He was going to be a daddy. As for the wife that had royally screwed up by not telling him as soon as she knew, he would find it in the heart she owned lock, stock, and barrel, to forgive her once more. But damn, she'd better never pull such a boner again. Patience was one thing; enabling destructive patterns of behavior, another.

He was in no rush to reach his car, so he lingered on the sidewalk fronting her apartment where yellow stripes of division and painted numbers to mark their ownership pulled their perfunctory duty. Even the huts in third world countries with open fires to cook by felt more family friendly. People almost always did the best they could with what resources they had, especially when children were involved, and he didn't doubt there were good families doing their best here, and no telling how many other such complexes that stretched across the globe.

But the hell if he and Whitney would start their own family here when they—yes, *they*—had the good fortune of providing more, but not too spoilage much, to their offspring.

His parents and Grandmother Ming had taught him that good parenting came with the responsibility of avoiding over-indulgence, of disallowing a sense of entitlement for what you had not personally earned. Hard work and not taking the easy way out were all part of building character. There was no free lunch in the real buffet of life.

What he had left behind for Whitney to do with as she chose was quite the buffet. The kimono on the mattress, next to the open luggage that still had him reeling. The important jewelry—ring, neck- lace—was on her nightstand, along with their marriage papers. But perhaps most significant of all was the note he had penned and folded into an origami stork that stuck out from a crocheted baby bootie.

He dawdled long enough to worry that either Whitney hadn't found the note, wasn't coming, or the manager might call the cops to check out a loiter.

So much for the perfect exit. He had more than a little pride and point making on the line so maybe a quick run to the local Krispy- Kreme was in order while he cooled what was left of his smoking jets.

Might not be a bad idea to pick up some ice cream along with a fresh jar of Clausen's best while he was at it.

Eric was about halfway to his relegated Visitor parking spot when he heard a door slam and Whitney yelling, "WAIT!"

He turned to see the most amazing vision he could hope for coming straight at him: Kimono flapping past pumping legs; necklace bouncing between unbound breasts that would nurture their child; the envelope containing their marriage documents waving wildly in the air—

From his peripheral vision he saw a racing Camaro with no place to go but into its allotted slot heading straight into Whitney's path.

Eric reversed direction; ran faster than he ever thought himself capable as he shouted, "Whitney, look out!" and flung himself in front of the screeching wheels before they could connect with his wife, his child, everything that mattered in his life.

And the world went black.

CHAPTER 30

*W*hitney paced the white tiled linoleum, chafing her arms against the chill that wouldn't go away. She was still wearing the kimono, covered in Eric's blood. She couldn't stop replaying the horrific sight of his whole body connecting with chrome and metal, then spiraling through the air before landing with a sickening *thud* on the asphalt near her feet.

The wail that had ripped from her throat was soon joined by the endless loop of sirens. Eric was strapped onto a stretcher the medics couldn't pry her from until they literally had to push her away to resuscitate him in the ambulance.

She looked at the clock she couldn't stop watching in the surgical waiting room. Midnight. One a.m. Two.

Had Adam gotten her frantic message? Had he contacted Eric's parents, Grandmother Ming?

How could this happen? What had she done?

With palsied hands she held Eric's message that had been folded into a stork and tucked inside a baby bootie. If only she had seen it sooner. If only she hadn't watched him shut the front door, then wasted precious time staring dumbly at all the treasures he had left behind on the nightstand, the kimono on the bed. She'd thought he must be giving her a taste of her own medicine, leaving her to wonder where he had gone until he decided to show up again.

She should have known better. She should have known Eric better. *"For Chrissakes, Whitney, don't you know me at all?"*

Of course he would never leave her the way she'd left him. Of course what he'd left behind was an entrusted responsibility for her to pick up, not for him to escape.

And of course any note he wrote wouldn't remotely resemble the one she had left him.

Whitney touched the rice paper he had put his bold script to and re-read what was already committed to memory:

```
Pack the robe. Put on the necklace. Bring the
ring so I can put it back where it belongs. I am
incomplete without you, yuan-pao. You are my
greatest treasure; my greatest weakness; my
greatest strength. We'll get this right somehow.
Meet me at the car. Our future, and the family we
will create together, starts now. I love you
forever.
Your husband, Eric
```

She traced each word yet again with a trembling fingertip. What if this was all she had left of him? She had to take extra good care of his note, her prime treasure. She couldn't get it wet or damage the paper.

Very carefully she returned it to the pocket hidden inside the obi belt.

"Whitney, I got here as soon as I could."

"Thank God you're here."

Adam embraced her and Whitney managed not to fall apart while she told him all the horrible things about the actual accident. Somehow she couldn't bring herself to share the private details of the confrontation that had led up to the unthinkable, or what she had kept from Eric.

It was nearly dawn when they were joined by the lead surgeon in blue scrubs, pulling down a surgical mask from his mouth, as if he'd just left the operating room. She noticed there was sweat on his forehead that his scrub cap hadn't soaked up.

For some reason she looked at the clock again, a big round orb with black fingers pointing to timely numbers that called it 5:12 in the morning with a second hand ticking.

"Mrs. Townsend?"

"Yes. That's me."

"I'm Dr. Bekz. Your husband is out of surgery."

"Then he's alive."

The surgeon nodded but was momentarily silent.

"I'm Eric's brother. Tell us what we need to know." Adam, sounding so much like Eric. Cool head in the midst of a crisis.

"We almost lost him a few times. His injuries were quite severe. Multiple fractures. Internal bleeding. Trauma to the head. But we have his vital signs under control. For now."

"What do you mean 'for now'?" She barely managed not to grab the doctor by his scrubs. "What do you mean by that? He's going to be a father. I need him—our child needs him—to be okay."

Adam's grip around her shoulder tightened.

"I wish I could tell you that, Mrs. Townsend. As it is, we're taking him directly to ICU. He's in critical condition. There could be brain damage. It's too soon to tell. We have him on life support."

Eric. With his brilliant mind possibly damaged. His beautiful body broken. Reduced to even breathing at the behest of a machine.

He would hate it.

"Can I see him?"

"I wouldn't usually permit it this soon, but...we'll make an exception. Visits are limited to ten minutes. Just prepare yourself before you go in."

The doctor's acquiescence told her that the only thing he was sure of was that Eric might not make it.

She had been in ICU before, right at the end with Mama. Whitney steeled herself, having a good idea of what she was walking into...

But she was wrong. Oh. So. Wrong.

Eric was on a ventilator; a tracheotomy tube at his throat. There were multiple other machines that beeped and glowed with lights, along with drips and IV tubes that were doing their duty. His head was wrapped in gauze and so much of the rest of him was held together by splints and pins and surgical tape there wasn't a single exposed part that could assure her it was Eric. Except for his mouth. Lax and never more beautiful.

Adam grasped her hand as they stood beside the bed.

"Maybe it's not him," she whispered. "Maybe this is a nightmare and when I wake up he'll be beside me in another bed."

"He'll wake up," Adam said gruffly. "He's too stubborn to die. Aren't you, bro?"

The machines continued to beep. An alarm went off nearby. Whitney jerked at the sound of "Stat!"—then relaxed when several nurses raced into another room.

"I wish I could put my head on his chest, so I could hear his heart. I wish he could put his head on mine."

Adam squeezed her hand. "He'd love that. He's crazy about you, you know."

Leaning down she whispered, "I should have told you about the baby sooner. I'm so sorry, Eric. Please don't leave me." She tried so hard not to cry. But she failed. She failed so badly that she wept.

"Hey. Hey, now." Adam held her, providing the kind of brotherly support she'd never had growing up. "You're not alone. The rest of the family is on their way. We are all in this together."

"I'm sorry, but time's up," an ICU nurse quietly announced. "You can come back in four hours."

Whitney lightly touched her lips to Eric's. "Don't leave me," she whispered. Then she remembered she wasn't alone. "Don't leave us."

Once outside ICU Adam grabbed a box of tissues and knew his first and foremost priority was to keep it together for his brother.

"Here," he said gently, handing Whitney a wad of white while he herded them into a private waiting area. "Sounds like I'm going to be an uncle? Wow! I had no idea. Eric didn't tell me."

"He just found out himself...right before the accident." Whitney blew her nose. Adam had to agree with his brother—her eyes were an incredible shade of blue; maybe they did make the Caribbean look dull on a crystal clear day. "I'm sure you would have been the first to know, Adam."

"Nah." He shook his head, managed to pull out a smile from his bag of modeling tricks. "Grandmother Ming. Then the parents. I'd get third place. Pecking order. That's okay."

Adam thought of Eric saying he wanted to expedite their wedding because Whitney had no family and he still wanted to look after her if anything happened to him. Brother, had it. Eric looked like road kill. His wife was covered in the evidence of it.

"Listen, we can't do anything here right now, so I think the best thing we can do is take care of you. First, let's go find you something else to wear—"

"No!" She gripped the kimono protectively tight. "I don't want to take it off. Eric gave it to me on our honeymoon. It was really important to him that I put it back on after he..."

Her voice trailed off.

"After he found you?"

Whitney nodded haltingly. There was definitely a story behind this kimono thing and whatever happened between Whitney disappearing and Eric getting totaled by a car. Well, maybe he'd get enough bits and pieces to put it together in time, but he wasn't probing now.

"I understand you don't want to change out of something important that Eric gave you, but Whitney, do you think he would want you wearing this when you see Grandmother Ming?"

Slowly, she shook her head.

"When was the last time you ate?"

"I...I don't know. Yesterday, lunch?"

"Okay. Then after we take care of the clothes, it's time for breakfast."

"I'm not hungry."

"Neither am I. But you've got more than one to feed now, and my brother would be very pissed off if I didn't make sure his kid was being well fed. In fact, just to make him happy, let's see if we can order his favorite breakfast."

"But I'm not sure what that is. He always seemed to be cooking for me and making my favorites."

"Red eye gravy on a buttermilk biscuit. Eggs over easy. Hash browns extra crispy. Salmon absolutely, with bacon and sausage on the side. Fresh berries on a nice slab of French toast with real maple syrup. And on special occasions, a beer to chase it all down."

"Really?" Whitney actually smiled. "That's a lot of breakfast. I had no idea."

"I'll drink the beer. You can eat the rest." Maybe he should have thrown in a loaded omelet, too.

"Thank you, Adam. You're a really good brother...in law."

"And I'm glad you're my sister-in-law." Placing a protective arm around her, he moved them towards the elevator. "C'mon, he's not going anywhere. Let's get you cleaned up and feed that baby. Otherwise, when Eric wakes up, he's gonna kick my ass."

Thanks to Adam she was clean, she had eaten for the baby's sake, and she wasn't a complete wreck when Eric's parents and Grandmother Ming arrived at the hospital.

Would they blame her for this? No need, she blamed herself enough.

Adam kept his arm around her as he made the introductions.

His arm didn't stay there long.

Eric's mom, Dorothy, immediately took her hands. "Oh my darling girl. Whitney..."

She didn't say anything more, nor did she have to, as Eric's father wrapped the three of them into a group hug. All he said was, "We're here now. We'll get through this."

The four star general and his wife were such an incredibly handsome couple there was no question as to where Adam and Eric got their looks. Or, their character.

But it was Grandmother Ming that Whitney couldn't take her eyes from as she stood apart, silently watching.

Adam cleared his throat. "It's visitation time. But only two are allowed, and only for ten minutes."

As much as she longed to race back to Eric, to put herself first, as she so clearly had in their history together, Whitney said, "General and Mrs. Townsend, go see your son."

They exchanged a look that reminded Whitney of how she and Eric had come to communicate with a glance, a touch, some facial expression that conveyed what the other one was thinking.

"Call us Mom and Dad," they said in unison.

A kiss to her cheek and off they went.

Grandmother Ming nodded to Adam. "Leave us."

Adam made himself scarce.

That left Whitney face to face, alone, with Grandmother Ming.

She was all of five feet, if that. All of one hundred pounds, if that. And yet her regal bearing filled the entire space surrounding them, make that the entire hospital.

Actually, Grandmother Ming looked ready to rule the whole world. In style.

She wore a sleek couture dress with her straight silver hair draped over her shoulders. Her fingernails were painted dragon red and even nearing ninety—though who would believe it!?—she could stop traffic with a bat of her dark, amber flecked eyes.

Eric's eyes.

Whitney bowed. She bowed low, since the lower you bowed the more respect was being shown. Eric had told her that many old traditions had given way to less formal forms of showing respect in Chinese culture, but his grandmother was Old School.

"You rise now."

Although she was a full head taller than Grandmother Ming, Whitney felt ever so small in her presence.

Grandmother Ming reached up, and with those dragon red nails tapped the family heirloom. Whitney prayed she wouldn't demand it back.

"You love my grandson?"

"More than anything, Grandmother Ming."

"Good. You call me that. I not so sure about you when I see him so upset. But then he so happy when he call me this week, saying you back together. Why you go away, do that to him?"

Whitney cobbled together the best explanation she could, leaving out the pregnancy, and managed not to cry while she did. Grandmother Ming was too stoic to suffer a fool's tears.

"I see." Grandmother Ming arched an eyebrow, tilted her head in a visibly shrewd assessment. "You have more to say."

"Yes," Whitney confessed, and for some reason she felt safe telling Grandmother Ming her worst transgression. "I'm carrying Eric's child. I didn't want to tell him at first, everything was such a mess, and I knew he didn't want to have a baby with Amy—"

"Amy?" Grandmother Ming practically spat out her name. "She a bitch. Spoiled brat. Have to control everything. He tell you she serve divorce papers while he in hospital? Guess not. Eric so smart, how he do something so stupid, marry her so young?" The shake of her silver head relayed the degree of grandmotherly disapproval. Then she shrugged. "Ah, we all make mistake. Eric. You. Me. It is how we learn."

Before she could say more, the Townsends emerged from their ten minute visit.

The pallor of their faces said it all as they silently gathered her into their arms and reached out to Grandmother Ming to bring her into their huddle.

So this was what a real family felt like, Whitney realized. Eric had given her the family she had always longed for. It was a tragic, precious moment that was somehow...better. Better than anything she had ever imagined.

"Now we make Eric happy," Grandmother Ming decreed. "We celebrate!"

Whitney whipped her attention to the grand matriarch clapping her hands. Twice.

Then Grandmother Ming bowed to her. She rose up with a conspirator's smile.

"We have new baby on way. Eric, smart man. Slow at first, but he learn his lesson."

~

Two weeks later Eric was breathing on his own. That was huge. But there were still various measures being taken to keep him stabilized.

He was in a coma.

Everyone was so worn out. Adam had a photo shoot he reluctantly flew out for but would be back in a few days.

Dorothy and Four Star—now Mom and Dad—were taking their turns bedsitting. They were exhausted, too.

Even Mr. Andrews had pitched in and offered all the support he possibly could.

Whitney was so grateful for them all, but she especially loved her time alone with Grandmother Ming. They had spent hours talking. Hours in shared silences, reading their books.

And hours sitting across from each other while Grandmother Ming taught her mahjong. Instead of cards, small delicately engraved tiles were used—a whopping 136 tiles to be exact.

"How old was Eric when you taught him this game?"

"Three. He beat me at five."

Whitney looked at the complex array of symbols and characters with Wind tiles and Dragon tiles that were laid out on the hospital table near Eric's bed.

Then she looked at him, so still and silent, except for the sound of his breathing. Did he dream? Would he ever play this game again? Ever hold their child? She had already made every bargain with God she could think of and sent up ten thousand prayers. Where did she go from here?

"He strong, Whitney." Grandmother Ming reached over the tiles and firmly clasped her hand. "But you strong, too. More strong than you think."

"I hope so, Grandmother Ming, because I don't feel strong."

"You must be. No choice."

Whitney nodded. She had her marching orders. She would not let Eric, or Grandmother Ming down.

"I have a procedure tomorrow. It's an ultrasound. I was supposed to have it before now but…" The way Grandmother Ming tilted her head, raised a brow, it was all Eric. So were the eyes that held hers in a steady gaze. "I'm supposed to hear the baby's heartbeat for the first time. Since Eric can't be there, will you come with me instead?"

Grandmother Ming rose from her chair. She came around the table and led Whitney's left hand, now bearing the ring she would never take off, to her own abdomen.

"I give life to one child. I lose one after her, and it bad—no more babies. Eric, he like baby boy I lost." She nodded in Eric's supinely still direction. "Life hard. But life so good, too. Yes. Tomorrow we go together."

Grandmother Ming smiled a secret smile.

As Whitney smiled back she squared her shoulders and sat straighter. She could do this. No choice.

CHAPTER 31

*T*he first thing he heard was Adam's voice, saying, "Whitney, please go get some rest. My brother would be very unhappy with me if he thought I wasn't watching out for you."

Next he heard Whitney saying something about...

And he faded into nothingness again.

Until the sound of his parents' voices filtered his consciousness and he heard Grandmother Ming from what sounded like a tin can with a long string to his ear, saying in her sweet, sing-songy accent that reminded him of wind chimes, "Eric, Eric...you wake up now. Your wife, she need you. Babies need you, too..."

Babies? He struggled to mind his grandmother, to wake up, to remember...babies?

And then, after what seemed a very long time, he heard soft weeping. Something wet and warm kept falling like raindrops onto his cheeks. He felt a familiar hand stroking his, and close to his ear, clear as a bell came Whitney's voice.

"We had another appointment with Dr. Clark today. The twins are doing great, heartbeats are strong, and they're kicking like crazy. Here, you can feel them."

He felt his hand being moved, his palm pressed against a hard lump, like a little foot or a fist, and the lump jumped.

"See? Big and strong just like his daddy. Or maybe it's the girl." More rain, sniffles. "Sorry, didn't mean to drop my snot on you like that. Here, let me clean that up."

Something that felt like a tissue was being patted on his face. He tried to open his eyes but it wasn't easy, so he tried harder and managed a slit.

He could see the yin-yang pendant that had belonged in the family for generations dangling between some really big boobs.

His throat felt super dry, and sore, like something had been lodged down his esophagus. He swallowed to see if there was a blockage, but no, all clear, he just needed...

"Water," he croaked.

"Eric?"

Her ear was close to his mouth and her hair tickled his nose.

He really wanted the water, but through the fog in his brain, there was only one thing he wanted more.

"Whitney."

He didn't mind the cane. Beat the hell out of a wheelchair. What bothered Eric the most was being literally comatose for so much of Whitney's pregnancy.

"Ready?" she asked, all aglow as she patted the back of the wheelchair he had no intentions of riding in, even if it was just to the hospital exit.

"I can walk," he countered stubbornly, and moved her way to prove it. "In fact, once we're out of here I'll prove how fast I can chase you."

"I can't run very fast." She laughed that amazing laugh of hers and pointed two index fingers at the cause of her own physical limitations.

As much as he wanted to get out of here, Eric pushed his door shut before they had the usual company of hospital personnel. He'd been here so long that they'd even gotten an invitation from one of his nurses to attend her wedding.

"Sit with me for a moment." He put aside his cane and took a seat in the big chair that could make out into a bed—one that Whitney had slept in many a night while he was in traction. Eric patted his lap.

"I'm afraid I'm too heavy." Her laughter stilled and those bluer than blue eyes turned somber. "I don't want to hurt you."

"I won't break." Insistently, he patted his lap again. "Sit."

Whitney's obliging was so hesitant and then so careful that Eric pulled her down and into his arms.

"Much better." Better enough that he didn't mind the slight discomfort. It had taken three months for his broken pelvis to heal. He wouldn't be doing any Elvis dance moves for a while but there was a slow tango he was looking forward to beneath the sheets. That still worked. Thank God. "Before we get out of here, I just want to lay some ground rules we can both agree to. Number one: Do not treat me like an invalid."

"I'll try not to, Eric. I'll really try, but—"

"No ifs, ands, or buts. I'm not broken. My bones are intact." He gave her a slight nudge to prove there was one in perfectly fine order. "Number two: We find another place to live ASAP. We've got a nursery to put together and less than two months to do it."

Whitney gave him a sheepish grin. "I wanted it to be a surprise but...we've already moved."

"What? Really?" Would she ever cease to amaze him? Not in a million years. "Where?"

"It's not exactly a house," she said excitedly. "It's more like a house on wheels. A really, really nice RV that Grandmother Ming helped me pick out. I've already learned how to drive it."

A vision of Whitney plowing through a rain forest in a jeep while he shouted his love to the Caribbean sky tightened his throat. He loved her so much then, so much more now.

"I'll just bet you have." He lifted her left hand and kissed the pearl that was held by two reaching hands—so symbolic of the balance of life, suspended by the joined forces of woman and man. "And might I

240

ask whatever prompted you to go out and buy an RV, Mrs. Townsend?"

"Well, Dr. Townsend, it's like this." Placing his hand over her heart, close to where their family heirloom rested, Whitney explained, "After the accident I couldn't stand to see that parking lot, and I couldn't imagine us ever living there...if you lived. I had a lot of soul searching to do and I realized that staying in one place to raise a family only provides so much stability, and it certainly doesn't guarantee a happy home. I finally got it, and maybe too late, that anywhere I was with you, that was stable, that was solid, and that was home. Only, if I didn't have you, then how would I raise our children? Did I want them to grow up like me, with a limited view outside a window that never moved, or did I want them to see the world through their father's eyes? So I bought the RV and told myself if you didn't make it, once I had the babies, I would take them to Portland and we would live on your houseboat—a not so little houseboat as it turns out. We would take trips to spend time with their Great-grandmother Ming, and we'd spend lots of time with their Uncle Adam, and two of the most wonderful grandparents they could possibly have. We would go to national forests and we would go to all the mountains their father had written about and tended and..."

She looked so deep into his eyes and in hers he could see forever. "And Eric, what I realized was that if you did pull through, I wouldn't try to keep you from doing the work you love. Because, after all, if you had been working with Marcia on a crater in Ecuador, you would have been safer than you were in a parking lot trying to save me."

For a moment he held his silence. With their twins, Taiga and Lily, on the way, the various offers he had received were mighty tempting —particularly the endowed Deanship that would enable them to start their family on his not-so-little houseboat. Of course the position at Stanford, sweetened with an enormous research grant, would put them only an hour away from Grandmother Ming....

Something for them to further discuss in the RV tonight.

"You know I'd do it all over again," was all he said.

"I know." She knuckled his jaw. "But I have a better idea."

241

As he tilted his head, studied his wife, Eric knew for a certainty the best idea he'd ever had in his life was to marry her. Whitney had taught him so much about life, about love, and all its hard, beautiful lessons.

Laying his hand over her stomach that felt like a wrestling match was going on in there, he asked, "And just what might that idea be?"

With a kittenish grin, Whitney escaped from his lap. "Why don't we find out how fast I can run and whether or not you can catch me?"

The End

LOVE GAME

RISKY LOVERS, BOOK 3

"I'll turn off the lights," Chris offered, needing some distance from their close encounter of the comforting kind. But Greg's hurt spot, his sense of failure as a father, stuck with her. Trying to escape it, she hastened her pace and snapped out a silent order. *Sleep with him, laugh with him, anything. Just don't let yourself start to care.* An emotional entanglement she had to avoid at any cost. *Especially* with Greg. Audrey aside, he was too tempting and too lethal, like cheese baiting a steel trap.

Chris stopped in her tracks as he kicked off his shoes. They landed on top of the heels she'd shucked off. With his arms stretched out on the sofa's back, his easy posture reminded her of a…"Family man," she whispered.

"Did you say something?" he asked, looking away from the opening credits.

"I said that I'm glad you thought this up. A relaxed evening has a certain charm for a woman who's got a sore rear end and ate leftover fries at the skating rink today." *Good,* she told herself. *Hook it to the kid and make him bring it back to the bed where this whole crazy thing belongs.*

"Then it's okay if we don't cancel the movie and go embarrass ourselves on the dance floor?"

"The older I get, Greg, the slower I go."

"That's good to hear. Otherwise, I couldn't keep up."

Chris frowned. He was too easy to be with, too easy to talk to. She couldn't seem to quit telling him things—little things that were somehow more revealing than big secrets. Her affection for him was genuine and that was fine. But what she *could not* do was let herself think of him as more than a good time on the fly.

His fly was where she angled her gaze since she deemed it safer than his couch-potato slouch.

"Sit with me?" He patted the sofa and looked even more dangerously domestic. "I won't bite."

"I'm disappointed." Her retaliatory defense got the reaction she needed to put Greg in his proper perspective. A dark brow rose over a darker glitter in his eyes. "Wouldn't you be more comfortable with your shirt off?" she prompted, ignoring the prickling sensation on her neck.

He tapped his fingertips together, as if contemplating his answer. Suddenly, he pushed the coffee table away.

And then, he worked loose the knot of his tie. Slipping it off, he slowly, suggestively, ran its length over his palm.

"Come here." His voice was smooth but rough around the edges.

Her feet were slow to acknowledge the command. Once she stood where he had indicated, between his spread legs, her lungs shut down, her stomach rolled over, and the sound of her thrumming heart filled her ears. The only thing that seemed to be in working order was her vision, locked in on the thin red silk he continued to feed through a loose fist.

What was he planning to do with it? Why did he keep staring at her that way, saying nothing, and making her imagination leap in these crazy directions?

His slide of the tie around the small of her back caused her to breathe out in a rush. Using it as a pulley, he drew her forward until her knees met the couch. Thank goodness for the couch, something solid to keep her knees from hitting the floor.

He gave a quick yank and she felt herself falling, guided by his hands on her waist until she was spilled over him. Her head against the crook of his neck, she felt his fingers twisting into her hair, then pulling until he stared at her, hard. His voice emerged gritty, challenging and...amused?

"What did you think I was going to do with it?"

"I—I didn't know."

"Were you curious?" When she jerked out a nod, he said, "Curious, that's good. What about...excited? Were you?"

She was shaking, even her lips were shaking. Forcing them to move, she answered, "I was."

"Excellent." He led her hands from his shoulders to the first button of his shirt. "Anything and everything you can imagine...I *want*."

Available in paperback from your favorite online retailer or bookstore.

ALSO BY MALLORY RUSH

The Risky Lovers Series

Love Trade

Love Lessons

Love Game

ABOUT THE AUTHOR

Mallory Rush believes in true love's ability to elevate all of our lives from the ordinary to the transcendent. As Olivia Rupprecht she has written and edited fiction and non-fiction, and was series developer for the True Vows reality-based romance series from HCI Books. Writing as Hart Rivers, she is also co-author of the bestselling Murder on the Mekong series of psychological thrillers. But when it comes to romance, she considers it to be more than a storytelling genre—it's as essential as breathing for a truly rich life. Mallory loves to hear from her readers.

www.MALLORYRUSH.com
www.murderonthemekong.com

www.ingramcontent.com/pod-product-compliance
Lightning Source LLC
Chambersburg PA
CBHW022029260626
47156CB00017B/956